# THE WORLD'S FINEST ASSASSIN

### Gets Reincarnated in Another World as an Aristocrat

**† Tarte**

Lugh's personal retainer and his assassination assistant. She cares deeply for Lugh because he saved her life.

**† Maha**

The proxy representative of Lugh's cosmetics brand. She provides logistical support by collecting funds, information, and more.

**† Dia**

A noble lady from a foreign country. She is among the strongest mages in the world.

† **Cian**

Lugh's father and the strongest man in the history of the clan of assassins. He is both a loving husband and a coldhearted killer.

† **Lugh**

The oldest son of the clan of assassins, who is often called a boy genius. He was the world's greatest assassin in his previous life, and he combines that knowledge with the magic of his new world.

† **Esri**

Lugh's adoring mother. She can be a bit of an airhead, but she's clever in her own way.

# Contents

The World's Finest Assassin
Gets Reincarnated in Another World as an Aristocrat

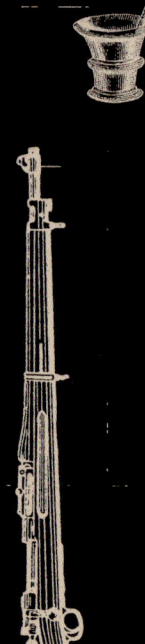

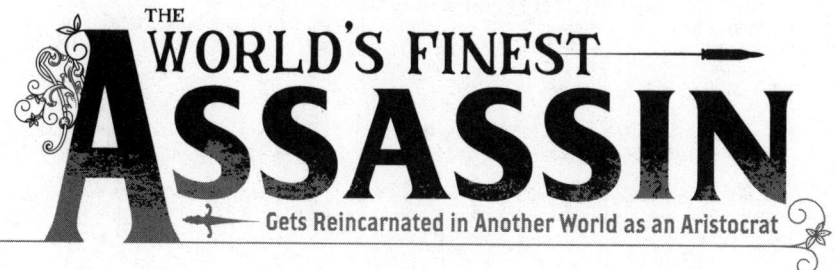

# THE WORLD'S FINEST ASSASSIN

### Gets Reincarnated in Another World as an Aristocrat

# 1

## Rui Tsukiyo

Illustration by **Reia**

YEN ON

New York

The World's Finest Assassin Gets Reincarnated in Another World as an Aristocrat, Vol. 1
Rui Tsukiyo

Translation by Luke Hutton
Cover art by Reia

SEKAI SAIKO NO ANSATSUSHA, ISEKAI KIZOKU NI TENSEI SURU Vol. 1
©Rui Tsukiyo, Reia 2019
First published in Japan in 2019 by KADOKAWA CORPORATION, Tokyo.
English translation rights arranged with KADOKAWA CORPORATION, Tokyo through TUTTLE-MORI AGENCY, INC., Tokyo.

English translation © 2020 by Yen Press, LLC

Yen On
150 West 30th Street, 19th Floor
New York, NY 10001

Visit us at yenpress.com
facebook.com/yenpress
twitter.com/yenpress
yenpress.tumblr.com
instagram.com/yenpress

First Yen On Edition: December 2020

Yen On is an imprint of Yen Press, LLC.
The Yen On name and logo are trademarks of Yen Press, LLC.

The publisher is not responsible for websites (or their content)
that are not owned by the publisher.

Library of Congress Cataloging-in-Publication Data
Names: Tsukiyo, Rui, author. | Reia, 1990– illustrator.
Title: The world's finest assassin gets reincarnated in another world / Rui Tsukiyo ; illustration by Reia.
Other titles: Sekai saikou no ansatsusha, isekai kizoku ni tensei suru. English
Description: First Yen On edition. | New York : Yen On, 2020–
Identifiers: LCCN 2020043584 | ISBN 9781975312411 (v. 1 ; trade paperback)
Subjects: LCSH: Assassins—Fiction. | GSAFD: Fantasy fiction.
Classification: LCC PL876.S858 S4513 2020 | DDC 895.6/36—dc23
LC record available at https://lccn.loc.gov/2020043584

ISBNs: 978-1-9753-1241-1 (paperback)
       978-1-9753-1242-8 (ebook)

10 9 8 7 6 5 4 3 2 1

LSC-C

Printed in the United States of America

I was reclining comfortably in my seat on a passenger plane. Having finished my work overseas, I was on my way back to Japan.

Assassins exist only in fiction. I'm sure that's what most people believe. Take a moment to really think about it, though.

There's no quicker or more efficient means of disposing of an enemy than murder, and the more money and influence a person has, the more enemies they'll need taken out of the picture. Where there is a demand for a service, a supply will rise to meet it...and that's how assassins like me came to be.

"My last job went off without a hitch." It was going to be my final day as an assassin. I had a retirement plan and everything.

I came to be known as the world's greatest assassin, having been responsible for the sudden "death by illness" of numerous major figures, including several presidents. But in the end, even I was unable to defeat Father Time.

My next job was already lined up. I was going back to work as an instructor at the facility where I long ago learned the tricks of my particular trade.

Training assassins required an extreme degree of highly specialized knowledge and skill. Finding qualified personnel wasn't easy. From that day forward, I was going to be turning promising youths into seasoned assassins like myself.

Or at least, that's what I'd thought. Unfortunately, it seemed this job was nothing more than a fabrication designed to have me let down my guard.

The passenger plane shook violently with the sound of an explosion, then the aircraft rapidly began to lose altitude.

"I can understand the desire to dispose of a tool that has out-lived its usefulness, but to go this far just to kill one person... It seems I've built up quite the reputation, haven't I?"

Now I really felt old. I should've guessed this kind of thing would happen.

I stood up and pushed my way through the panicking pas-sengers, hurrying toward the source of the sound. I hacked the security for the door to the cockpit and forced my way in. A few crew members tried to stop me on the way, but I kindly put them all to sleep.

When I entered the cockpit, I was greeted by the headless bodies of the pilot and copilot.

*This is fine. Nothing I can't handle*, I told myself.

Assassination demands a great many skills. Piloting a passen-ger plane was no problem for me.

...Or at least, it wouldn't have been a problem if the console hadn't also been blown to smithereens along with the heads of the two pilots.

"I've taken the lives of a great many people in my day. I fig-ured my time would come eventually, but I never imagined I'd have such an extravagant grave prepared."

No matter the situation, I always tried my best to survive, even if the odds were stacked against me. That had always been my policy. I made use of all the knowledge and experience I'd gained over the years and pushed my mind to the limit in order to find a means of escape.

…*There's still something I can do.* Saving the plane and its passengers was a tall order, but there was still a chance I could save myself.

"Well, this certainly came sooner than I expected. Their preparation was flawless… Looks like I'm done for."

Outside the window, I could see a fighter jet armed with missiles quickly approaching.

The plane was currently flying over a metropolitan area. If it were to crash in the city, the damage would be catastrophic. It seemed that the plan was to break my plane into tiny fragments before that could happen.

By my estimation, the plane was supposed to reach its destination in about ten minutes, though that seemed less likely now.

The jet fired a missile.

It was an annoying complication. I would've been able to save myself if I only had the impending plane crash to worry about. The missile was an AIM-92 Stinger, an air-to-air model capable of so thoroughly destroying a passenger plane of this caliber that not even a scrap would remain.

…*How unfortunate*, I thought.

A lifetime of acting as an emotionless tool for my organization, and this was how I was being repaid. I was so loyal that I wouldn't have hesitated to kill myself if given the order. Such a betrayal instilled doubts in my mind about my employers and my line of work for the first time in my life.

As death approached, I imagined that if I had another shot at life, I wouldn't spend my days as someone else's servant. I'd live only for myself. If I utilized my skills, knowledge, and experience purely for my own sake, then surely...

Holding on to that hope, I fought for my life until the very last second, using every means at my disposal.

When next I opened my eyes, I discovered I was in a temple. It appeared to be an ancient structure made of white stone. If I had to compare it to something, it'd be the Parthenon. There was no escaping that plane, and a part of me wondered if I'd dreamed the whole ordeal.

"Nope, that wasn't a dream. Everything you just experienced was real. You were the world's greatest assassin, but in a moment of carelessness, you allowed *yourself* to be assassinated. Ah-ha-ha... ha-ha-ha-ha!" A woman with white hair, dressed in an equally white tunic, burst out laughing. Actually, not only were her hair and clothes white, but so was her skin, her eyes—everything about her was that alabaster hue. To top it all off, she was strikingly beautiful.

Whatever she was, it was clear she wasn't human. Her beauty was *too* flawless, as if she'd been carved by a master sculptor. The frank tone she was speaking with could not have been less appropriate, however.

"...Um, would you mind explaining what's going on here?" I asked.

"You're dead, and I summoned your soul to this place. Oh, I'm a goddess, by the way!" she explained.

"Do you bring every single dead person in for an idle chat? If that's the case, then considering the number of people who die every day, there must be as many gods as there are stars in the sky. Either that or you have way too much free time. Or perhaps you had a special reason for summoning me here."

"You got it on your last guess. Typically, souls are immediately wiped clean and recycled. We gods are very busy, after all."

Throughout the conversation, I'd been trying to ascertain the validity of this odd woman's statements by paying careful attention to the movements of her face, the intonation of her voice, her perspiration, and anything else that could've betrayed a lie. Unfortunately, everything about the way she carried herself was normal to the point of abnormality, almost like the so-called goddess knew what I was going to do before I did it and was having a bit of fun. It was unsettling, to say the least.

I knew how to play her game to a certain degree, but she was far superior, to a point where it extended beyond the capabilities of a human being. That's what convinced me she really was who she claimed to be.

"If that's the case, then may I ask why I was summoned here?"

"Wow, you're a quick one. I'm giving you a choice. You can have your soul wiped clean so that you'll be reborn as a brand-new person. You'll be a cute little baby without any idea of who you used to be! Or, in exchange for taking on a little request of mine, I can transport your soul into another world and allow you to be reincarnated with the knowledge and experience from your previous life intact."

So, if I went with the former option, I wouldn't be me anymore. I'd become an entirely different person. The latter option would, in a sense, allow me to continue my current life. That seemed like a far more appealing proposition.

Spending my entire life as a weapon only to be betrayed and

killed by my master in the end was an incredibly painful way to die. Starting again with my memories intact was a good chance for a do-over.

However, I could think of only one reason why I was handed this offer. The goddess's "little request" was obvious, and I knew I wouldn't like it.

"So, regarding the condition for the second option... Who do you want me to kill?"

"Ever the sharp one, aren't you? That'll make my job much easier. Though I'd expect nothing less from the soul I set my eyes on. I want you to assassinate a hero in a world of swords and magic. I need it done within eighteen years of your birth in that new world."

"A world of swords and magic? A hero? Are you making this up?"

No sooner had I asked the question than knowledge of that world flooded into my mind. Instantly, I knew about the structure of that place, the art of "magic," the culture, and the level of technological advancement. I even learned about the concept of "heroes," such as the one I had been tasked with eliminating.

It was a world completely different from my own.

"This hero we're talking about saved the world, didn't he? Why does he need to be killed?" I asked.

"Sixteen years from now, after this hero defeats the Demon King and saves the world, he will use his power for his own selfish desires, plunging the world into chaos on a scale that will far surpass the reign of the Demon King. Then, two years after that, or eighteen years from now, that world will fall to complete ruin. I would like you to kill him before any of this comes to pass."

"In other words, once the hero overthrows the Demon King,

he'll have outlived his usefulness," I surmised. Somehow, I felt an affinity for that man who would become a villain.

"We would have left him alone if he didn't cause any trouble, but he just had to go and make such a mess of things that I had to get involved. Ugh, how annoying!" the goddess whined.

This was a world where magic existed, and a good number of people possessed physical strength that far surpassed what was possible in my world. Their level of technology ranged from as far back as the Middle Ages to as recent as the mid-eighteenth century, though magic likely supplanted a lot of the more advanced science my world had.

My soul was to be transported there for the sole purpose of assassinating a hero.

"So I'm to dispose of this hero once he kills the Demon King and is no longer needed. Will I have to worry about suffering the same fate once I kill him?"

"Didn't I just explain this? It's only because he's causing so much trouble that we have to get involved. Plus, you lack his power, and if you had the capability of obtaining it, I wouldn't have chosen you in the first place."

The goddess put a hand to my chin and gave me a bewitching smile.

"We chose an assassin because no soldier, knight, or sorcerer would've been able to kill the hero while staying within the bounds of normal human capability. Only a highly skilled assassin is capable of carrying out this job."

"So I have to kill this hero, who happens to greatly exceed the strength of an ordinary man, while remaining a humble human myself."

The reason for our difference in strength had been placed

into my mind along with the information I was given earlier. The humans born in that world of swords and magic had a certain limitation placed on their abilities. From a very young age, heroes were able to break through that limitation and could become far more powerful and superior to other human beings.

The goddess, or whoever else was in charge, allowed only one hero to exist at a time.

Thus, if a hero went rogue and decided to rampage across the world, there'd be no one who could stop them. No other person could hope to best the hero in battle. That's why this situation called for assassination.

"I understand the nature of this hero, more or less. He's a monster. Given what I know, I'm sure I can kill him. However, I'm going to need abilities on the very high end of the human spectrum," I said.

"Sure, I can help you out there. You'll be equipped with the strongest possible specs a human can have, though still within reason. You will also be allowed to choose skills that would otherwise have been assigned to you at random," the goddess explained.

Suddenly, countless skill options flooded my mind. In the world of swords and magic, people were assigned, at most, five random skills at birth. Being given the ability to choose freely from a seemingly infinite pool of skills was no small task.

Rather than simply choosing the most powerful skills, I thought it best to choose skills with strong compatibility. That way they'd add up to more than the sum of their parts.

"...You can't choose the skills for me, can you?" I asked.

"Aw, is critical thinking not your strong suit? It would be thrilling to watch you struggle to complete the job with the weakest skills I could possibly give you, but... How about this? I'll give you three days to mull it over, so choose wisely. Of course, that is only on the condition that you accept my request."

"I have a number of questions I'd like to ask first. From what I've gleaned, it seems you're not able to interfere excessively in worldly matters, but isn't that exactly what you're doing right now by sending my soul to this other world to do your dirty work?"

"You're not wrong. Occasionally, however, it just so happens that a world is short on souls and needs an influx from another world. Then there are cases where, *coincidentally*, the soul-cleansing process goes wrong and memories and knowledge are accidentally left intact, and *coincidentally*, that person is born with great strength and powerful skills. That is the limit to which we can interfere. Unfortunately, this hero situation isn't one where the world can be saved through conventional means."

Evidently, the goddess was doing the most she could within her limited framework.

"Next question. I have to kill him within eighteen years, right? Can I just off him as soon as I'm ready?"

"Ah, no, that won't do. Wait until he kills the Demon King, at least. Only the hero is capable of defeating the Demon King, so offing him before he gets the chance would doom the world in a different way."

"I see. How many other souls have you lured here and enticed with this same proposition?"

It was hard to imagine I'd be the only person being sent to the world of swords and magic with their memories intact in order to try to assassinate the hero. If I were in the goddess's position, I would try to up my chances by placing as many pieces on the board as I possibly could.

"Oh, now that's a shrewd question. I can see how you were

able to become your world's most notorious assassin... The answer is none. For now, it's just you. Even if I am a goddess, there's no way I can pass off multiple assassins being reincarnated with all with their memories intact as pure coincidence."

*For now, she says.* I made a note of that remark.

"Last question. Which is more important to you: saving the world or killing the hero? If it's the former, then in the event that an opportunity to save the world without killing the hero presents itself, would that be good enough?"

"Saving the world is the primary goal, of course. Yes, if there was a way to secure a bright future for the world that didn't involve the hero's death, then that would be fine... If you really think you can make that happen, you're more than welcome to try," the goddess said with an unnerving smile.

"Got it. I accept your request. I'll be reincarnated into the world of swords and magic. I do have one request of my own, however. I would prefer to be born into a family of moderate wealth. I'll need an environment where I can train to the fullest."

"Ah, there's no need to worry about that. You're being reincarnated as the scion of House Tuatha Dé. They're that world's greatest family of assassins. You will have every resource you need available to you, so please work hard to raise your abilities to the maximum of human potential. Once you choose your skills, I will transfer your soul to your new world."

The goddess disappeared, and I broke into a bit of laughter. I couldn't believe that even after being given a chance at a second life, I was still going to be stuck as an assassin.

I'd sworn to myself that if I got a second shot at life, I would live only for myself. Now I actually was getting another chance, with my memories of my past life intact no less, but I'd be a tool right from the get-go. The irony wasn't lost on me...

Still, I wasn't about to complain. I'd been given eighteen years to kill a single person, and I'd get to continue living as myself despite having already died.

This time, I promised to live for myself and find happiness.

My first day was spent sorting through all the skills that had been shoved into my mind.

It was critical that I had not only a deep understanding of the skills themselves but also of the world I was going to be reborn into.

The total number of skills was absurd. To be exact, there were 123,851.

In the world of swords and magic, people were assigned skills randomly at birth. There were many skills that didn't seem to have any practical uses: Animal Cry, Dishwashing, Speedy Dressing, and Cross-dressing, to name a few.

Skills were divided into five ranks: S, A, B, C, and D, and I could choose only one from each.

S: 1/100,000,000 chance

A: 1/1,000,000 chance

B: 1/10,000 chance

C: 1/100 chance

D: 1/1 chance

The likelihood of being given a skill differed depending on the rank. Theoretically, it was possible to be born with a skill from every rank. But the odds of getting an S-Rank skill alone were one in one hundred million. That meant the probability of being born with a skill from all five ranks was...

…one in one hundred quintillion.

Considering that, I felt extremely fortunate to be given the privilege of choosing my skills. Most people were born with only a single D-Rank skill.

I decided that the best way to choose my skills would be to select a skill from the most powerful category, S Rank, and then select subsequent skills that would best complement it.

"As one would expect given such low odds, each of the S-Rank skills is a force to be reckoned with," I muttered.

Merely possessing an S-Rank skill was enough to put someone among the strongest people in the world.

**Magic Blade Summon:** Allows the user to summon and wield a magic blade that adjusts to the user's strength.

This one seemed a little plain at first, but the magic blade was outrageously powerful. You could cleave a mountain in half with this skill.

**Holy Vigor:** Envelops the user in a shining golden aura that substantially increases strength, defense, and agility.

The word *substantially* was a bit vague, but I was willing to bet that even an infant could take down a tank with their bare hands using this skill. It had great versatility. If I was unsure of what skill to pick, this one seemed like a solid choice.

**Seal of Subordination:** Enables the user to control their opponent by placing a mark on the target's forehead.

With this skill, you could create your own personal army of people under your complete control. There was a catch, however. When the mark is made, the target has the chance to resist its influence by using their mana. Simply put, the user's mana needs to be greater than the target's.

**Monster Creation:** Allows the user to create monsters using a great variety of materials, and command them in battle.

This skill would allow you to create the monster army of your dreams. It seemed monsters were primarily made using corpses and magical stones. I could think of countless uses for this one.

These were just a few of the S-Rank skills available to me.

When choosing my skill, the first thing I needed to confirm was that I would have enough firepower. The hero far surpassed all standards of human strength, so even if I found him in a defenseless situation, I'd no doubt lack the necessary strength to even put a scratch on him. This meant I'd need to make sure I had the ability to kill him with a single strike to some vital point.

My chosen skill was also going to need a great deal of versatility. Any number of unexpected developments could occur during my attempt to assassinate the hero. Flexibility would be required if I was to recover from unforeseen circumstances and carry out my mission.

Taking all of that into consideration, there was no better choice for my S-Rank skill than Rapid Recovery.

**Rapid Recovery:** Increases the recovery rate of stamina, mana, healing, etc. Recovery rate is increased by a factor of one hundred. This multiplier can be further increased with training.

At first glance, this ability didn't seem all that impressive, but he who can run the farthest will always survive. Being able to easily replenish your mana, which seemed to be the closest equivalent in that world to reloading a gun, was also attractive. Plus, it could be used to recover quickly from illness or injury.

I'd also be able to function on very little sleep, and my stamina recovery rate would allow me to train for extended periods of time. After considering the rules of my new world, an accelerated rate of recovery seemed best.

If the goddess hadn't given me a rundown of the world I was headed to, I doubt I would've chosen this skill.

"This is easily the best choice for my A-Rank skill," I said.

**Spell Weaver:** Grants the ability to create new spells.

In the world of swords and magic, spells were magical abilities bestowed upon people by the gods. There were only about one hundred standard god-given skills that could be used.

However, Spell Weaver allowed me to make my own spells, allowing for infinite possibilities. Figuring that I'd be able to use my world's superior knowledge of science, I reasoned that I'd make great use of this skill.

"After choosing Rapid Recovery, this one's a no-brainer for my B-rank skill."

**Limitless Growth:** Enables one to break through natural limitations.

While this skill sounded really strong, it was pointless on its own. Normally, removing growth limits would be meaningless. Limits are often so high that most people don't reach them even if they spend their entire lives training. However, it formed an excellent combination with the inexhaustible supply of stamina afforded by Rapid Recovery.

For my C-Rank skill, I prioritized versatility and chose Martial Arts.

**Martial Arts:** Grants superb hand-to-hand combat capability and heightened reflexes.

This skill had inferior strength compared to weapon-specific skills such as Sword Arts or Spear Arts. But as an assassin, I already knew how to handle just about any type of weapon, so martial arts seemed like the best choice for me. I had no reason to choose a skill that limited myself to a particular weapon.

"I'm not sure the gods are aware this D-Rank skill even exists."

For my D Rank, I decided to go with a rather amusing skill. It wasn't particularly strong, but its effectiveness could vary greatly depending on how I used it. While all outward appearances pointed to it being boring, I was confident it would become my trump card.

In addition to skills, I also needed to choose my elemental affinity, which determined what kind of magic I could cast.

In the world of swords and magic, people were born with one elemental affinity; on rare occasions, a person could be born with two. There were four basic elemental affinities: earth, fire, wind, and water. These were joined by a pair of rarer elemental affinities: light and dark.

Spells were awarded by the gods after repeated use of your elemental affinity.

The elemental affinity I went with was Total Affinity.

Total Affinity allowed you to use all four of the basic elemental affinities, but neither of the rarer ones. This wasn't without a drawback, however. As a trade-off for being able to use so many kinds of magic, the improvement rate for each of them was halved.

"If my improvement rate is cut in half, then I'll just train twice as hard. That shouldn't be a problem, since my recovery rate is increased a hundredfold."

I decided the merit of being able to use four elements out-weighed the demerit of a slower growth rate.

After only two days into my allotted time, I'd chosen all my skills and my elemental affinity, but I decided not to tell the goddess yet. It was better to spend any time I had left considering my choices and looking over all the skills to see if there was a better combination.

After spending my final day thinking through my options, I decided to stick with what I'd chosen the previous day.

I'd use Rapid Recovery and Limitless Growth to improve my fundamental abilities. Martial Arts would sharpen my movements. Spell Weaver and Total Affinity would greatly increase the tools at my disposal, and my D-Rank skill would be my ace in the hole.

"You seem to have found a combination that you are satisfied with," the goddess declared, appearing before me.

"Yep, this is the best I could come up with."

"Huh, you chose Rapid Recovery for your S-Rank skill. A bit dull, isn't it? Same goes for your A Rank. I'd forgotten that D-Rank skill even exists... Humans truly are fascinating creatures."

"Are you making fun of me?"

"Far from it. I'm praising you. If you'd simply chosen the strongest skills without much thought, you would've had no chance of defeating the hero. He's got more than thirty skills after all."

On top of abnormal physical strength and mana, a hero was also born with thirty skills from the S and A Ranks. Of those thirty, a minimum of five were S Rank. Given the ridiculous strength of those skills, I could certainly see why defeating the hero in battle was borderline impossible.

With enough training and careful preparation, however, assassination seemed doable.

I chose my skills specifically for the purpose of killing the hero, whose many abilities had granted him monstrous strength from birth.

"Okay, time for your reincarnation. Full disclosure: It's going to be awkward for a while. You're going to have to live as a baby while retaining your current knowledge and personality. Just try to bear it, okay? I'm sure being born into the Tuatha Dé clan of assassins will be anything but boring. Your mother is beautiful, you know. And thank goodness for that! I can only imagine how uncomfortable it would have been if you made a repulsed face every time you had to breastfeed! That'd be a pretty nasty shock for any parent. Oh, one more warning. I recommend you change your manner of speech. It'll be off-putting to hear a child speak the way you do now."

Without waiting for my reply, the goddess snapped her fingers.

My body transformed into particles of light.

I was about to begin a new life.

Hopefully, the Tuatha Dé clan of assassins would provide me with everything I needed to prepare.

I felt someone wipe my body and wrap me in a soft blanket.

*Oh yeah. The goddess said I should be careful with my vernacular to avoid making people uncomfortable. I'll keep that in mind.*

I tried to move, but I was even weaker than I'd expected.

When I opened my eyes, I found my vision extremely blurry. The world steadily came into focus.

I was in the arms of a beautiful silver-haired woman. She'd been thumping me on the back for the last few minutes in order to make me cry. I felt something welling up inside me. Abandoning myself to the impulse, I began to cry violently.

The woman held me tight.

"My precious little Lugh."

Evidently that was to be my name.

My neck movement was still fairly restricted, so I couldn't get a good look at my surroundings, but given the health of my mother, the quality of the blanket, and the furnishings within my field of vision, I could guess that I'd been born into a wealthy family.

*Come to think of it, the language of this world should be entirely different, right? How am I able to understand it? I wondered.*

With superb timing, words from the goddess echoed in my mind, saying, *"This is a special gift just for today so you can get your bearings. Make sure you study hard and learn the language!"*

I heard footsteps approaching, and a number of people entered the room.

"How's the child, Esri?" one voice asked.

"He's a healthy boy... Cian, are we going to bring this child into the clan, too?"

"This country needs House Tuatha Dé. With our skill as assassins, we are the only ones who can remove the malignant tumors that plague our land."

"...I don't like it. I'm terrified of losing him like we lost Ruff."

"We'll raise him to be strong so that doesn't happen. We won't repeat the same mistakes. Trust me, Esri, I don't want to lose a second child, either."

This man, Cian, spoke sternly in a voice that brooked no argument, but there was a tangible hint of warmth behind his words.

It sounds like Ruff was either my brother or my sister. Apparently, they'd died in the family line of work.

Even so, there were plenty of benefits to being born into a family with such a dangerous profession.

All the tricks and knowledge I gained as an assassin in my previous life were for killing the people of that world, where magic didn't exist. The Tuatha Dé clan, on the other hand, had been operating in the world of swords and magic for generations. They'd have the know-how I needed to become an assassin here.

Noble status meant I'd enjoy all the things that came with considerable wealth, and I'd have no trouble finding enough time to train.

"Very well. I'll abide by your decision. But know that if I lose this child, I don't think I'll be able to bear the pain again..."

"I swear to you, I will not let Lugh die."

Still hugging me tight, my mother kissed my father.

Then they both leaned in to kiss me.

When I'd heard I was going to be born into a clan of assassins, I didn't exactly expect such a wholesome family environment. My parents seemed to genuinely love me.

As far back as I could remember, I'd only ever shown affection as an act. It was merely a simple bargaining tool to help with my work.

I wondered why my parents' affection made me feel so strange... Perhaps this was what true love felt like?

*Living here may give me a chance to study the concept of love.*

Assassins didn't need love, but I knew it'd be essential if I was to live as a person and not a tool.

Before I knew it, five years had passed since my reincarnation.

Learning how to read and write took a long time because of my youth. Two of those years were spent waiting for my brain to develop enough for me to be able to study at all. Still, my rate of learning was extraordinarily quick for a child my age.

As a result, my parents and the family's servants were all beside themselves in shock at my progress. To them, I must have seemed like a prodigy. At first, I tried to slow my development so that others wouldn't grow suspicious of me, but acting mature for my age seemed to delight those around me, so after a while, I stopped holding back.

I did make sure my speech and mannerisms matched those appropriate for a child.

I played the part of a perfect son for my parents to ensure an ideal training environment. Surprisingly, I came to truly love them over time, and I genuinely wanted to make them happy.

Around the time I turned five, the number of things I could do greatly increased.

Rapid Recovery was a boon.

My young body tired easily, but because I quickly recovered from fatigue, I could stay active for long periods of time. As my muscles continued to develop, my strength far surpassed that of others my age.

On one particular day, I found myself in the library. This great study was truly impressive, even by the standards of nobles. Collected on its shelves were innumerable records gathered by the family as well as many more volumes amassed from every corner of the world. Just about anything I could have wanted to learn was written in one of the books in that library.

"My new family has a lot more red in their ledger than I'd expected," I muttered.

House Tuatha Dé was a noble house of the kingdom of Alvan—itself one of the four major kingdoms on the continent— and the head of the house claimed the rank of baron.

Baron was one of the lowest ranks among nobles, and as such, they didn't hold much land. But despite that, Tuatha Dé was extremely wealthy.

On the surface, House Tuatha Dé was a respected family that possessed the best medical knowledge in the kingdom. It was well known that they'd used their superior curative methods to earn themselves great rewards and the favor of the royal family as well as many other lauded houses.

It was hidden from the public eye, however, that the Tuatha Dé clan headed a group of assassins that carried out requests for the royal family and a certain dukedom. They used murder as a tool to remove those who had become a liability for the country.

Life and death. With control over both, House Tuatha Dé had come to possess great wealth and political influence, despite their outward appearance being rather humble.

"...I have an impressive heritage. Successfully operating as a family of killers for seven generations is no small feat."

What's more, they had done so while holding on to a secret that would flip the country on its head if it were to ever come to light.

The kingdom would probably jump at the chance to dispose of House Tuatha Dé if it meant the public would never learn of the arrangement it shared with the royal family. It was likely that the Tuatha Dé lineage held secrets that prevented such a thing from happening.

"All right, that seems like enough for today." Right as I closed the book, there was a knock at the door.

"Master Lugh, my lord wishes to see you," someone called.

*That time already, is it?* I thought.

From early childhood, members of the Tuatha Dé clan were given training comprised of magical drills as well as regular physical exercise adjusted for one's current strength. It was a very efficient training regimen.

However, once you turned five, the *real* training began, and the difficulty was upped significantly. I did my best to learn what I could from my father. As the head of the clan, he was as good a teacher as I could've asked for.

On that day, it seemed we were using an underground facility for training. Entry into that place was normally forbidden.

"Lugh, from this day forth, I am going to begin sharing with you the secrets of our unrivaled medical and assassination knowledge. But first, repeat to me the family creed."

"The Tuatha Dé clan's skills are only to be used to ensure the prosperity of the kingdom," I parroted.

"How does our medical technology benefit the country?"

"By saving the lives of major figures."

"That's exactly right. Our family has little political power. However, if we can save the lives of those above us, they will be able to make our country a better place. Next question. For what purpose does the Tuatha Dé clan carry out assassinations?"

"To eliminate those who have become an unhealthy presence in our lands. We remove people who are of foul mind in order to prevent them from causing excess damage."

Without falter, I recited the Tuatha Dé family principles that my father had repeated to me countless times.

We existed to keep those who were beneficial to our country alive, and we killed those who would cause harm. Our family brought prosperity to the country through our control over life and death.

"Right again," said Father. "If, for example, a noble was to go mad with ambition and start a rebellion, even if such an uprising fell, the toll it would take would be felt throughout the kingdom. Our fellow countrymen would be made to fight and kill each other. However, we have the ability to prevent such a situation from occurring before a single commoner dies. No matter how cunning a person is, no matter how above the law they may seem, they die at our hand just as sure as any other."

The blade of the Tuatha Dé clan was most commonly turned toward the nobles of this country.

In the Alvanian Kingdom, the nobility had significant sway

in matters of the court. With that power, they were often able to escape punishment. They'd built such a safety net for themselves that even the royal family had trouble going after them. However, all the political power in the world couldn't save a man with a dagger in his throat. Such was their fate when the Tuatha Dé clan was called upon to dispose of them.

As my more intense training was finally about to begin, it was from then on that I would gain the strength needed to fulfill my family's long-standing duty.

"Lugh, in what way are martial artists similar to doctors?" asked my father.

"Hmm. In order to efficiently best a person in combat, you need to understand the human body."

Martial artists had a good understanding of anatomy. Such knowledge allowed them precise control over their movements and gave them the information necessary to aim for an opponent's weak points to quickly subdue them.

"Very good. From my point of view, though, the techniques of martial artists are mere child's play. They don't have a thorough enough understanding of the human body. We Tuatha Dé are different. No one knows how to end a person's life more efficiently than a doctor."

My father came to stop in front of a massive dungeon full of prisoners.

"These are prisoners both native and foreign. All have been sentenced to death and were therefore offered to the Tuatha Dé clan as human subjects," he explained.

"I see. No one will care if we kill these people. I can't imagine a more useful resource than human subjects, both for medical study and for assassination."

Truly, my family was impressive. They had used the study of medicine to improve the killing arts as well. There was no more efficient way to study both how to save lives and how to end them than by experimenting on actual living people.

Whether they'd admit it or not, I'm sure the doctors in my previous world would feel a pang of jealousy were they to hear about this. I'm sure they would like to test new medicines and surgeries on people, but they have no choice but to use guinea pigs instead. If doctors were able to use living humans for all of their experiments, medicine would be hundreds of years more advanced.

"...You don't seem fazed by this in the slightest. I was terrified when I was brought here at your age. I even cursed my own father's name," said Cian.

"I do feel some reluctance, but it makes sense to me from a logical standpoint," I replied.

"You truly are a gifted boy. To think you already possess this level of logic and reason at such a young age. As your father, I'm looking forward to seeing the kind of man you become. To commemorate this event, the task for your first lesson will be to commit murder. I would like you to kill five people. Take this knife. I'll leave the method up to you, so kill them however you like. They've all been administered a muscle relaxant, so they won't be able to put up a fight. But before you begin, I have one more question. Why do you think I'm asking you to do this?"

All I had to do was off a few people who couldn't even fight back. Even at the age of five, that was fairly easy with a knife in my hand. I wondered if perhaps my father wanted me to memorize efficient killing techniques, but that didn't seem like the answer.

"To get used to killing? You want me to kill people for practice so I don't hesitate when it comes to the real thing," I answered.

"Correct. Humans are extremely reluctant to take the lives of others. This resistance to killing is so great that soldiers sent to war will often hesitate in eliminating their targets. An acquaintance of mine in the army once told me that only one in three people are able to do what needs to be done on their first campaign."

"Understood. I'll get used to killing now to avoid hesitating during my first assassination."

Without delay, I moved toward the many jailed criminals who'd been condemned to death.

"Before I kill them, I have a question," I said.

"Go ahead," my father urged.

"Why did you raise me to be hesitant to kill? The picture books that Mother reads to me all speak of the preciousness of life, and you've taught me to 'love thy neighbor.' These emotions will only distract from my job," I explained.

In my previous life, my organization taught me that human lives were meaningless. As a result, I'd never once hesitated to take lives, nor had I ever felt guilty about it.

As if in opposition of their very profession, the Tuatha Dé family had raised me to hold virtuous ideals and keep a wholesome heart. These were both new to me, as I'd lacked them in my previous life.

I couldn't help but worry that such feelings and ideals would only serve to dull my inner blade.

"If you lack a normal human value system, you'll be incapable of understanding how other people think," my father replied. "Knowing how to think and behave like a normal person is an essential weapon for an assassin. Also, never forget that we are people first and foremost, not tools. We don't follow orders blindly. Only accept a job after you are sure it is in our nation's best interest. I want you to keep that in mind. I'm raising you to become a capable assassin who can do what needs to be done, but above all else, I want you to have a heart," Cian detailed.

"I half get it and half don't. I'll have to think about that," I said in reply.

The warmth that would dull my mind would also make me stronger somehow. It seemed illogical, and yet, I could already feel changes within myself. Surely my father's words would help me be happy. After all, I was going to live as a person this time, not a weapon.

*All right, time to do what I have to do.*

For the first time, I felt hesitation and guilt over killing, but even so, I didn't run away.

This was an essential step to begin my life as Lugh Tuatha Dé.

By the time I was seven, my physical strength had increased significantly thanks to my father's training regimen and my own personal practice. The improved stamina provided by Rapid Recovery had helped me last longer at both.

Cian had discovered the presence of my Rapid Recovery skill during one of my regular medical examinations and had been assigning me extra strength drills that took its effects into account.

One day, I was sent to a mountain within our territory for a mission where I would practice hunting.

While called "hunting," that was not to imply the purpose was simply to gather food. Trekking through the dangerous terrain would help hone my stamina and agility, and through hunting, I was to sharpen my techniques of pursuit and stealth and my ability to kill quickly.

Beasts had much sharper senses than humans. If I was able to sneak up on a wild animal and kill it in a single strike, then assassinating a human would surely be a piece of cake in comparison.

The mountain itself was free of human development. As such, there were no roads. Wading through the thick, overgrown grass was a trial in itself.

Having set a route, I carefully examined the ground for the faintest sign of potential prey.

"Looks like I've found my target for the day."

Rabbit droppings—and fresh, at that. There were also foot-prints that led through the grass. At a glance, I could tell they belonged to an Alvanian rabbit, which are known as arte rabbits. They're big enough to consume large dogs if given the chance.

I dashed swiftly through the trees, cloaking myself in mana and becoming as quick as the wind. I still didn't know how to use magic, but I had been studying how to manipulate mana.

About halfway to my prey, I jumped into a tree and began to leap from branch to branch. Normally, they would've broken under my weight, but my use of mana kept me light enough that such a thing didn't happen.

It was a nice feeling to manipulate mana as easily as breathing.

In only a few moments, I sighted my prey. Roughly thirty meters ahead, a massive rabbit was digging up some yams and hav-ing a feast.

With me situated downwind, the creature wouldn't pick up on my scent. Rabbits had excellent hearing, however, so it was sure to notice me if I got any closer.

Taking care not to do anything that would give myself away, I hung upside down with my legs hooked over a branch I had been perching on and drew the bow that was slung over my back.

The custom-built bowstring was strung so tight that even adults would've had difficulty drawing it back. This was a weapon that required enhanced physical ability.

I released the arrow, and it immediately found purchase. I pierced the large rabbit's head in a single shot, killing it instantly.

"All right, that concludes this morning's training."

I leaped down from the tree and approached the animal's

corpse. After draining the blood and butchering the body, I covered the pieces I wanted in tree bark and placed them in the basket on my back.

On the way home, I also gathered some berries, herbs, and mushrooms.

"Come oooooon, Lugh, won't you let me do the cooking today?"

"You promised to let me cook on days when I hunt. Please have a seat, Mother."

After I returned to the estate, I headed straight for the kitchen and began to prepare lunch using the rabbit I'd butchered this morning.

Not only did my meal promise to be delicious, but it would also help me grow stronger. In order to build a tough physique, I needed to understand nutritional science and take great care with what I ate. Back in my old world, athletes were often given a personal nutritionist from a young age for that very reason.

As advanced as House Tuatha Dé was in many fields of study, their understanding of nutritional science was rather lacking. This was why I tried to cook for myself at least once every few days to ensure I was getting the balanced diet I needed.

Normally, I did my best to obediently do as my mother, Esri, said, but I refused to concede to her this time. I was cooking for my own benefit after all.

Building a strong body was my number one priority. No matter how skilled I became, it wouldn't mean much if I didn't have the proper power to back it up.

"Boooo, that's not fair." My mother pouted, puffing out her cheeks. As I was trying to think of a response, my father walked into the room.

"Esri, it's no trouble if Lugh wants to cook this time, is it? Lately, I've been starting to think he's just as promising a chef as he is an assassin. I'm sure whatever he makes will be good. After all, it's thanks to your wonderful teaching that he's become so acquainted with the kitchen in the first place," he said.

"It's not the food I'm worried about. My mouth is watering already just thinking about how good it will be. As his mother, it fills me with pride that our little Lugh is such a skilled cook. The problem is all his brilliant ideas are putting my cooking to shame," Esri responded, glaring daggers at me.

"Mother, you're giving me too much credit. I still have a ways to go before my cooking catches up to yours," I said.

"Oh-ho, seems he's not just skilled as a chef but also as a flatterer!" My father guffawed.

"Oh, enough, Cian!" Mother snapped.

This was the scene of a truly happy family. Mother always got this way, and when Father wasn't working or training, he was always smiling and cracking jokes.

At times, my father even got so cheery that you couldn't see a hint of the cold-blooded killer he really was, further evidence of his status as a master assassin. His targets would never suspect him before they met their end. He was exceptionally skilled at playing the part of a generous and sociable person who put others at ease. I'd come to wonder, though, if that wasn't an act at all. Maybe he truly was the kind of person who genuinely loved his wife and hopelessly doted on his son.

I decided to make cream stew.

Rabbit meat had a mild taste similar to poultry and went well with thick seasoning. The main sources of flavor in this stew were a mellow soup stock prepared with homemade dried mushrooms, and fresh goat milk and butter.

With mushrooms, root vegetables, milk, and ample meat, this stew contained all the nutrients I needed, making it perfect for my growth.

"This pot you made sure is convenient, Lugh," my mother said. "I can't believe you were able to make such a thick, delicious stew in just thirty minutes. Are you sure you're not cheating with some kind of spell? Oh, the long hours I've wasted laboring over my own broths in the past!"

"There's nothing magical about a pressure cooker, Mother. I happened to find out about this technique in a book from the study and thought I'd try it out," I lied.

The principles behind pressure cooking were straightforward. All you had to do was seal the pot so liquid and vapor couldn't escape. That caused steam to build up and raise the pressure in the pot, which in turn helped cook the food inside faster. It wasn't particularly complicated.

"Well, it looks like magic to me!" Cian exclaimed. "You really are smart, Lugh. I have long known that pressure causes this type of phenomenon, but I never would've thought to use it for cooking. This flexible way of thinking will serve you well as an assassin, my boy!" my father extolled.

It could, admittedly, get a bit embarrassing when my parents praised me for every single thing I did.

Before long, my cream stew was finished. It was thick and white and looked every bit as decadent as it smelled.

Last year, the family had purchased a large number of goats.

Since then, we had plenty of goat milk and butter to use in our cooking.

"Father, Mother, please sit. Let's eat," I said.

Thus, we sat down to eat a family lunch.

Mother and I did most of the cooking in the Tuatha Dé household, which was quite rare for nobility. The reason for such an anomaly was rather simple: My mother loved to cook.

When I was five, I'd told her that I'd wanted to start cooking, and she'd been positively thrilled to teach me. Recently, however, my mother's fear of my cooking ability overtaking hers had stoked a strange sense of competitiveness within her.

Perhaps it's strange for a son to say this, but something about that combative spirit made her look youthful and cute.

That said, I could've done without some of the moments when she babied me. Even though I was now seven years old, she'd recently asked me if I wanted to suckle.

I set the food down on the table. In addition to the rabbit stew, we were also having some salad and bread.

The dining table was quite modest, given the Tuatha Dé family's noble status. Our meals typically consisted of a main dish, bread, various side dishes, salads, soups, and the occasional dessert.

"This stew is stupendous, Lugh. You would have to be a genius to come up with something like this," praised my mother.

"Too true! You can't find stew like this in the capital, even. I bet we could sell this for quite the profit," my father added.

"That's a bit of an exaggeration. This isn't anything to get so excited about," I said.

"You're too humble, Lugh. Ah, I have an idea! We should serve this stew at this year's harvest festival! Everyone will love it!"

"Hmm, I think that's a great idea. The ingredients are cheap, so we'll stay under the festival's budget even if we make enough for everyone in our domain. Perhaps this could even become a specialty dish for our land that our people will come to be proud of!"

Seeing Father dote on me as he did, I sometimes started to doubt if he was actually the head of the renowned Tuatha Dé clan of assassins... But it didn't bother me. It wasn't so bad to have such loving parents.

I was certainly having more fun with cooking than I ever had in my previous life.

Truthfully, I'd always been a decent cook. One of the easiest ways to infiltrate any venue to reach a target was by working as a chef. I'd learned the culinary arts because it was convenient for my job as a hired killer. The food I'd made back then, along with the many cuisines I'd sampled for research, had probably all tasted objectively better than the stew.

Curiously, this dish I'd prepared for my parents somehow tasted better than anything I'd known in my previous life. Perhaps it was because I was experiencing feelings my former self had never known.

After we finished eating, my mother began to gather up the dishes and take them to the kitchen. It was a rule in this household that those who didn't cook had to clean up.

With a serious expression on his face, my father looked me up and down. Once a week before afternoon training, he'd check to see how much I'd grown. Based on that assessment, he'd choose the contents of that day's training accordingly.

"You've grown enough to be able to handle surgery. Today you will receive your Tuatha Dé Mystic Eyes," he declared.

I gulped.

*So it's that time already, huh?* I'd seen the term "Mystic Eyes" show up in various documents in the study.

While I'd been born with the same silver hair as my mother, I had the eyes of neither parent. Mother's eyes were a vivid shade of blue and Father's eyes were the color of ash, but my eyes were black.

As it happened, my father's eyes were black at birth. His eyes had turned gray later in life. That ashen color was proof that one bore the Mystic Eyes of House Tuatha Dé.

The implant surgery had been tested on hundreds of prisoners on death row. It was highly difficult and required mana to perform, but if successful, the patient would gain incredible perceptive ability.

"I'm ready, Father," I said.

"Are you scared?"

"No, I trust your skill."

He may have acted like a total sap when it was just the family, but when it came time to act as the head of the clan, Cian Tuatha Dé was a true professional.

"You have no need to worry. I promise you the surgery will be successful," he assured me, and for good reason. This was not the first time he'd performed this procedure.

When I awoke, I was greeted by total darkness. Father had wrapped a bandage around my head after finishing the operation.

Once he'd judged it safe to remove the gauze, which was only moments later thanks to my Rapid Recovery skill, I did so and opened my eyes. Immediately, I was overtaken by just how much my vision had been altered.

There was a marked increase in my perception. My long-distance vision had improved as well. Objects in motion appeared far clearer, and it seemed I'd even acquired a stronger sense of depth.

I'd also acquired the ability to see mana. Normally, mana was something one could only sense, yet now I could faintly make out its flow within my body.

Being able to see an opponent's mana would allow me to predict their movements, a major advantage in any fight. These new eyes of mine were basically cheating.

Unfortunately, such a sudden increase in capability was more than my brain could handle at first, and I was struck by a massive headache. I knew that, before long, Rapid Recovery and Limitless Growth would help my mind adapt and process this new information. For the time being, I would just have to endure.

"Father, it worked. I can see more than ever before," I said.

"That's a relief. One day, Lugh, I'll teach you how to perform this surgery so that you can pass it down to your child."

"I understand."

Developed three generations ago, this implantation surgery was one of House Tuatha Dé's greatest secrets.

"With that business finished, I have good news to share with you. I'm finally able to grant you something that you've desired for a long time," my father revealed.

"Did you find me a mentor who can teach me how to use magic?!" I excitedly asked.

Learning how to cast spells without a teacher was impossible. As such, I've wanted a proper instructor since birth. Both Mother and Father were quite used to using mana, but neither knew how to cast proper spells, so they couldn't teach me. I'd been wanting to learn how to use magic for a long time so that I could finally put my Spell Weaver skill to use.

"That's right. Your mentor will arrive next week. I suggest you devote yourself to preparing for their arrival," my father instructed.

An absent element in my previous world, magic, I thought, was likely to end up being a key to the successful assassination of the hero.

My work aside, I was earnestly interested in learning how magic worked. I could hardly contain my excitement.

Chapter 4 | The Assassin Studies Magic

Over the years, I came to realize that my mother was an unusual person in a number of ways.

Despite her status, she loved to cook. She preferred typical home cooking to the fancy foods more commonly associated with high society. Luxurious things like jewelry and dresses didn't seem to catch her interest very much, as she possessed few of either. Often, she would try her best to avoid the many invitations she received for tea gatherings, parties, and other such social assemblies. To top it all off, she spent her free time sewing.

"I think these clothes would look great on you, Lugh," my mother said.

"...Ha-ha, they're definitely cute, but they look like girls' clothing, and they'll be difficult to move around in," I responded. The outfit was rather frilly and had an excess of decoration. I had no interest in dressing like a girl. Still, I didn't want to upset her, so I tried letting her down as gently as possible.

"What? Lugh, you really don't want to wear this?" my mother asked.

"Well...sorry."

"I worked so hard on this for you, though... It would be such a waste if you didn't wear it. Please try it on!" Putting her hands together in a begging motion, my mother bowed her head.

"They look like something a girl would wear, though." It seemed my point hadn't gone through the first time, so with this rebuttal I tried to be more direct.

"But I really think they'd look great on you!"

"Mother, you're not even denying that they look like girls' clothes…"

"If you wear them, I'll make your favorite roast duck for dinner tonight."

Growing up in the Tuatha Dé household, I'd been raised with love, and I'd come to understand what it meant to love others. For that, I was very grateful, and it's why I tried my best to be a good son for my parents.

Even so, some things were just too much.

Unfortunately, my mother was looking at me as if she was about to cry, and I caved. "Fine, I'll wear it. But you'd better make the roast duck like you promised."

"Of course! I'm going to call a painter while you're changing. The image of you in this adorable outfit needs to be captured for posterity!"

"…Now, that I won't agree to. My new mentor is arriving today. I can't make them wait."

"Oh, you're right. How disappointing…"

I'd been eagerly looking forward to the arrival of my magic instructor all day. Originally, my impatience had been because I just wanted to learn magic, but now I suddenly found myself with an even more pressing reason for hoping they'd arrive soon. No sooner had my mother started using me as her personal dress-up doll than my teacher arrived. I was saved.

"Are you satisfied yet, Mother? I need to change back to go greet my mentor," I said.

"What are you talking about? Just keep on what you're wear-ing now. I made that outfit for this very occasion, after all," she replied.

After I gave her a look of shock, Mother suddenly moved back and held the clothes I'd previously been wearing tight to her chest to keep me from retrieving them.

In my mind, I knew she was teasing me. There was no way my mother wasn't enjoying this rare chance to see me so flustered.

At the call of a servant, I made my way to the reception room, where I was greeted by a girl and her attendant. The girl was wearing a robe that could not have been more fitting for a prac-titioner of magic. As she removed her hood, silver hair tumbled down to rest at her shoulders.

I'd never seen anyone other than myself or Mother with silver hair before. This girl was exceptionally beautiful.

Her age, however, was somewhat concerning. She looked to be only around ten years old, but I knew better than to judge based on physical maturity. One look at myself was all I needed to know that making snap decisions based on how young one looked was unwise.

I could tell right away that the strength of the mana surround-ing her greatly surpassed Father's.

Just the fact that this girl was a mage had to mean she was either a noble or a knight. Given her high mana capacity, it was more likely that she was descended from a lineage of the former.

A mage was a person who possessed mana. Parents who didn't possess mana themselves rarely give birth to children who did, and as one might've expected, parents with strong mana often sired children with strong mana as well.

The country my family lived in had traditionally placed great value on people who possessed mana. Thus, it was unsurprising that a high-ranking noble family likely also bore children with greater mana.

That's exactly the reason why it fell to a noble family like House Tuatha Dé to become a clan of assassins. Only a noble was capable of killing one of their own.

My father entered the room and invited the girl to sit on the sofa before seating himself. I followed their example and sat down as well.

A servant brought us all herbal tea.

"I'm sorry for making you travel all the way here. You must have a busy schedule," my father apologized.

"No need to worry about that. The Viekone family owes much to House Tuatha Dé, in spite of your thievery," the girl replied.

"Ha-ha, calling me a thief is a bit harsh, no?" my father asked.

The girl seemed to be referring to something I was unaware of.

Whatever it was likely referred to my family's secret trade. Yet the number of people who knew about our status as assassins was very limited. Furthermore, there shouldn't have been any nobles in the Alvanian Kingdom with the name Viekone.

*Just who is this girl?* I wondered.

"So is this kid my new apprentice? I was told he was a boy," the girl inquired.

"...I am a boy," I stated.

I knew this would happen. I resolved to speak with my mother about this later.

"These clothes were made by my wife. Sewing is a hobby of hers," my father explained.

"Oh, really? Now that you mention it, she... Ahem. Anyway... Isn't he a little young to be learning magic?"

"Lugh is a special case. You may not believe me, but at seven years old, he's already more capable than most of my subordinates—on both sides of the Tuatha Dé coin, so to speak. He's a genius of your level, Dia."

"If this wasn't Cian Tuatha Dé speaking, I would've dismissed this simply as a parent being overly fond of their child. All right, I'll teach him the basics in the two weeks I've been allotted. However, if I judge him to be unworthy of my training, I'll declare this a waste of time and discontinue my instruction."

Finding the deal agreeable, my father nodded. If I was judged unworthy, I'd lose the mentor I'd waited so long for... I needed to give this my all.

Instead of the indoor training room, my teacher and I ended up using the courtyard for magic practice.

"Allow me to introduce myself. My name is Dia Viekone. I'm ten years old, but it would be unwise to underestimate me. I'm far more proficient with magic than any adult," stated the mage with considerable confidence.

"I'm Lugh Tuatha Dé. I'm seven years old. I look forward to your guidance," I answered in kind.

"Nice to meet you. First, I need to measure the strength of your mana. This training will be pointless if your mana is below average," Dia said, and she prepared a transparent marble.

"Lugh, you know how to manipulate mana, right?"

"Yes, ma'am. I learned from my father."

"You don't need to be so polite. I don't want this to feel so stiff."

"But you're my mentor."

"That's true, but…be more relaxed. Magic is tiring enough, so it would be foolish to waste energy on your speech."

Something about Dia's attitude felt curiously familiar.

Her silver hair, her facial features, and, above all, her personality reminded me of my mother.

"All right. I'll be less formal. So what am I supposed to do with this ball?" I dropped formality and started to speak in the natural voice I usually kept hidden from my parents.

It felt far better to talk that way, and Dia gave a satisfied smile.

"Hold it and fill it with mana. Continue until your mana is fully depleted. That way we'll be able to measure your mana capacity."

I directed my mana into the ball and was surprised to discover the marble really did have the ability to store it all.

Single-mindedly, I focused on transferring my mana into the marble. At first, Dia was nodding as if impressed, but after a minute passed, her expression shifted to disbelief. She even began to sweat.

"Releasing that much mana for over a minute is not normal!" she exclaimed.

"I still have plenty to spare." It wasn't a lie. I'd had yet to use even 20 percent of my mana. The fact that my mana was still vigorously flowing into the marble was proof of that.

"I-is that so? Then continue," Dia instructed.

"Understood," I replied.

By the time I passed the three-minute mark, Dia's face had totally stiffened.

My mana capacity was close to a thousand times higher than the average person's because of the amount of training I'd done. It was thanks to the information about this world from the goddess that I'd known how best to increase my capacity, and I'd worked hard to make good use of that insight.

The more you use mana, the more your maximum amount of mana will increase. This is a very slow process, however. Your maximum increases by a factor of only 0.01 percent each time you fully exhaust your mana. Complicating things further was that it took the average person around three days to fully recover their mana after exhausting it.

Even if you spent a year repeating this process fully as often as you could, it would take a year to grow your mana capacity by a single percent. Following that ratio, it would take ten years to increase it by 10 percent. Maintaining a steady release of mana in this manner until you run out was also extremely tiring, so there weren't many people who were capable of the discipline required to stick with that sort of rigorous exercise.

In my case, Rapid Recovery allowed me to recover my mana at one hundred times the normal rate, which increased a hundred-fold the efficiency with which I could train my mana. My stamina also returned to me at a similar rate, so releasing mana didn't tire me out at all.

With that in mind, I reasoned that I could increase my mana capacity by 330 percent every year. On top of that, my recovery rate from Rapid Recovery also increased as I trained, compounding the process and making it even more efficient.

Thanks to my making sure I constantly discharged mana, my

capacity had already swelled to a thousand times higher than what it was at birth. If I hadn't chosen the Limitless Growth skill, I surely would've hit my natural maximum a long time ago. That was precisely the reason I chose both Rapid Recovery and Limitless Growth.

"No matter how you look at it, this amount of mana is not normal!!!"

"I have what I have. There's nothing abnormal about taking this long to release a large mana capacity."

I had managed to multiply my mana capacity by one thousand, but that affects only the amount of mana I can store. The amount of mana you can release at once, known as instantaneous mana discharge, increases at a much slower rate through training than capacity. Instantaneous mana discharge takes longer to increase the higher your mana capacity is, so right now it takes me five times longer than the average person. That's why I'm so interested in this marble.

If I filled several of these marbles with a vast quantity of mana and built up a collection of them, I could use them in times of need to instantly release a much higher amount of mana than my instantaneous mana discharge was capable of.

As if it had heard my thoughts, the marble suddenly made a high-pitched noise and began to crack. Dia's face went pale, then quickly turned dark red.

"Throw it! Now! Throw it up as high as you can!!!" she cried.

I shifted my mana toward upping my physical strength and threw the marble into the air, as instructed.

I may only have the body of a seven-year-old, but thanks to the combination of my special Tuatha Dé training and Rapid Recovery, my physical strength had increased significantly, and I could use my abnormally high mana to increase my strength even more.

I threw the marble so high it disappeared into the sky. Seconds later, it erupted in a massive blue explosion.

Evidently, it was a good thing I'd thrown it with all my strength. If that explosion had happened anywhere near the ground, it would have wiped out the estate and everyone on it. Unfortunately, it'd still been strong enough to send a blast of wind back down, one strong enough to shake the mansion and shatter its windows.

Not a moment later, Mother and Father rushed outside to find out what had happened.

"Ms. Dia, what was that just now?" asked Father.

"I'm so sorry! I was trying to measure Lugh's mana, and...," Dia began.

"So you're telling me Lugh did this?" Father gave the young instructor a piercing look.

"A-ah, no, not really. I-it was my fault!"

"That's not what I'm asking. Is Lugh the one who caused that explosion?"

"W-well, yes. But it wasn't his fault—it was mine, so if you're angry, you should be angry with me!"

Despite her usual mature demeanor, Dia looked like any other child her age as she stood quaking, her eyes closed. Perhaps she thought my father was going to hit her.

That was not what happened, however, because Father was clearly not angry over this.

"That's incredible!!! Esri, did you hear that?!" he asked excitedly.

"Yes, as expected of our boy genius! To think he's already capable of such powerful magic!"

"Yes, but it isn't really suited for assassination," my father said. "No matter how you look at it, this is magic more suited for war. Ms. Dia, please teach him magic that will assist him as an assassin next."

"U-understood. Wait, huh?! Are you not mad?"

"Of course not! I couldn't have imagined a more splendid first show of magic from Lugh. Choosing you was the right decision, Ms. Dia."

Both grinning like the proud parents they were, Mother and Father returned to the mansion.

"Uh, sorry about that. They always get like that when it comes to me," I admitted.

"They're...quite something, aren't they?" Dia said, choosing her words carefully.

"By the way, Dia. Sorry to change the subject, but could you tell me where I can obtain more of those little balls? They seem very useful. I'd like a lot of them, if possible," I asked.

"These are prized goods from my domain. We're not allowed to give them to outsiders," the young mage replied.

I clicked my tongue in disappointment.

"What was that for?!" Dia snapped.

"Oh, I was just thinking that those balls would be really useful if I obtained a large quantity of them. They would make for amazing weapons."

To prepare as many methods for killing the hero as I could, I'd been looking into options outside of magic or training. I'd even gone so far as to consider developing firearms.

Obtaining the necessary gunpowder for that proved to be

difficult, however. Making gunpowder was easy enough, but making high-quality explosives more suited for firearms was too challenging.

That's what made this marble so incredible. With that kind of explosive power, I could create weapons that rivaled the strength of a tank cannon...no, even better, the cannon of a battleship.

"...This may be my parents' influence speaking, but as I said, I really can't give you one. *Ahem.* Anyway, your mana capacity turned out to be immeasurable, but it's enough just knowing that you'll have plenty of mana to deal with any situation. I'm curious; how much mana do you think you have left?" Dia asked.

"Hmm, I'd say about two-thirds," I answered.

"I'm so jealous... But mana capacity does not make a great mage alone! Let's move on."

"Hey, Dia?"

"What is it?"

"Are you sure you can't give me any of those marbles?"

"How many times do I have to say it? No!"

That was disappointing. At least I knew that I would be able to find some if I traveled to Dia's homeland. I resolved to make sure I got my hands on some, if at all possible. Being able to make weapons that could discharge a huge amount of mana all at once would be a huge boon toward killing the hero.

There would be time for that later, however. With the preparation complete, it was time for me to learn how to use magic.

Dia produced a new marble in place of the one I'd caused to explode.

Such an enormous explosion had resulted from simply attempting to measure my mana capacity. Magic was more dangerous than I'd expected.

Which meant it could be a very powerful weapon. Simply pouring enough mana into that marble had caused a massive explosion. Perhaps if I configured those little spheres to safely store mana, I'd be able to use them to discharge with even greater force... I was getting excited just thinking about it. I really wanted more of those marbles.

"Hey, are you daydreaming again? I won't give you any!" Dia said, as if reading my mind.

"It's a bit late to be asking this, but what are those balls called?"

"They're called Fahr Stones."

Dia said they were available only in her domain, but it was hard to imagine their material couldn't be mined elsewhere. I'd have to do some more research later.

"Lugh, I'm going to hand you another Fahr Stone, but it won't be yours to keep, okay? This time, just fill it with a little bit of mana and give it back to me. I would've used the stone we used to measure your mana, but since it exploded, we'll need to use a second one."

"Sorry."

"No, no need to apologize. That was an accident. All right, then, go ahead and infuse it with mana."

I did as I was told and handed it back.

Dia grasped it tightly. "Let's see, I'll try for fire first." She concentrated, and the stone turned from transparent into a shining red. "Your elemental affinity is fire. It's possible to have two elemental affinities, so let's try real quick to see if you have another."

The stone became transparent again, then turned an aqua shade.

"Ah, impressive. You also have an aptitude for water. You're the only person I've met other than myself with two affinities. This is very rare, you know. You should be proud."

"What did you just do?" I asked.

"I'm stimulating the mana stored in the stone to check for elemental affinity. The Fahr Stone will change color corresponding to each of your affinities."

"I see. Would you mind checking for the two remaining elemental affinities?"

"Sure, but I've never heard of anyone having three affinities… Wait, what? Earth affinity, too? And wind?! You can use all four elements?! Is that even possible?!"

The reason I had affinity for the four basic elements was because the goddess had allowed me to choose Total Affinity, which halved the rate of improvement of each affinity in exchange for allowing me to use fire, water, earth, and wind.

"Seems that way. We now know my mana capacity and my elemental affinities. So what's next?" I asked.

"…This is one unbelievable thing after another. But, whew, I guess I should expect the unexpected with you. I don't think anything you do could surprise me at this point. All right, now the real lesson begins. Time to teach you how to use magic."

Dia stood behind me and placed a slender hand on the back of my neck.

"Does this feel okay? You can already use mana, but magic is different. To use it, you'll need to perform an elemental conversion, which I'll help you with. Your first elemental conversion is an intense experience that will be burned into your memory forever. You might end up stuck with some unfortunate habits for life if you are led through your first conversion by an unskilled teacher."

"…You're not an unskilled teacher, are you, Dia?" I asked.

"No need to worry. I promise I'll give you the best first experience you could ask for," she replied.

I felt a strange power flowing into my body from my nape. It seemed the mana within my body was being directly converted, similar to that which had been contained within the Fahr Stone earlier.

"Don't lose focus. We're going to do earth first, my strongest affinity. Feel the conversion of mana in your skin. Engrave it into your heart," Dia instructed.

Just as directed, I closed my eyes and focused on the mana morphing within me. I could feel it shifting and beginning to change shape. It was a pleasant feeling. I'd never had anyone other than Dia do this to me, so I had no point of reference, but something told me she was most certainly skilled.

Shortly after the pleasant sensation came to an end, Dia removed her hand.

"You've had your first experience. Now go ahead and try it yourself," she directed.

"That was nice. Thank you... I think I understand how it works, more or less. Like this, right?" I changed the colorless mana in my body to earth mana, just as Dia had demonstrated.

"That was a little rough. You might have a large capacity for mana, but if you can't properly convert it, that will be meaningless. A typical conversion rate sits around sixty percent, but because *I'm* your teacher, we're going to aim for eighty percent."

You could cast magic only by using mana that had undergone an elemental conversion. In other words, any mana that wasn't properly converted was wasted energy. I could see why Father had been so careful with his selection of mentor.

If a mage was saddled with bad habits because their first conversion was performed by a poor teacher, they'd struggle with losing mana during conversions for the rest of their life.

After trying it myself, I now understood how skilled Dia's elemental conversion really was. Clearly, she was the best of the best. I tried again, this time following her example as best I could.

"Well, you're not going to get there easily. You'll have to train for years to— Hey, wait! H-how have you improved that much already?!" Dia exclaimed.

"I just followed your example. I still have a long way to go to become as good as you."

"My pride is going to be in shambles if you overtake me on your first day! And people call *me* a genius... Elemental conversion is one of the quintessential skills for casting mana. Make sure to practice it every day. Hmm-hmm-hmm, this isn't going to be easy for you. Since you have four elements, that's going to make your training four times as difficult."

Although I wasn't quite sure how I knew it, I was certain I understood how to convert my mana to all four of the elements after only changing my mana to earth.

I'd have to set aside time every day to practice this.

After gathering some earth mana, a collection of symbols I'd never seen before suddenly appeared in my mind.

"Ah, that face must mean you've just learned some magic, right?" asked Dia.

"So this is magic...," I said.

"Yep. Once you fill your body with a higher amount of elemental magic than normal, you receive a divine revelation from the gods and learn your first spell."

"...I see the spell in my mind, but how do I use it?" I had no idea what these mental characters meant, to say nothing of how to read them.

"You need to chant the words while boosting your converted mana... I'll demonstrate using the spell you just learned. Watch closely."

With a beautiful singing voice, Dia strung words together in a language unlike any I'd ever heard. The pronunciation and accent sounded completely different from the local language. When the incantation concluded, a lump of lead formed in her hand.

"This is the first magic that you learn from the earth affinity. A spell to produce lead. New spells will appear in your mind as you use magic, bestowed upon you by the gods. This spell only produces lead, which is relatively soft, but if you train, you'll be able to produce harder metals like iron!" Dia explained.

Iron did have a higher degree of hardness, but that didn't necessarily make it superior to lead. Regardless, learning new spells through repeated use of my elemental affinities sounded fun.

"I'd like to try myself, but I can't read these weird characters, if that's what they even are. Can you teach me how to read these?" I asked.

"Yes, that is one of the fundamentals of magic. Proper pronunciation of the magic characters, referred to as runes, means everything! The accuracy of your pronunciation has an effect on the precision and force of your magic."

"So elemental conversion and incantation are equally important. This sounds tough."

"There are many people who decide to never use magic because of how troublesome it is to learn. There are other drawbacks that dissuade people, too."

"Really? Magic seems really convenient, though. Even the spell for producing lead that you just showed me could have any number of uses."

A lump of iron on its own could be fashioned into an acceptable weapon, and I had to imagine there were plenty of other spells that were far more useful.

"Like I said, there are obstacles. Possessing magic gives you the strength of a hundred soldiers on the battlefield because you can use mana to increase your physical strength and defense. However, when you cast a spell, you have to divert mana to your incantation, which results in your strength and defense falling to that of a normal person. This makes you very vulnerable if you're in the middle of a fight."

That definitely sounded dangerous. If you got caught mid-incantation within the striking distance of a foe, it'd likely be the end.

Even with such a weakness, magic held so much potential. It

also would be a waste not to use it given my Spell Weaver skill, which allowed me to create new spells.

I already had a spell that could produce lead, and there was also one that could apparently produce iron as well. I wondered if perhaps it was possible for me to then use Spell Weaver to alter the formula and produce metals more suited for combat.

Titanium, for example, would be quite useful. It was just as tough as iron but considerably lighter. The hard and heavy tungsten could also prove useful.

I could use titanium to make light and sturdy slashing weapons, while tungsten could be fashioned into piercing armaments like spears or bullets. Magic held many possibilities to increase my combat capabilities.

Given the technology of this world, most weapons were made with, at best, low-quality iron possessed of high levels of impurities. Using weapons made from high-quality metals would give me a big advantage over others.

Just the fact that I could produce metals from thin air was incredible on its own, as the metal itself could make for a useful weapon. For example, if I jumped up high in the air and then produced a metal with a high atomic mass and hurled it back down, I could create an incredible amount of kinetic energy.

As I pondered even further, I hit upon the idea of producing a makeshift gun by propelling bullets created from my earth affinity with explosions produced by my fire affinity. There was also the question of if I could create Fahr Stones via magic. If so, I could fashion bombs with massive explosive power.

After learning only one spell, I was already overwhelmed by

the many possibilities. Surely more spells would only lead to further inspiration.

"Um, Lugh? What's going on? You've been standing there grinning to yourself," Dia said.

"Ah, sorry. It's nothing."

In truth, I was getting rather excited at the many prospects.

Studying runes in order to perfect my incantations would need to be a priority. Once I mastered the art of casting magic, I'd have a whole new world of options at my disposal.

Thankfully, I had Dia as my teacher. I was certain to master the language of magic in no time.

My lessons with Dia on how to read runes soon began in earnest.

There were thirty-six characters. After learning the pronunciations of each, I then had to study how their pronunciations changed when lined up with other characters. It didn't seem like Dia knew anything about the meaning of each individual symbol, which was a little disappointing.

Creating new spells with Spell Weaver looked like it was going to be really hard.

There was no way I'd be able to write new spells without understanding the meanings of the runes or the rules behind the language.

Despite such a complication, Dia was a wonderful teacher. Her pronunciation of the language was beautiful. She read the most difficult of words without falter.

Altogether, the thirty-six characters of the magic language combined to make 114 sounds. Dia was having me learn them all through repetition. She read some runes to me, and I repeated back what she said.

"How are you able to memorize these after hearing them just once?!" she exclaimed.

"I have confidence in my memory. My tongue is having trouble keeping up, though," I replied.

There were certain methods that existed to help improve one's memory. I knew of them from my previous life and had put them to good use with learning runes.

That's not the only reason my memory was so good, however. My Tuatha Dé eyes were continually sending massive amounts of information into my brain. Thankfully, Rapid Recovery and Limitless Growth were also allowing my brain to adapt to handle such a burden. As a side effect, my level of retention also increased.

Compared to Dia, though, my pronunciation was still quite rough. The runic language required the use of facial muscles that I didn't normally rely on, so it was going take practice to improve my intonation.

"That doesn't make me feel any better! I had to study super hard to learn these... Anyway, once you learn how to pronounce the characters, you can move on to incantation. You can currently only use one spell, so I'll read that one to you first," Dia said.

Dia chose the first earth spell, the one that produced lead, and wrote it down. She slowly chanted it while tracing the characters with her finger, and a clump of lead appeared in her palm. With a motion, she bade me to try next. Nodding, I read the spell.

With some effort, I was able to produce lead. It took no small amount of concentration, however.

With my Tuatha Dé eyes, I was able to see the movement of mana as Dia and I cast spells. Far more of my own had been wasted than Dia's, and for the amount of mana I'd spent, the lead I produced was small and full of impurities.

"So this is magic. It's fun," I commented.

"I was excited the first time I used magic, too. It's so much fun being granted new spells as you use more magic."

"Wouldn't you be able to skip waiting for spells to appear in your mind if someone just wrote one down on a piece of paper and handed it to you? Shouldn't using mana and reading the formula be enough?" I asked.

"Want to give it a try? I'll write another earth spell... Should I demonstrate it for you first?" offered Dia.

"No, that's fine. I just want to see if anything will happen."

The one Dia had written looked to be about the same length as the formula for creating lead. Upon closer inspection, I realized that around 95 percent of the characters were the same. Dia had probably intentionally chosen a spell that would be easy for me to read.

I recited the spell, and a piece of metal appeared just like before. This time, it was iron.

"No way, it actually worked... That's so weird. Now that I think about it, it seems obvious that this should work. I can't see why no one ever thought to try it until now."

As Dia had said, it was baffling that nobody had ever tried this method of casting spells before. In this world, you could use only spells given to you by the gods. Perhaps, as a way to enforce that rule, there was some kind of contrivance in place preventing anyone without the Spell Weaver skill from coming up with that idea.

Having just produced two different metals, I was struck by a bolt of inspiration. The formulas for lead and iron were 95 percent the same. From that, it seemed natural to conclude that the remaining 5 percent of the formula was what specified the material produced.

...*So by adjusting that 5 percent of the formula, can I produce whatever type of metal I want?* I thought.

The trouble was that even if I knew which portion of the spell formula to change, I didn't know how to change it. I didn't yet understand the language or how the formulas actually worked. There was a way to narrow that down, however.

"I have a request. Can you write down all of the formulas you know, demonstrate them, and teach me what they do?"

I could guess the meanings of two formulas to an extent by studying them side by side, but it would be much more efficient to compare their similarities and differences by seeing them in action.

With a bigger sample of spells to work with, I could quickly gain a far deeper understanding of how the formulas worked.

"Hey, this isn't going to be easy, you know," Dia warned.

"That's all right. After comparing the formulas for lead and iron, I noticed that they're almost entirely the same. It was only a small difference in the formulas that changed the metal that was produced... If I'm right about that, then if I analyze and compare more similarities and differences between spells, I'll be able to figure out how magic equations work. I might then even be able to adjust formulas and create entirely new spells. So, please, it'll help me a lot. As thanks, I'll do anything you want," I pleaded.

"...Fine. But I'm not doing it for your thanks. I just think unraveling the meaning of the formulas and creating new spells sounds really exciting. I want to try creating new magic, too." Dia wrote down the nine earth spells and the seven fire spells she could use. She explained each and performed all of them for me, taking occasional breaks to recover mana.

After she finished, we pored over the formulas together for similarities and differences. Dia's cognitive ability was impressive—her intuition seemed very well honed. She even spotted a number of rules that I'd missed myself.

While debating the rules of the formulas, we continually came up with new ideas, a process that only served to drag us further into our work. The sun had set before we'd noticed.

Though it had taken a great amount of effort, it was also a lot of fun. Watching Dia's face light up as she passionately argued her own theories, I suddenly realized how cute she was. I'd never experienced a feeling like that before.

"Lugh, are you listening to me?" Dia asked.

"U-um, yeah, I'm listening," I stammered out, embarrassed that I allowed myself to zone out while thinking about her like that.

"I think the part that differs between the formulas for producing lead and iron represents numbers. Look at these three formulas here. This section makes sense if you substitute numbers for the characters. If we assume that's the case, then in the lead formula, the numbers are 11.3, 327.5, and 207.2. Iron is 7.8, 1,540, and 55.8... I don't know what this means, though. I have no idea what we would even change the numbers to."

As I thought about what Dia said, it began to help me understand other parts of each formula, too. It was clear enough that the numbers written in the lead and iron formulas were anything but random.

"Lead is 11.3, 327.5, 207.2. Iron is 7.8, 1,540, 55.8... This can't be a coincidence. Nice catch! Can you make a conversion chart for runes and numbers?" I requested.

"Of course. All right, here you go," Dia answered, handing me a quickly drafted sheet.

Consulting the chart, I altered the formula for producing lead. I changed 11.3 to 10.5, 327.5 to 961.8, and 207.2 to 107.9. All I did was change the numbers in those three columns, but if my assumption was correct, it was likely to produce the result I was looking for.

Dia began the incantation, cast the spell, and produced a cube of silver.

"Is this silver?! I've never heard of magic that produces silver," she said as she examined the conjured object.

"Just as I thought. These three numbers designate the parameters of the metal you want to produce," I said.

"Explain that to me in a way I can understand," Dia requested.

"These numbers represent density, melting point, and atomic weight. Which means all you have to do is change the parameters of lead to silver, and the spell will produce it," I explained. There were still some points I was unclear on. I thought these units of measurement were created in my original world, but if they were really created by the gods here, then how did they exist in my old life, too?

A feeling that there was a deeper secret hidden within this discovery needled at the back of my mind.

That was the only part of the formula I understood at that point, but I made sure to make note of it. It could very well have been an important key to unlocking how the rest worked.

"Yeah, I'm still totally lost...," Dia admitted.

My excitement was building. Ignoring Dia's confusion, I altered the formula two more times and performed the incantations.

"Ha-ha, it worked again. Titanium and tungsten, two metals I never thought I'd be able to obtain in this world... You had spells that allow you to reshape metal, too, right?"

Searching Dia's list, I found the spell I was looking for. Rather easily, I shaped the titanium into a knife and swung it at a tree in the garden. It proved to be both sharp and comfortably light.

I now had a knife made of titanium in an era where the most

common metal was iron filled with impurities. While titanium was harder than iron, it was also 40 percent lighter and very resistant to corrosion. Possessing such a resource gave me enough of an advantage that you may as well have called it a magic blade.

Next up was tungsten. It was a very strong metal with high weight and hardness, and it was known for being very rare.

"Just as I expected, I was able to produce the exact metals I wanted. Dia, you try these incantations, too," I said.

"All right, I'll try... Ah, I actually made silver. I can't believe this!" she exclaimed.

While my theory proved true, something about the situation still troubled me. To successfully write new formulas, you should've needed Spell Weaver. If Dia could also use these new spells, I was beginning to worry that I didn't need the skill after all.

"Hey, Dia. Want to see if we can make gold? I know the parameters," I proposed.

"Yeah, let's try it. If you know the numbers, I should be able to do it, too!"

Dia wrote down the new formula with the numbers I gave her and began the incantation. Suddenly, her face turned red, and the girl collapsed.

"Are you okay, Dia?!"

"Y-yeah, I'm okay. I just suddenly got a massive headache and became really nauseous," she explained.

I looked at the formula. Everything was correct. Dia had written the density, melting point, and atomic weight just as I'd told her.

I wrote down the exact same formula that Dia did, and unlike her, I successfully conjured gold.

*...So this is what Spell Weaver does.*

If anyone other than me tried to create a new spell and cast it, their body would suffer a kind of adverse reaction to the incantation, preventing them from using it.

If I wrote the equation, however, it seemed that anyone would be able to use it. At the moment, that was only a hypothesis, though. I'd need to make sure.

"Dia, if you don't want to do this, that's fine. I wrote down the exact same spell that you did. Try reading it now. This is essential for finding the criteria for creating new spells."

"You know if you word it like that, I can't say no, right? I'm too curious now."

Pale, Dia chanted the formula that I wrote down. This time she got through the incantation without faltering, and she successfully produced some gold.

"That's strange. I suppose this means I can create new spells, too, just by having you write them down for me. This is really exciting. Let's work hard to discover all the rules we can! If we do that, we'll be able to create even more amazing magic!"

"Glad we're on the same page. We should divvy up the work. The first problem is that our list of spells to sample from is too small right now. I'm going to cast as much water and wind magic as I can in order to learn new spells. Dia, you take fire and earth," I said.

"Of course!" she agreed.

We firmly shook each other's hands.

My ability to create new spells was really something I should've kept a secret. Enlisting the help of another was something my first self would never have done. Dia was truly skilled, however, so working with her served to speed up my process.

If I was being honest, though, spending time with her was

fun. Far more so than anything else I'd ever done. That's why I asked her to stay, despite my better instincts.

Thus, I took my first important step toward creating spells.

But mindlessly and carelessly creating new kinds of magic would only lead to trouble. I knew I needed a goal to focus my efforts. Today I'd been able to devise a way to create whatever metal I wanted, and I learned how to shape it. If I could learn some sort of explosive magic, I could create firearms.

Bullets would never be an issue because of my large supply of mana. My other abilities would help me ensure an accuracy that would rival the guns of my previous world.

Once mastered, I'd be able to produce a weapon with significant range and destructive force at any time, even while being empty-handed. I couldn't think of a weapon more suitable for assassination, nor could I imagine a better first goal to work toward.

The thought of how much I could achieve by working with Dia had me the most excited I'd ever been in my new life.

It had been nine days since Dia's arrival. The mage was mature for her age, but I'd noticed she was prone to bouts of loneliness and acting like a spoiled child.

The day before, she'd told me it was too lonely for me to sleep by myself, despite my age. Then she immediately climbed into my bed and used me as a body pillow.

Because of how young we were, there was nothing sexual about it, but for some reason, it still set my heart racing. When Dia hugged me, I became strangely aware of her sweet fragrance, her softness, and her warmth.

"Lugh, you'd better make sure to listen to your big sister today."

"…When did I become your little brother?"

"Ah, Lord Cian hasn't told you about that thing. Well, regardless, this is an order from your mentor: You're now my little brother!"

*That thing?* I wondered. *Is Dia saying she's a child of my father's from another woman? No, that's impossible.*

Since Dia was my mentor, I'd gathered as much information on her as I could. Dia's last name was Viekone. There was no noble family in Alvan with that name. There was, however, a count in a neighboring country with that name.

My mother was purported to have been a commoner, but she had mana, and her elegant demeanor and etiquette were too refined to have been adopted later in life. Everything about her would've made you think she was born into a wealthy family.

Dia reminded me a lot of her. They both had the same distinct silver hair, a similar physical appearance, similar habits, and they both spoke with a slight accent to their speech that you otherwise didn't hear anywhere in Alvan.

I'd been wondering if maybe Mother was born into House Viekone and had disguised her social status before marrying Father. Were that true, there was a good chance Dia was my cousin.

"Got it. I'll follow my mentor's orders," I responded.

"Hmm-hmm, I'm glad we have an understanding. Man, Tuatha Dé food is delicious!" Dia said through a mouthful of gratin.

Yesterday I'd brought home another rabbit and served cream stew again. Today I took the leftovers and used them to prepare gratin. I added pasta and spice to the stew, then I further altered the taste by sprinkling in some dried tomatoes. After that, I added ample amounts of cheese and baked it in the oven. The mixture quickly became a delicious gratin.

"Sorry I couldn't make anything fancier," I apologized.

"I'm sick of that kind of stuff. Gratin has a really nice taste. I love it," Dia replied.

"I'm glad."

"…How are you able to do all this at just seven years old? You seem to have an extensive knowledge of just about everything, and you're smarter than me despite being younger. Everyone called *me* a genius, but you're on another level."

"It's all thanks to my parents' education. Oh yeah, I need

to go grab something for dinner later. I know you're going to like it."

It was almost the season when the pheasants fattened up for the winter, which made them really tasty. Once today's magic research had ended, I'd have to go hunt some. That way I could treat Dia to a delicious pheasant roast for dinner.

Dia and I went out to the courtyard.

Over the last ten days, we'd been splitting up the work and recording a wide variety of new spells and rules.

If it hadn't been clear before that Dia had a talent for magic, it certainly was now. I had been fairly self-assured in my skills of analysis, but Dia had discovered way more rules than I had.

"This should complete the spell you've been working on, Lugh," she said, passing me a note with something scribbled on it.

"Amazing. This is exactly what I was looking for. You're really good at this," I praised.

"I'm your big sister, after all!"

*That doesn't have anything to do with it*, I thought. It would've been annoying to have Dia get upset with me, so instead I merely nodded and added the new piece to the formula I'd been working on.

"If we can pull this off, it'll dramatically increase the value of magic," Dia surmised.

"Yeah, you're right. This long-range magic with explosive firepower should have very low fuel consumption. It'll be incredibly convenient," I said.

Before long, it was time to test some magic fit for assassination.

The spells we were developing were extremely dangerous, so Dia and I decided to perform our tests on a hill behind the estate.

After exchanging a nod with my mentor, I performed an earth elemental conversion and began my incantation. I produced iron from thin air, morphed it into the shape of a cylinder with a handle, and then carved out the inside of the cylinder.

I continued to chant, loading the cylinder with a tungsten bullet.

The first step was complete. Next, I performed a fire elemental conversion and once again began to chant. I filled the inside of the cylinder with fire mana until...

*BOOM.*

An explosion propelled the bullet forward. The little projectile spiraled rapidly thanks to the rifling I'd carved into the barrel.

Instantly, the bullet broke the sound barrier. With impressive aerodynamic stability, it traveled four hundred meters, where it knocked down a large tree.

"Wow, it worked! This new magic we're developing could change the way people use spells. You can reach distances impossible with a bow, and it's so accurate and so strong! This is amazing!" Dia exclaimed, excited.

"With this kind of range, you won't have to worry about being defenseless during the incantation," I said.

Up until now, incantations had to be cast relatively close to your opponent. But with this firing range, you'd be able to safely chant from a distance where not even arrows could reach you.

Dia performed the same incantation that I had and tried firing a bullet.

"Whoo-hoo! I hit that boulder! It was massive, but it was blown to pieces."

"Let's practice a bit more. It's clearly powerful, but we need to ensure that it's accurate, too. I prepared these for that purpose." I motioned to a large collection of bullets I'd created in advance.

Making a bullet every time you wanted to fire was inefficient. Instead, it was better to have many of them ready and simply load them by hand before propelling them with the fire explosion. This method was sure to work better in battle.

"Good thinking. Let's practice!"

We became engrossed in practicing this new magic. I felt like we got more accurate the more bullets we fired. Reducing recoil was going to be important for improving accuracy even further.

Now that we were capable of firing bullets using fire magic, my first goal was complete.

There were some complications, though. It was important that you used mana to increase your physical strength right before the explosion, and the timing to do so was precise. Without enhanced strength, you wouldn't have the power necessary to keep the muzzle from rising. It was likely you'd also be knocked to the ground by the force of the explosion.

The barrel of the gun greatly resembled that of a matchlock, but the firepower and accuracy were on another level. Magic combustion was capable of much more force than gunpowder ever was, and even more important, my bullets were of a much higher quality.

The harder a bullet was, the denser a surface it'd be able to penetrate. Tungsten was one of the hardest metals known to man, giving it a huge advantage over iron bullets.

Back in my original world, tungsten was often used in the shells of tanks, and it could easily cut through steel plates.

The aerodynamic shape of the bullets I'd made gave them low air resistance, and the rifling ensured high accuracy as well. There was no denying this was incredibly useful magic, but I was still going to need more firepower if I was to kill the hero.

My current level was probably more than enough to handle the average mage, but against the almighty hero, it was unreliable at best. That guy's abnormal strength meant something on this level wouldn't even scratch him if I shot him at point-blank range while he was napping.

With that in mind, I'd prepared something even stronger for today's test.

The fundamentals were the same, but this magic was on a different scale. Such spells would be impossible to use for someone without my mana capacity.

"Lugh, what is th—? HUUUUUUUUH?"

My new magic began to take shape.

First, I produced the barrel. This one was much larger than the matchlock-sized original. Its size was around that of a tank cannon.

The barrel was about two meters long and very thick. Even the sight of it was intimidating. As it was impossible to carry by hand, it would have to be placed on a pedestal and staked into the ground.

The cannon was too big to create all at once, so I was forced to make it in three parts and combine them together using a transfiguration spell.

Next, I produced the ammunition that the cannon would fire. Much like the barrel, the bullet was also quite massive. It

ran around 120 mm in diameter, a common size for tanks. That was roughly fourteen times as long as a bullet used in a pistol. It was enormous, roughly the size of a milk bottle.

I took a deep breath, then cast the fire spell. When the smaller gun had fired, I'd tried my best to repress the force so the barrel wouldn't rupture, but that wasn't an issue with this cannon. Even if I put all my strength into the explosion, the barrel was thick enough to withstand it.

The inside of the cannon surged with a force that put the gun to shame.

"Dia, cover your ears," I instructed.

"O-okay!"

A thundering shock tore through the air, and the cannon fired. Such firepower made the gun look like a child's toy by comparison.

Despite being fixed in place with spikes, the cannon ended up being propelled backward, tearing up the ground along the way. The impact left a crater on the surface of the mountain where it landed.

"I knew that increasing the mass of the bullets and strengthening the explosion would create force on another level...but I didn't expect it to be *this* strong," I said.

In my previous life, I'd operated tanks and even fired shells, but this was an even greater power.

Unfortunately, I knew this still probably wouldn't be enough to kill the hero if he used mana to withstand the explosion or if he had some kind of skill that enhanced his defense at all times.

Even then, there was a chance it could kill him if I caught him off guard. That meant I now had a card to play that could get the job done.

"What the heck do you plan on shooting with this?! This is clearly overkill!" Dia shouted.

"I might one day have to face an opponent who can't be killed without this level of force," I answered vaguely.

I checked the barrel and immediately spotted a problem. A crack had formed in the metal. I'd thought it would be thick enough to prevent that.

*Should I use something other than iron for the barrel? ...No, there's no metal that makes more sense. Tungsten is much harder than iron, but it's brittle. I need a hard metal with high tenacity.*

This was going to be a problem if I could produce only raw metals. Alloys and processed metals would surely be stronger. As I thought about it, I reasoned that it should be possible to create alloys using magic. Were that true, I would have access to even more durable materials.

"I got the force I wanted, but there are still a lot of kinks to work out," I explained.

"This is ridiculous... But firing that thing looked like it felt really good," answered Dia.

"Want to try it?"

"Hmm, I hate to admit it, but I can't. It would be impossible without your insane level of mana," Dia said reproachfully. She wasn't wrong; firing the cannon did consume a very large amount of mana.

"I now know the issues I need to work on with this magic. All right, how about some practice?" I proposed.

"Okay! Hmm-hmm-hmm, if I use magic like this, those barbarians won't stand a chance!"

I wasn't sure exactly what Dia meant, but it seemed there was some sort of enemy she wanted gone.

"Oh yeah, Lugh. You haven't named these spells yet," she added.

"Right. I'll call the one you're holding 'Gun Strike' and the big one 'Cannon Strike.'"

"I'm not really sure what those words mean, but they sound cool!"

I could feel my past intuitions with firearms returning as Dia and I continued firing practice until she ran out of mana.

With no wind interference, it should've been possible to strike an immobile target from over three hundred meters away without issue. Normal assassination jobs would be a piece of cake with a gun like this.

In this world, where the concept of a gun didn't even exist, being sniped from a distance would seem impossible to defend against.

"Only four more days... I want to stay here and do this forever," Dia muttered solemnly.

It was true—there wasn't much time left with her. There were still a number of things I wanted to do before she left.

In the blink of an eye, Dia's final day arrived. She was to leave that evening.

On the mountain behind the estate, we were testing magic designed to create alloys.

Up until now, we'd been able to produce only metals on the periodic table, but through modifying the formula for transfiguration, we succeeded in combining multiple metals—a very meaningful development.

Titanium was a high-quality metal. Its solidity was about the same as iron, and it was 40 percent lighter. It possessed a high melting point, enabling it to withstand very high temperatures, and it was very resistant to rust and corrosion.

It was just too bad that it wasn't much harder than iron. On the other hand, harder metals were often either too brittle or too heavy. Thus, if you were to try to think of a better metal than titanium, finding an answer would be difficult.

A titanium alloy was a whole different story, however. It would allow you to keep all the strong points of titanium while increasing its hardness and sharpness.

By adding vanadium and aluminum, you got the beta titanium alloy.

While being twice as hard, it was still very light. It was

also tough and degradation-resistant. In other words, it was the dream material. No other alloy could serve you better in a harsh environment.

Using magic, I combined titanium, vanadium, and aluminum into one. Just as I'd hoped, I produced beta titanium. I then trans-figured the beta titanium into the shape of a knife. I wrapped the handle in leather and passed it to Dia.

"Dia, this is the fruit of our labor," I said.

The girl slashed at a nearby tree.

"It's light and really sharp! If we made swords with this and distributed them to our soldiers, we'd be unbeatable in battle!" she exclaimed.

"That would be a bad idea. We probably won't cause much of a fuss if we use this purely for ourselves, but mass-producing them for others could lead to serious trouble... Worst-case scenario, we could end up being made slaves to produce those swords for the rest of our lives," I refuted.

The majority of weapons in this world were still made of iron. If word got around that swords this strong existed, everyone would be scrambling to get their hands on one.

"Now that you say that, I get your point...but what if I only give one each to three knights whom I trust? I'm confident they can keep a secret, and I want them to have good weapons. I don't want to see any of them die on the battlefield."

Strong weapons to prevent people you care about from dying... I understood the feeling, and I was also a little jealous of those knights Dia valued so much.

"Even if you trust those knights, they likely have people they can't lie to. The secret will definitely get out... But if you don't tell anyone that they were made with magic, it should be okay.

I'm repeating myself, but I want to keep these new spells we've developed a secret. Only use Gun Strike if you feel your life is in danger," I cautioned.

"Okay, sounds good!" Dia nodded, then followed my example and performed the same incantation to produce the alloy. Her attempt turned out to be a failure, however. "Wh-what happened?" she asked.

"If I had to guess, I'd say it failed because your mental image of the alloy wasn't strong enough. Unlike the spells where you simply produce a metal, when making an alloy, it's important that you know exactly how you want to change the metals and exactly what you want the finished product to be," I advised.

Unlike other spells, a caster's mental image was important when creating an alloy. This was more complicated than simply changing a metal's shape. It required a knowledge of the chemistry behind the concept.

"That's impossible for me. I have no idea what to mix with what to create strong metals...," Dia said dejectedly.

"I'd like to teach you, but first you'd have to know the basics of physics and materials science, so it would take a really long time. A month, at the least."

That was taking into account Dia's genius intellect. It would normally take five times as long.

"Aw, but I'm leaving today...," she said with a frown.

"Can you extend your stay?" I asked.

"...I would if I could. I asked numerous times, but the answer is always no. I really want to stay here and keep making magic with you."

I was happy to hear those words, so I decided to give Dia

a parting gift. Conjuring up more titanium alloy, I shaped it into three copies of a kind of straight-bladed sword that was common to the region. As a bonus, I also created scabbards for them.

"You can take home the knife I gave you and these three swords as souvenirs. We'll have to come up with an explanation for how you got them, though. Father will probably help us. Your father will likely find it strange that you brought home magic swords from the Tuatha Dé domain, and he'll contact my father to ask if you stole them."

"Hmm, yeah. That probably is what my father would do," Dia replied. "Thank you so much for making these for me. You're a really good kid, Lugh." Happily, Dia hugged the swords.

"...They're just a thank-you gift. If you hadn't been my mentor, I wouldn't have been able to become this skilled at magic in the first place," I said.

"You have my thanks as well. If I hadn't met you, I would've never thought to try creating new spells. I don't think I've ever loved magic more than I do right now. I'm going to keep making new spells after I return home. You're going to have to write them all down for me when we meet again!"

"That sounds like it'll take forever, but I'd be glad to do it. I look forward to seeing what you come up with."

I was certain that Dia's ideas would be very different from anything I could ever imagine. It was sure to result in some really interesting spells. With her help, I would definitely be able to grow even stronger.

"Don't think this is a one-way street, though! You have to teach me the spells you write, too!" Dia said.

"For sure. I'll make new magic that'll knock your socks off...

Actually, I think I can use the eleventh spell you learned to make one with four hundred times the force of Cannon Strike."

The idea was still in the theoretical stage, but if I could realize it, I'd be able to produce a very useful spell far stronger than anything else Dia and I had created thus far, and all it would require was an instantaneous discharge of my mana.

"…That spell already far surpasses the strength of ceremonial magic cast by a hundred people pooling their mana together, but I'm excited to see it. This was probably the most fun I've had in my entire life. I don't want to leave, so let's promise this won't be the end for us." Dia held out her pinkie finger, and I joined mine with hers. She smiled.

She was adorable. Perhaps this was love, or longing, or some other emotion I'd never experienced in my life. Whatever it was, the thought of Dia leaving pained me greatly.

I wanted more of these feelings that had been so absent in my first life.

Dinner was slightly earlier that evening, as the meal was meant to double as a farewell party for Dia.

Mother and I prepared a feast for the occasion, featuring the gratin Dia loved. A look of pure joy spread across the young girl's face as she dug into the food.

"Dia, thank you so much for teaching our son magic over the last couple of weeks," said my father.

"Lugh is a genius. He did most of the learning on his own. This is the first time I've ever felt jealous about someone else's magical ability," Dia replied.

"So Lugh is a naturally gifted mage as well. Our boy never ceases to make us proud." My father laughed jovially and drank from his glass of wine.

"Um, Uncle Cian, while exploring the mountains with Lugh, I found these swords. Lugh said I can take them home as souvenirs. Would that be all right?" asked Dia. She and I then proceeded to explain to my father how we came by the weapons, sticking to a script we'd decided on earlier.

"Oh, that's an unusual place to find swords. Mind if I take a look at one?" Father asked.

"Please," Dia responded, handing him one of the blades.

Father removed the titanium-alloy sword from the scabbard and carefully examined it. His keen eye likely discerned the value of the magic weapon in mere moments.

"Huh, to think there was something so interesting just waiting to be found on that mountain. Perhaps there are more of them out there, maybe even buried in *different* mountains." The intonation made it clear that my father was implying something.

Grasping the intent of my father's words, I spoke up in answer. "Father, there are plenty more buried in that mountain. We should go search for them together next time. But I can guarantee you they are only on that one mountain."

"I see. Only that mountain. If that's the case, then I see no issue. I permit you to share these with these people you value, Dia."

Essentially, my father had asked a coded message that inquired if I'd made the swords myself, if I could make more, and whether or not I was the only one who could make them. I'd answered affirmative to all.

"Wow, Lugh is giving a present to a girl! Our little boy is becoming so mature. Dia is so cute, too."

"...Please, Mother, stop saying things like that."

"Hee-hee-hee, I won't stop. You've been getting cheeky lately, Lugh, and watching you squirm in situations like these has become too much fun. How about you become a child of this household, Dia?"

"U-um, yeah, I think that would be amazing." Dia blushed and looked down. Mother was getting overexcited and saying embarrassing things again.

Still, I wasn't about to object.

Dia was sure to grow into a beautiful woman, and she was superbly talented. Our development of new magic would progress much faster if we were together.

"I personally feel like that would be a bit hasty. In any case, I'm glad you became Lugh's friend. The boy never goes outside, so I worry about him sometimes," my father admitted.

He had a point. When I wasn't training with my father, I was either studying or practicing my skills on my own. That was great for my physical and mental development, but it did nothing for my social skills. Perhaps making an effort to go outside and befriend other kids my age wasn't such a bad idea.

"I'm happy to be Lugh's friend. I'll write to him after I return home, and I'll visit as much as I can," said Dia.

Mother and Father smiled pleasantly at us both, evoking a bit of bashfulness from me in the process.

With that, our last meal before Dia's departure came to an end.

Later on, as the four of us were enjoying some tea, a servant approached and announced that Dia's carriage had arrived.

The four of us went outside, and I watched as Dia climbed into the carriage. The horses took off at a slow trot.

"This was really, really fun! I'm definitely going to be back!" Dia shouted after poking her head out the window.

"I'll be waiting for you," I called back.

"Also, take this! Make sure not to forget me!" she said, and she threw me a pendant she often wore around her neck.

Attached to the necklace was a transparent stone. It shone with the purple mana stored inside it. I'd spent more than enough time with Dia to know what this was. She'd given me a Fahr Stone filled with her mana, even though the girl had previously said such a thing was forbidden.

"I won't forget you!" I shouted.

"One more thing. Remember when you said you would do anything I want as thanks? I'm asking for that favor now. If I ever need to see you, promise you'll drop everything and come running to me!" Dia proclaimed.

It was certainly no small ask, but I had no issue with it.

"I promise! I'll come to you as quickly as I can!"

Standing outside, I watched the carriage until it had gone out of sight.

In these last two weeks, I learned how to use magic, developed my skill significantly, and acquired some very powerful new tools.

Resolving to do my very best, I was confident I'd create some really incredible magic that was sure to surprise Dia the next time I saw her.

That did raise the question of when I'd get to meet her again, though… Years could pass before we ever got the chance.

I didn't want that. Regular meetings were better for my research. Also, I was going to miss her terribly.

The Viekone domain was over three hundred kilometers away, and the journey took you across two separate mountains.

Not only would I have to travel that distance on foot, but I'd also have to sneak across the border and then sneak into Dia's estate without anyone noticing. Such a feat was sure to be difficult, but I knew it wasn't impossible for me, and I could think of no better training.

This was something my first self would never have even considered doing, but I was beginning to enjoy this new side of me. I was no longer just a tool that lived to obey the orders of others. I did what I wanted of my own volition.

Winter was nearing, and I could feel the chill as I stalked over the mountain. Before long, this region would be buried in snow. Once that happened, this mountain would be impossible to cross.

We had to act soon to either stock some dry meat or store it salt-cured. Otherwise, dinners in the winter were sure to be depressing.

To make my tenth winter enjoyable, I'd been searching for something to keep myself occupied, but all I'd managed to turn up were animals.

"I can't believe I couldn't even find one person… If only my search had gone as smoothly as hunting."

There was a limit to what I could do on my own, so lately I'd been searching for an assistant. The only requirement I had was that they needed to be a mage.

The trouble was that very few people not of noble birth or some offshoot lineage possessed mana, and convincing someone of high birth to be my assistant was difficult.

For that reason, I'd been searching for a commoner with mana, something that occurred only at a ratio of about one in ten thousand.

It was possible for a person to be a mage but live without being aware of it because they didn't know how to use their mana.

While difficult, finding that kind of person should have been possible by way of my Tuatha Dé eyes. Unfortunately, I hadn't found a single mage, even after searching every nook and cranny of this region.

"...Maybe I should search other domains," I muttered.

The sooner I could find an assistant, the better.

My assistant's necessary education would likely take two years, and then they'd need another year of combat experience, meaning it would require three years to acquire a full-fledged aide.

Snow began to fall. I knew it had been cold, but I hadn't expected snowfall this soon.

"Maybe I'll go see Dia tomorrow."

Not even I was capable of crossing two mountains and over three hundred kilometers on foot once the snow had piled up. I'd been going to see Dia around once a month, but that wasn't going to be doable in the winter. I wanted to see her at least one more time before the weather made that impossible.

Suddenly sensing a presence, I drew my bow, then quickly realized it hadn't been a beast I'd detected but a human.

To avoid other people, I'd chosen a dangerous part of the mountain known to be the home of bears and wolves. Wondering who in the world could've been traveling in such a dangerous area, I got a closer look.

It was a young girl, about the same age as I was.

Despite the cold weather, she was wrapped only in a thin layer of ragged cloth, and she was barefoot. Her shivers were obvious, and she was clutching her arms to her bony body as hard as she could.

The girl looked deathly fragile, and her skin and golden hair were thin and ragged. It seemed likely that she was suffering from malnutrition, but right now that was the least of her concerns. Death by starvation seemed right around the corner. I imagined she would've been quite pretty had she been healthier, though it was difficult to tell for sure.

*How did she get this far up the mountain all by herself and without any equipment? It's a miracle she's still alive.*

What was more surprising was the mana emanating from the girl's body. I thought I'd checked every single person in the Tuatha Dé domain, but it turned out the mage I was looking for had been right here.

Judging from a few factors, it seemed like she didn't know how to use mana, and as a result, it was secluded deep within her body. She herself hadn't even noticed the gift she possessed, which effectively made her no different from a normal person.

"U-u-um, I—I haven't done anything wrong, so please don't hurt me," she stammered.

"...Who are you? What are you doing so deep in this forest?" I asked.

"M-my village is very poor, and I was forced to leave so there would be fewer mouths to feed. If I try to return, I'll just get driven out again... I remembered hearing a traveler say that the Tuatha Dé domain across the mountain is well-off, so I thought maybe if I made it there, then..." In the middle of her explanation, her stomach growled, and she staggered. I caught her before she fell to the ground and helped her stand.

She smelled terrible and was impossibly light.

"I want to hear your story, but first, please eat. You look like you're going to collapse." I smiled and produced a sandwich I'd prepared for my lunch.

The girl's eyes widened. Having lived in a village so

impoverished, she was driven out for the sake of others' survival. Receiving food from another person probably seemed like an unthinkable act of kindness.

While she was standing there at a loss for how to respond, I poured warm soup in a cup, filled it with the contents of the sandwich, and broke up the bread on top to make bread porridge. The girl's stomach was undoubtedly weak from not having eaten in a while. Preparing the food for her this way would make it easier on her stomach.

Eagerly, the girl grabbed the cup and held it tightly to her chest as if to prevent me from stealing it back. I let go of her, and she sat down on the ground and began eating the porridge.

There'd been rumors that the lord of the neighboring domain was incompetent, greedy, and heavily taxed his citizens, but I had no idea that the situation was this bad.

After she finished eating, the girl made a happy, content expression.

Her face flushed when she noticed I was looking at her. Now that her belly was swollen full of food, it seemed she had the energy to be self-conscious.

"So you say you were heading to the Tuatha Dé domain. I happen to be the son of the head of House Tuatha Dé."

"...Th-that's amazing. This means the fated encounter the goddess told me about in my dream turned out to be true," the girl replied.

Had she really just said "goddess"? Was this overly convenient encounter the goddess's doing? The idea that such a thing could've been true irritated me, but I wasn't about to overlook such an opportunity.

"If it's okay with you, how would you like to become my retainer? I have need of your strength," I said.

Aside from the fact that she was a mage, I'd been evaluating her other potential uses. Her decision-making after being thrown out of her village appeared quite good.

She'd reasoned that returning to her home was a waste of time and energy, so instead she'd searched for a chance at prolonging her life. Being able to decide on the proper course of action in a crisis situation was an essential quality for an assassin. It wasn't something you could learn later in life.

The girl looked up at me, and tears began to trickle down her cheeks.

"What's wrong?" I asked.

"I'm so happy. No one has ever told me that they needed me before. I've always been told that I'm worthless, that I'm nothing more than a hindrance. I was even abandoned by my home...but you say you *need* me..."

All of her pent-up emotions burst forth, and she began to weep uncontrollably.

I hugged her tight.

"I-I'm filthy," she said.

"Yes, you are. But once we get you cleaned up, you'll shine like new."

"I-I'll do my best. I really, really will..."

"That's great. I need someone like you, so I hope you'll work hard for me."

The girl may have been disheveled, but to me, she was a diamond in the rough, yet to realize her potential.

She was a great find, and I would have to be sure to raise her carefully to mold her into the assistant worthy of an assassin like myself.

I awoke to somebody shaking me.

"Lord Lugh, please wake up!"

The hands gripping me were soft and warm.

When I opened my eyes, I saw a young girl with vibrant golden hair. She was twelve years old and wearing the clothes of a servant. Officially, she was my personal retainer.

The girl carried a charming presence about her that attracted the eyes of many visitors. Especially male ones.

"Lord Lugh, i–if you don't get up, I'll play a prank on you," she said in a quiet voice while shaking me.

*Well, that makes me want to get up less*, I thought.

"Morning, Tarte," I said.

"Good morning, my lord. It's unusual for you to sleep late."

"I pushed myself a little too hard yesterday."

I hardly ever needed rest because of Rapid Recovery, but yesterday I'd gotten a little ambitious and tried something even my skills couldn't keep up with.

"Breakfast is ready. It's one of my best dishes yet!"

"I'm looking forward to it. Let's go."

"Yes, my lord!"

Together, the two of us walked to the dining room.

"Tarte, I had a dream last night of when we met two years ago."

"…Th–that's so embarrassing. I was only skin and bones back then. Plus, I was really unhealthy."

"When I picked you up on that mountain, I never would've thought you'd become this beautiful."

"...! I'm gonna run ahead and put some fruit in your yogurt, my lord!"

Over the last two years, that skinny little girl had gained a healthy physique and become quite lovely. She'd thankfully put some real meat back on her bones and was admittedly quite physically developed for her age.

As I sat down, Tarte served my breakfast and then stationed herself behind me.

"You don't need to act as my retainer all the time. It's really just an excuse to have you at my side," I reminded her as I ate. The breakfast Tarte had prepared consisted of bacon and eggs, with yogurt on the side. It was a favorite dish of mine, made up entirely of ingredients from the Tuatha Dé domain.

"No, that will not do. I am your retainer! I do my best every day so that you can live a comfortable life!"

I'd designated Tarte as my retainer only because I needed her to be at my side at all times to support my work as an assassin. Her acting as a proper attendant was the best way to avoid others getting suspicious.

Despite the fact that I didn't really expect it of her, Tarte had been giving both her jobs her utmost effort.

"Tarte, you've been doing an amazing job."

She wasn't particularly gifted in any one area, nor did she possess strong intuition. What she lacked in such areas, however, she made up for with hard, honest work. It was this aspect of her personality that allowed me to place my undying faith in her.

"I would've died if you hadn't found me in that forest, my

lord...and you said that you needed me. My life is yours, now and forever."

The words were more than mere flattery. Tarte was speaking from the heart.

I stood up and lightly patted her golden hair. She took the opportunity to lean into me.

"It makes me happy to hear you say that. I do need you, Tarte." She seemed to light up whenever I said that I need her, and it helped motivate her to push through even the most difficult training.

In just two years, Tarte had grown a lot as an assassin, and she'd put in no small amount of effort to become a fitting retainer for a noble.

When I'd first explained to Father that I was taking her in and raising her as my assistant, he'd made me promise two things.

The first was that I had to take full responsibility for Tarte's upbringing. My father was not going to involve himself in her education. The second was that because I was going to have to share top secret Tuatha Dé knowledge with Tarte, I'd have to be the one to kill her if she ever went rogue.

It was likely that the first condition had been set knowing that I'd deepen my own knowledge through Tarte's education. Agreeing to the second condition wasn't much of a problem, either. It was dangerous to share family secrets with an outsider, after all.

It hardly mattered anyway, because I had full confidence in Tarte's loyalty.

She was devoted to me because of the circumstances of our meeting. Additionally, I'd been using some techniques from my previous life over the last two years to help ensure her allegiance.

Tarte worshipped and depended on me.

"Lord Tuatha Dé asked for you to meet him in the study once you finish eating. He has an important matter to discuss with you," Tarte said.

"Got it. Let's go."

I could think of only one thing such a request could entail.

Feeling a little tense, I met with Father.

"Lugh, how's it going with Tarte?" he asked.

"After two years of training, she's now around the same skill level as the best of the branch family. She's not especially talented, but she is a very hard worker," I explained.

"I see. Her training seems to be progressing smoothly, but that's not what I'm asking."

"...At this point, I've found nothing. I've been monitoring her consistently over the last two years, and discreetly searching through everyday conversation, but she really seems to be nothing more than a simple villager's daughter," I said.

"Perhaps I was overthinking things. I feared she may have been a spy sent to our family to steal our knowledge and technology," my father admitted.

No matter how you looked at it, my first encounter with Tarte was definitely too good to be true.

I searched the entire domain for a mage and hadn't turned up anything, but then a girl suddenly appeared out of nowhere. Father had been right to suspect a setup.

The possibility that Tarte was a spy planted by someone who knew I was searching for a mage had also occurred to me.

More than anything, I thought back to what Tarte had

said—that a goddess had appeared in her dream and told her that she would meet me.

Over the past two years, there'd never once been any reason to doubt Tarte's intentions. If she really was a spy, her ability had to surpass both my father's and my own.

"Father, is that the only matter you wished to discuss?" I asked.

"No, that's not the main reason I called you. Your next training session will be a special one, because it's also a test. If you pass and overcome one final extended period of training, I'll acknowledge you as a full-fledged member of the clan, and you can start taking on real jobs," he said.

"I'll gladly take the test. What do I have to do?"

"You will fight me. Winning or losing is irrelevant. Just show me what you're capable of."

What an appealing idea it was. At last I was going to put all my training to work and come at my father with everything I had.

The test began.

The stage for our duel was the forest, a suitable environment for assassins.

This was not a head-to-head fight of physical strength. The format of the duel was to use stealth to search for your opponent and catch them using a surprise attack. That meant that whoever found their opponent first would have an overwhelming advantage.

While doing my best to stay hidden, I concentrated as hard as I could on not leaving even the slightest trace of where I'd been.

I leaped to the side just as an arrow pierced the ground where I'd been standing a moment before. It was a short projectile, the kind shot from bowguns.

Shiny black poison was spread onto the surface of the arrow. The concoction was a powerful mixture that was strong enough to knock a normal person out for as long as three days if it so much as grazed the skin. Evidently, my father was quite serious about this test.

"…I was really confident in my stealth, too."

I wasn't even able to hazard a guess at how Father had detected where I'd been hiding.

However, judging by the trajectory and angle of the arrow, I was able to pinpoint the location he'd shot it from. It was a spot roughly fifty meters southeast from my current position.

Not wanting to miss this opportunity, I enveloped myself in mana and ran. My mana capacity and instantaneous mana discharge were off the charts. Which meant my speed and strength were equally overpowered.

Normally, the mountain vegetation grew thick and made running difficult. I overcame this with a signature technique of mine. I kicked off a tree trunk and used a branch to propel myself into the air. The branch I landed on should've broken under my weight, but I covered it in mana the moment I landed, which was a highly advanced technique.

*There he is.* As soon as I spotted my father, I drew forth two knives from my pockets and threw them.

Knives were my primary weapon. I always walked around with multiple titanium-alloy knives on hand. Over the years, I'd come to shape them specifically for throwing.

The knives soared the through the air at nearly the speed of sound because I'd hurled them with mana-enhanced strength.

Father dodged one knife and knocked away the other, but I was still able to close the distance between us. I slashed at him with my reserve knife, but he blocked me by picking up and using one of the knives I'd thrown. He immediately chopped at my throat with his hand.

I narrowly dodged, then kicked. Father read me perfectly, catching my leg between his elbow and his knee and breaking it all in one motion.

Stifling a scream, I squirmed and threw him off me.

If I'd been unable to shake him off, that would have been the end of the test for sure. Scanning around, I was dismayed to discover that my father had vanished again.

I focused mana on healing my broken leg. With the help of Rapid Recovery, it would take only a minute to reconnect the bone.

"…He's seriously a monster," I muttered.

My strength and speed were both superior, plus I had the knowledge of two worlds at my disposal. Even with such advantages, my father held total control over the match, and I knew the reason. It was because he could read my movements.

Thanks to his total understanding of the human body, he could predict what I'd do next by following the motions of my muscles, heartbeat, pupils, perspiration, breathing, line of sight, smell, and the flow of my mana. Such was the power granted by the Tuatha Dé clan's medical knowledge, purported to be the best in the world.

He was every bit as skilled as you'd expect the head of House Tuatha Dé to be.

Having trained under him for years, however, I could use all the same tricks. Given that I was able to combine what I'd learned in this world with what I'd learned in my previous life, my knowledge and options surpassed his.

Even so, my father was able to trick me with a fake-out that I should've seen coming. Conversely, he'd seen completely through my attempt to trick him. Though I was loath to admit it, we were likely separated by a wide gap in experience.

This was enough to shake the confidence I had in myself for having been the greatest assassin in my previous world. That just served to confirm how much I still had to learn and how much stronger I could become. I was definitely lucky to be the child of Cian Tuatha Dé.

"Get it together," I said to myself. "I'm going to win."

I closed my eyes and focused my senses. Pursuing my father would be playing right into his hands. Instead I was going to wait for him to make the first move.

We were both ready to kill.

As I'd hoped, he acted first this time.

A knife came flying at me. It was one of the titanium-alloy knives I'd thrown earlier.

I knocked it aside, but a second one instantly hurtled toward me from my blind spot. With incredible timing, I angled my body into a near-impossible position, just barely dodging.

I had no idea how Father was able to throw two knives from completely different directions at nearly the exact same time, but I did know that they were only meant to be a distraction.

The true strike came from above. While the previous two attacks had been detectable, Father had erased his presence completely before launching this one.

Father swung underhanded with my knife. I had no way to avoid it because of the awkward position I was in from dodging the first two blades he'd tossed. Thus, I didn't avoid it. I twisted to make sure my father wouldn't hit any vital points, and the knife pierced my shoulder. Ignoring the pain, I drew my hidden third knife and put it to Father's throat.

"I win." My declaration couldn't have come any sooner. I was suppressing a violent nausea and dizziness. The knives Father had used were coated in poison. If I hadn't built up a tolerance, I would've been knocked unconscious before I had a chance to strike back.

"Seems you're right. I can't believe I lost to a twelve-year-old… and you went easy on me, too. So much for my ambitions of being the most powerful Tuatha Dé in history."

Father removed the knife, poured an antidote down my throat, and tended to my wound.

"I wasn't going easy on you," I said.

"Is not using magic and strengthening yourself with only the minimum amount of mana required to win not going easy on me?"

"That would have rendered the match meaningless. You said it before. This is a test, but it was also training. If I'd used my full strength and simply overwhelmed you, I wouldn't have learned anything. That wouldn't have been training."

Before the match, Father had said I should think of this as training and that it made no difference whether I won or lost. It was clear he was telling me that it wasn't winning that was important, but learning and improving my skills through practice.

A jovial smile broke through on my father's face.

"That's right, you got my message exactly. Seeing that winning wasn't the most important thing was part of the test... It's important that an assassin never loses sight of their goal. If you'd only been thinking of defeating me, I would have judged you unqualified in that aspect... With this, I have nothing left to teach you."

"No, that isn't true," I refuted. "I'm still unable to match your skill. I only won because of a lucky gamble."

"I've taught you everything I know, and you have shown me that you can put it into practice. Now all you need is experience. From here on, you need to move forward on your own two feet. I suggest you take initiative in searching for ways to become stronger... As promised, I will soon give you one last trial. It's one that will grow your capabilities for use outside of battle."

Whatever this final trial was to be, it likely wouldn't involve medical science or assassination. Perhaps there was some other essential component of being a member of the Tuatha Dé family business.

After training, I took a bath, changed, and went outside with Tarte.

I was off to greet the citizens of the domain. As its future lord, I'd begun making an effort to do this with some regularity as of late.

"I made fertilizer and spread it over the fields just as you said, my lord. We had a bountiful harvest this year," a commoner named Ruck said.

"I'm glad to hear it. I was wondering if you'd be willing to trade next time if I have any extra game, Ruck? Your green onions are delicious."

"That would be great! But first, please accept these as a thank-you gift for the fertilizer. I would be honored for you to have some, my lord." Ruck passed me a bundle of fresh green onions, which I accepted with a word of thanks.

More commoners came running in our direction.

"Mah cow...," one man said through heavy panting. "Mah cow broke its back leg. Couldja please heal it for me?"

"Yes, lead the way," I said.

We rushed over to the man's cow. The treatment was simple, and I performed it free of charge.

In this world, the nobility held a lot of power. This was largely because they were the only ones who possessed mana, and they used that strength to protect the domain from monsters and other threats. Such great strength and protection often led to a near-religious devotion from citizens, which was why people obeyed the laws set by the ruling class and why they paid taxes.

Winning hearts took more than power alone, however. Earning my way into their good graces was important if I was to ever rule.

The sun had set by the time Tarte and I returned to the mansion.

"Nice work today, my lord. You're always so popular," Tarte said.

"I'm grateful for that, but I received way too many gifts. I'm not sure I can eat them all before they go bad..."

My basket was full of items given to me by local citizens.

Many had come to depend on me because of my elemental magic and what little I knew of agriculture from my past life. The former of which I'd been using to help out with some manual labor.

Just recently, I'd used my water affinity to refill a reservoir that had dried up due to drought, and afterward I'd ended up being treated like a god. There were nobles who taught their people that magic was sacred and never to be used for things like agriculture, but I didn't see any reason not to use such a convenient power to help out.

"This bag is full, too."

I opened my own bag, which was packed full of Fahr Stones.

Mana capacity increased the more you used mana. Knowing this, I'd always made an effort to discharge mana constantly at the rate that my Rapid Recovery allowed me to recover it. That seemed like a waste, however, which is why I started carrying Fahr Stones around.

Half a year ago, I'd conducted a thorough study on the Fahr Stone that Dia had left me as a parting gift and successfully created a spell to produce stones of my own. Since then, I'd been making as many as I could and storing mana in them.

Depositing the filled bag into storage, I started to load a new sack with yet unused Fahr Stones. I was confident that this large supply of weapons I was stockpiling would come in handy in the future.

After I'd passed the test, Father started taking me along on jobs. I began assisting with both our public medical jobs and our top secret assassination missions.

This likely meant that he judged me capable enough to not be a burden during real jobs. My father's brilliance in the field was incredible to watch, even more so than during training. Although he told me there was nothing left that he could teach me, I was sure I had more to learn from him.

In my previous life, I was never once captivated by the skill of another person, but every time I saw Father at work, I had to fight to contain my shouts of wonder.

What I was aiming for was a perfect marriage of the knowledge I brought from my previous life and the new knowledge I gained in this one.

"You performed amazingly on that job, too."

"Yeah, it went well... It seems like you have a good understanding of why I'm taking you along on both medical and assassination jobs, Lugh."

"Yes, it's to get a sense of work in the actual field. It also provides good chances to study the composition of buildings, the placement of guards, and the strength of our targets, all of which may become useful during future assassinations. It's not too often you get a chance to enter a noble's estate."

The estates of nobles were more than simple living spaces. They also served as fortresses to repel attacks from thieves and other threats.

If we were to one day sneak into a noble's home as assassins, knowing the layout of their estate beforehand would be an incredible boon. Our role as doctors was convenient for this reason, as it allowed us to be invited into estates for a legitimate reason. Even if the noble we were visiting wasn't our target yet, they could become one in the future.

"That's correct. You really were made to be an assassin. To an almost scary degree," my father said.

"I am your son, after all."

For a second, I saw a somber expression cross Father's face, and I was confused. Surely he couldn't possibly have been troubled over raising his son to be an assassin. There's no way someone as skilled as him would've allowed himself to have that kind of doubt.

We were on a medical job today, but my father had put on such an amazing display during an assassination three days ago that I was still trembling a bit.

Being the experienced assassin that I was, I understood the greatness of that performance. My father had made the whole thing look so easy that a normal person would've thought sneaking into a mansion and slitting someone's throat while they slept was the simplest thing in the world. That's what made Father so amazing. Jobs looked so effortless when he did them, no matter the difficulty.

"Lugh, I have yet to speak with you about your final trial, correct?"

"Yes. I've been curious about it."

Back on the day of the test, my father had said that there would be one more trial.

"The Tuatha Dé clan receives many assignments like the previous one, where all we have to do is sneak into the target's home and kill them. Those jobs are simple because it's easy to avoid leaving behind any evidence. However, there are nobles who are more cautious and make infiltration more difficult by setting up many barriers and employing a strict security system. In these types of situations, we get near the target through other means, such as falsifying our identities to do things like attending a party that our target is sponsoring. Occasionally, there are also times when we can gain entry to a place because the target invites us there willingly."

I often did the same things in my first life. I'd disguised myself as a chef, a college professor, a pianist, a coordinator, an architect, a card dealer, and more, all to get close to my mark.

"There are also cases where we are given an opportunity to enter a residence as doctors, which allows us to make it look like our target died of an illness. However, our target conveniently becoming our patient is a rare occurrence—and not something we can count on. For that reason, we have false identities. The most commonly used identities are chefs and merchants. Nobles usually have a personal chef, but if they are throwing a large-scale party, they will need more staff and will reach out to the culinary association. The culinary association will then dispatch top-class chefs to the noble's estate... And we have a connection in the culinary association who can get us in as one of those chefs."

"I'm surprised. I've never once seen you cook, Father," I said. If he could pass for a cook at a noble party, he was probably more skilled than my mother. She'd surely be upset to know something like that. "So that means I will have to improve my skill as a chef."

"There's actually another practice that should take precedence. I want you to become a merchant. Nobles are creatures who are always seeking satisfaction, and they have the power and wealth to obtain anything they want. As a result, they have a habit of constantly wanting new things: a treasure from a land across the sea, a jewel more beautiful than anything anyone has ever laid eyes on, or a transcendent work of art. If a merchant carrying such items were to visit their estate, the lord or lady of the manor would welcome them with open arms...especially if they held a famed reputation."

"And you have a connection who can help me obtain this reputation, Father?"

"Correct. I have three names: Cian Tuatha Dé, a baron of the Alvanian Kingdom; Tori Bahara, a chef from Alster; and Dowaf Garner, a merchant and head of the Calrad Company. All are entered in the family register and exist in records as though they were all real people. If someone decided to check for one of my fake identities and found that the family register was falsified, my secret would be out. It is for that reason that the moment I was born, Tori and Dowaf were born as well."

"Does that mean I can assume I also have other identities in the family register?" I asked.

"Yes. The moment you came into this world, two other people appeared as well: Illig Balor, the illegitimate son of the head of the Balor Company, born of a prostitute, and Saphir Ogma, the son of a blacksmith."

Falsifying the family register later would've led to too many inconsistencies in the records.

That's why two false identities had been fabricated the moment I was born. This way, if someone checked the records, nothing would seem out of the ordinary. An unfortunate complication was that taxes needed to be paid for the fake identities, and my father likely owed large sums of remuneration to those families to not end up in their debt.

It was surely difficult, but going that extra mile was part of what made the Tuatha Dé clan the best of the best.

"Ogma the blacksmith aside, that's impressive you got the head of the Balor Company to cooperate with falsifying the family register. The Balor Company is one of the most prominent trading companies even in the large commercial city of the Milteu domain," I said.

Milteu is directly south of the Tuatha Dé domain, faces the sea, and houses the largest port city in the Alvanian Kingdom. It is the liveliest center of trade in the country.

Given the number of influential trading companies situated there, Milteu was a more powerful region than Tuatha Dé.

"He owes me a debt from long ago. I want you to live there for two years, until you turn fourteen. You will live as Balor's son and train as a merchant. As far as the public knows, Balor put your other identity, Illig Balor, up for adoption to avoid upsetting his wife. You are returning to your father because his legitimate son has fallen ill and he needs you to take over his son's duties... That's the story."

It was a perfectly natural excuse for Illig to suddenly return to his father. Spending two long years living there and studying commerce was a concerning request, however. Still, I trusted that my father wouldn't have given me a pointless order. There had to be some deeper meaning to this.

"I will learn about the world, build personal connections, and prepare an information network. I will grow Illig's name to be famous beyond the Balor Company, enabling myself to freely visit the homes of nobles. That is what I should try to accomplish during my two years at the Balor Company," I stated confidently.

Father gave a satisfied smile. Milteu was the country's largest center of trade thanks to its ports. Goods were brought there from around the world, and people gathered from all over the country seeking them. It was a place where I could gather all kinds of information. In many ways, Milteu was more the center of our country than even the royal capital.

Spending two years there would surely broaden my view of society, and I'd gain a deeper understanding of how the world worked.

Living as a merchant would be a great opportunity to make a variety of connections and grow my personal network.

Trading companies build up large communication webs as a way to ensure successful business. Such a resource was equally useful for an assassin.

If I was able to grow the reputation of Illig to the point where nobles delighted in hearing my name and would invite me into their homes without so much as a second thought, I would be free to use it as a pass to enter the home of any potential target.

This trial had four objectives. The first was to spend two years as Illig Balor and make him into a fully realized person. Second was to continue to acquire the abilities and tools necessary as an assassin to kill the hero. Third was to improve at gathering information from around the world. I still hadn't found the hero, and I didn't even know if he'd been born yet. The fourth and final objective was to gain capital, build information networks, and make personal connections, any of which were capable of being a more powerful weapon than pure combat strength alone.

After Father told me about the trial, it was decided that I'd depart in three days.

Now that I'd been deemed ready to take on real medical and assassination jobs, I was to undergo a trial away from home.

Before my departure for this last challenge, my relatives gathered for a commemorative banquet in my honor.

I usually saw people from the branch family only once a month, but I made sure to remember all their names and faces. They were a valuable source of fighting strength. While the bloodline was thinner among the branch family compared to the head family, its members still possessed mana. If war broke out, we would end up leading the branch family into battle.

To reduce the risk of our secret being exposed, only the head family performed actual assassinations, but the branch family could undertake medical jobs.

I'd always tried to be friendly with the branch family, but a certain someone had been glaring daggers throughout the night of the banquet.

That someone was Ronah, a cousin four years my senior. He hadn't so much as glanced at his food, but he'd certainly had plenty to drink.

Ronah suddenly stood up, downed the rest of his drink, and hurled the glass at me.

I'd been wary that he was going to try something all night, so I easily caught the glass and set it back down on the table. That only made him angrier, a vein now bulging from his forehead.

"I won't accept it! I won't accept that this little brat is the next head of House Tuatha Dé!"

It'd been obvious for a while that Ronah harbored such feelings. He'd always been quick to pick a quarrel with me during joint training sessions with the branch family.

Now that I was being celebrated like this, I thought it likely that his frustrations would finally boil over into some kind of outburst, and it seemed I was right. I felt a murderous rage emanating from Tarte, who was standing behind me. I signaled her not to act.

Ronah's father looked like he was about to shout at his son, but Father said that wasn't necessary, and he addressed Ronah himself.

"Hmm. Do you have some sort of objection to Lugh's inheritance, Ronah?"

"I was supposed to be the heir after Ruff! There's no fucking way a weak little kid like him can succeed you! I'm stronger than him! I should be the next head of House Tuatha Dé."

Ruff was my deceased older sibling. Mother and Father avoided talking about Ruff to a mysterious degree, and I couldn't even find any records, so I didn't know their age or gender.

It seemed Ronah thought that the house would fall to him next, and that was why he hated me so much. Being so despised was hardly a pleasant feeling.

"So that's what you have to say. Sorry, but you don't have

what it takes to inherit House Tuatha Dé. You're fundamentally wrong about what's necessary to succeed in the position. It sounds like you're arguing that physical strength alone should decide the heir, but the Tuatha Dé are assassins. Only a third-rate assassin allows themselves to fall into situations where they're forced to rely on combat. We only work on our combat prowess as insurance for the miniscule chance that something goes wrong." My father's words couldn't have been more correct. If you ended up in a situation where you had to fight, that meant your intent to kill had been discovered. The assassination was almost surely a failure at that point.

That wasn't to discount strength entirely, of course.

Strength could ensure a job got done even after being discovered. It also gave you a fighting chance of escaping if you were surrounded by guards, giving you the chance to recover and try again. No one would say it was worthless, but strength was not a top priority.

"Shut the hell up! What's wrong with killing your opponent head-on like a man?!"

Ronah was giving me a headache. Our job was to discreetly remove those who were causing damage to the country and could not be dealt with using lawful means. On the small chance that our role as assassins was ever exposed, the royal family would deny any culpability and we'd be tossed aside.

It was unbelievable that my cousin didn't understand that. Ronah's father was holding his head in his hands. I felt sorry for the man.

"Such a statement provokes a number of responses. If, hypothetically, Lugh proves to be stronger than you, will you recognize him as the heir of House Tuatha Dé?" my father asked.

"Of course I will. But if I'm stronger, I'll take that seat for myself!!!" Ronah declared. His eyes were sparkling, and the edges of his mouth were curled in a cocky smile. The young man was embarrassingly immature.

"Then so be it. See if you can defeat my son. Right now," my father stated plainly.

"Wha—? …GAH!" Ronah gasped pathetically. I'd pushed a knife enveloped in mana against his throat.

His skin was pierced slightly, and blood began to trickle down. If I'd wanted to kill him, I could have. He would've died before realizing what'd even happened, before there was ever a chance for a real fight. That's what it meant to be an assassin.

"Well then, it would seem that Lugh is stronger than you after all. Is this enough to satisfy you?" my father asked.

"U-u-uhhh…"

That was disappointingly abrupt. From where the conversation was heading, I'd guessed something like this would happen. I'd used the fact that Ronah's attention was focused on Father to creep over and lurk in his blind spot. Then all I had to do was attack as soon as Father gave the signal.

"Th-that was unfair!" Ronah whined.

"That's what it takes to be an assassin. We're not knights. I believe I already made this clear, but it seems you have the wrong idea about who the Tuatha Dé are… Lugh, please put away the knife."

I did as requested and placed the knife back in its scabbard. As soon as I did so, Ronah came at me again.

"WHO THE HELL SAID I LOST?!" He wound up for a punch, having now completely lost his temper.

*...This is absurd. Why does he think this will prove him worthy to inherit House Tuatha Dé?* I thought.

I dodged Ronah's arm, twisted him onto my back, then flipped him over with a shoulder throw. He tried to get up, and I put him in a choke hold. He thrashed with all his might but couldn't escape my grip. Tiring of his pointless resistance, I broke his arm.

"GAAAHHHHHHHHHHHHHHH!"

There really was no need for him to make such a fuss about all this. I'd made a point to break the limb cleanly so that it could easily be mended. With the use of his own mana and the Tuatha Dé medical treatment, a full recovery was likely to take only around two days.

"Surely you can see it now. Even in a normal fight, Lugh is stronger. I said strength isn't the top priority, but it is still necessary. You may be a third-rate assassin if you need to rely on combat, but it does allow you leeway to attempt certain risks," Father said.

An assassin should try their best to avoid contact, but your options were restricted if you weren't able to fight at all. With any luck, this demonstration had served to break Ronah's will and he wouldn't be causing any more trouble.

"How about that, everyone. Isn't my son impressive? I guarantee you all, he is a genius that tops me as both an assassin and a doctor. His actions just now were proof enough of that!" my father exclaimed, breaking the tension and lightening the mood in the room.

Ronah's parents wore clearly troubled looks, but everyone else praised me as a worthy successor. Perhaps Father had intentionally egged on Ronah so that he'd have a chance to boast about my skill.

I made a note to follow up with Ronah later. There was a good chance he'd end up serving under me one day, after all.

At last, the day of my departure arrived. I prepared a gift and went to visit Ronah.

"What the hell do you want? Come to make some snide remark, have you?" he said acidly.

"Not at all. I just thought you've seemed down the last couple days."

I chose to speak to him with a more casual tone, despite our age difference. It would've been unfitting to speak to him politely, given my higher rank.

"...I'm not feeling down. I'm just pissed at myself. I lost to a kid four years younger than me."

"If you want to put it like that, Father lost to a kid thirty years younger than him," I said.

"So the rumors were true, huh? The most powerful Tuatha Dé in history was defeated by a twelve-year-old. I never stood a chance." Ronah smiled self-deprecatingly.

"That's true. There was no way for you to defeat me in battle...but you don't have to. Once I become head of this house, I'm going to bring great prosperity to House Tuatha Dé. If you serve me, I promise to treat you well. You lost to me, but you're still strong. I watched the young knights' tournament in the royal capital last year. Of the twenty contestants, I can only say that four of them were stronger than you. I want your service, Ronah. I expect great things of you as a knight of House Tuatha Dé."

Knights were a standing army made up of second and third sons who didn't stand to inherit their father's seat, plus the occasional rare mage born as a commoner. In order to be made a knight, you had to overcome strict trials.

Their combat training was far more intense than that of nobles, who were only called to battle in times of emergency.

Not only was Ronah able to hold his own among those twenty young knights at the tournament, he was almost certainly better than most of them. While an overly simplistic thinker and not suitable for assassination work, he would surely be an asset to House Tuatha Dé in the years to come because of his strength.

"Hey, is that supposed to be praise?"

"Yeah, it is. And I'm inviting you into my service."

"You're an idiot, you know that? Who would be happy to be told that there are four people the same age who are stronger than them? I guess I appreciate the sentiment, though. I prefer that to flattery just meant to cheer me up."

"This is for you," I said, handing my cousin something.

"...This is a sword? It's unbelievably light. It's nice and sharp, too. Is this a magic blade or something?"

"Yeah, a sword suits you better than a knife. Both in terms of personality and physical makeup, you're more suited to a soldier's position than assassination. Our house has room enough for knights as well as assassins. One of these days, I'd like you to use that sword for me."

Ronah hung the sword from his hip and let out a deep sigh.

"Get out!" Ronah cried.

It seemed my entreaty had failed. Judging by the kind of man Ronah was, I'd thought for sure this sort of appeal would've worked. I put my hand to the door.

"When you return in two years, I'm going to be much improved. I understand now that I'm not fit to be an assassin. I'll become the knight you want me to be, so you go do your job," Ronah called as I made to leave.

"Sounds good. Let's both do our best," I replied.

Apparently, people like Ronah weren't good at speaking honestly about their feelings. I made a point to remember that.

At any rate, I'd just gained a talented young knight. I was sure to put him to good use once I became head of my family.

The next day, I was seen off by my parents and citizens of the domain before departing in a horse-drawn carriage.

"You don't need to come with me, you know. Even without me here, I can entrust your training to the branch family. And Milteu is a city of commerce. It's very different," I said.

"That doesn't matter! I am your retainer, my lord! No matter where you go, I will look after you."

Tarte had insisted on coming with me. She was panting after loading some heavy luggage.

As it happened, my mother called Tarte to her room and had a long talk with her last night. It'd probably been to discuss the mom of the identity I was slipping into. I'm sure my actual mother had filled Tarte's head full of nonsense.

Before I boarded the carriage, I'd used dye to conceal the silver hair I'd inherited from my mother. For the two years that I was going to be living as Illig, I couldn't risk showing any hint of my true self.

"I'm so excited for Milteu, my lord," Tarte said.

"Me too," I replied. My mind was abuzz with curiosity as to what kind of place Milteu was.

I'd promised Father that in these two years I would learn about the world, make personal connections, build an information network, and become a successful merchant.

The goal was to become such an exemplary trader that my rivals would hire assassins to try to eliminate me. It would be fun to be on the receiving end of an assassination attempt for a change, and it would give me an opportunity to learn something from my assailant.

Under normal methods, it was impossible to achieve such a level of accomplishment in only two years, but that's precisely what I found exciting. I'd already started to form a plan that would take Milteu by storm.

I vowed to do my best to leave my mark on the world as Illig Balor.

The first six months of my time with Tarte in the city of Milteu passed rather quickly.

I'd been living not as the son of the baron of the Tuatha Dé domain but as Illig of the Balor Company.

Hoping to further conceal my identity, I'd taken to wearing glasses in addition to dyeing my hair.

I'd also completely changed the way I dressed, my tone and voice, and my mannerisms and expressions. No one should've been able to tell that Illig and Lugh were the same person.

Truthfully, I did have some trouble adjusting to my new life at first. Tuatha Dé prospered thanks to its incredible medical capabilities, but that wealth really only extended to the head and branch families. Most of the region consisted of small villages that subsisted on agriculture.

The scale in Milteu was drastically different. Where goods gathered, all kinds of people converged.

Merchants, carpenters, alchemists, blacksmiths, and apothecaries all existed together in one place. With such a great variety of people came a great variety of goods, which rapidly grew the economy. That then led to more people moving to Milteu and continuing the cycle of constant economic growth.

After spending half a year in such a city, I'd come to like it.

My hope was that such a place would one day become an asset for Lugh Tuatha Dé as well.

If I managed to open a store in this city and did business in one of the world's largest markets, there was no doubt that the Tuatha Dé domain would enjoy greater wealth. Our cover as assassins could be blown at any point. If that ever happened, the family was going to need a new source of revenue.

I arrived at my destination, the office of the head of the Balor Company.

"Sorry for getting here late, Father," I said.

"No, no, that's my fault for calling you so suddenly," Balor replied.

"What kind of business do you have with me today?"

Illig was an illegitimate son who Balor put up for adoption to avoid upsetting his wife. Once Balor's legitimate son fell ill, Illig was called to offer support and was now undergoing education to become a merchant. Such is the story devised to explain how I, as Illig, came to work at this company.

True to the tale, Balor was giving me thorough training on the fundamentals of being a merchant.

For the first three months of my time in Milteu, I worked as an employee at the company's most successful store. The environment was so busy and hectic it may as well have been a battlefield.

I was yelled at often in the beginning, but I learned from my mistakes and got better at the job over time. I used knowledge from my previous life to improve my performance, and I came to be praised by my coworkers for my ability to smoothly handle any situation.

Once I got used to working in a store, I was transferred to headquarters.

The Balor Company owned a number of retail stores throughout Milteu, though the goods sold in all of them were largely the same.

It was the job of headquarters to judge demand and decide how much of each item each store should stock. Given the choice, I think I would've said that working at headquarters suited me better.

Predicting future product demand by using distribution and information networks spread across the world was extremely difficult work, but I found it very rewarding. Discovering attractive new products and negotiating with suppliers to procure them was exciting.

My improvement had been rapid because I enjoyed the work so much, and I'd even risen up in the company to work as Balor's right-hand man.

It was a good position to be in. I could procure information from literally anywhere. The world became a much smaller place when you looked at it from the perspective of the flow of commerce.

"I've been very impressed by you, Illig... So much so that I've found myself wanting to entrust the entire company to you," Balor admitted.

"That's out of the question. Beruid is heading toward recovery. My turn will surely never come," I said.

"Even that I owe to you. I brought you in to repay my debt to Cian...but you've become so skilled as a merchant while treating my son's illness. It seems I've only benefited further from this arrangement, and my debt has increased."

Studying as a merchant wasn't the only thing I'd been doing in Milteu. I'd also been treating the illness of Beruid, Balor's son.

An examination had revealed that Beruid was suffering from cancer. Thankfully, it was still in the early stages, so I was able to remove the cancerous cells from his body. He was well on his way to a full recovery. This world's level of medical treatment was rather primitive, and the Tuatha Dé were the only people capable of performing surgery. As a result, even something like appendicitis was regarded as an incurable death sentence.

Beyond the lack of proper medical technology, there was another reason why surgeries weren't performed in this country. Namely, because the bishop called putting a sword to skin in the name of treatment repulsive. Despite that, the Tuatha Dé still often performed regular surgeries, and I doubted that Beruid would complain.

"Father, I assure you I'm getting plenty in return. I've learned a lot here."

I'd seen many things here that I never would've been able to experience living as a noble in a remote region like Tuatha Dé.

I'd also been making use of merchant information and distribution networks to gather much-needed data and goods. If I had access to the distribution network of the world's leading trading company, there'd be nothing beyond my grasp.

"I'm glad to hear it. I'm a businessman through and through. I'd be ashamed if I had nothing to give you in return for saving my son's life and for helping so much with my business. It puts me at ease to know that this has been a valuable experience for you, even if this isn't exactly how I envisioned paying back that debt. All right, this preamble has gone on long enough. I've called you here today to give you a new job. Take a look at these." Balor handed me a map and the blueprint of a building. The location of the store wasn't far from the thoroughfare, and it was about the size of a large convenience store. It took an enormous amount of money to secure a shop of this size in Milteu, to say nothing of such a good location.

"The spot and capacity are great. You could do anything with a place like that," I assessed.

"That's right. The store we had there went out of business, unfortunately. So far, you've only been involved with our stores that sell daily necessities and foodstuffs, but the Balor Company is also expanding into other fields such as restaurants, weapons, armor, pharmacies, and more. This place was a liquor store, but it ended up failing."

The Balor Company had no other such alcohol specialty stores, which meant...

"This is a concept store. Did you use this to test breaking into the liquor business and try out experimental products not offered by existing competitors?" I inquired.

Aside from simply increasing their number of existing stores, the Balor Company was also attempting to pioneer new fields. This was probably one part of that effort.

If the entire focus of a business was simply to increase the number of locations without ever offering anything new, the growth of the company would eventually stall.

The concept store method allowed you to try your hand at new fields, and if the store failed, you could back out before there was any serious damage to your profit margins. If the experiment was a success, then more stores would be made based off that model.

"Yes, that's right. Competition among stores selling groceries and daily necessities is fierce, which makes growth difficult, and weapons sales have been slow because there's no war on. The same goes for medicine. Lately, monsters have been appearing more frequently, and if their numbers continue to increase, the demons will likely be reborn. Such an advent would produce a spike in weapon and medicine sales, but we can't afford to simply rest our hopes on that and do nothing. The Balor Company needs to expand into a new field with high growth potential. That said, we've already tried and failed three times. Expansion is easier said than done."

Balor's words reminded me that I'd recently heard someone in management had been demoted. The failed concept store probably had something to do with it.

"Can I assume you're about to hand this concept store to me?" I asked.

"That's right. I have a feeling you have what it takes to breathe fresh air into this company," Balor confirmed.

"I've only been here for half a year."

"Normally, I would never entrust something this important to someone so soon, but you've accomplished an extraordinary amount in your short time here. I'm going to share a valuable tip. While it's important for a merchant to have the ability to read demand and market prices, know how to negotiate and deal with customers, and the like, the most important thing is your ability to evaluate other people. We are not gods. There is only so much any individual is capable of. However, if you have the ability to evaluate the talent of others and entrust them with work they can handle, you'll find true success. Knowing you don't have to do everything yourself is what makes a true merchant."

They were meaningful words, especially so because Balor was the proof of that concept. If he'd been fixated on doing everything by himself, he probably never would've gotten beyond the success

of one store. Instead, he'd picked other people to entrust businesses to, and now he managed dozens of shops and had amassed
an enormous fortune.

"Thank you, Father. I'll keep that in mind. How long will I
have to prepare, how large will my budget be, and what kind of
personnel will I have?"

"You'll have one month for planning and one month for
reconstruction. The budget can be as large as you like. I'll prepare
the necessary personnel. I have one condition, however. Do not
damage the Balor name. Think you can handle it?"

I was very excited about this opportunity. I came to Milteu
to gain tools helpful for my work as an assassin while growing my
reputation as a merchant. Success with this opportunity Balor was
offering would assist with both of my objectives.

"I can. I'll do my best."

"I wish you luck. As a side note, if this project succeeds, we'll
expand the concept store into a chain. Five percent of the profit
from those stores will be paid to you in perpetuity. Don't mistake
this for special treatment. Compensating employees responsible
for breaking us into a new market is the Balor Company way."

"Now I'm even more motivated."

You could never have enough money, and I was going to need
a lot of capital to assemble all the goods, personnel, and information I needed to kill the hero.

"Then I'll pray for your success, O son I never knew," Balor
said.

"I won't betray your confidence. I know this is going to work."

"Oh-ho, it seems like you already have a plan."

"Of course I do. No merchant could live here for half a year
and not think about what kind of business they themselves would

start. I'd been working on a proposal for you even before I was given this opportunity," I admitted.

"...I really regret that I can't make you my proper successor. You couldn't be more gifted as a merchant," Balor replied.

After exchanging our good-byes, I accepted the documents and my sizable budget, then departed.

My store would be an unquestionable success, and I was eager to seize this opportunity to grow my name not just as a member of the Balor Company, but as Illig Balor the individual.

Pondering my new store and its featured product, I returned to my home in Milteu.

I'd been renting a middle-class house in the suburbs and living with two other people. It was a fairly spacious place considering the price. It even had a courtyard, which was incredibly useful for training.

When I opened the door, I heard two sets of footsteps come my way.

"Welcome home, Master Illig."

"Hello, dear brother."

One of them was Tarte, my retainer who came to this city with me from Tuatha Dé. The other was Maha, a rational and composed girl the same age as me. She was slender and had distinctive, shiny blue hair.

Even in the house, none of us used my real name, and I never removed my disguise or even dropped my adopted speaking tone. I got a lot of work-related visitors, so there was never a moment when I could let down my guard.

"Sorry for getting back so late. Father assigned me a new task. I'm being entrusted with a store. One that will be completely different from the other businesses the Balor Company runs. It's

going to be a challenge, but that's exactly why I'm so excited," I declared.

"You're amazing, Master Illig! You've only been here for half a year, and you're already being given such important work," Tarte praised.

"Your prowess makes me proud to be your little sister. I'll have to brag about this at the store tomorrow," Maha added.

"Actually, I'd rather you two keep this quiet until the project starts in earnest," I requested. The two girls nodded in understanding.

Maha calls me her big brother, but she didn't actually have any relation to the Balor family. She was a girl I rescued here in the city.

I'd been thinking for a while that I was going to need a team on my assassination jobs, and she was a candidate I'd picked out for that very purpose.

The minimum requirement for anyone on my team was that they had to be a mage.

Normally, mages were born only to two parents with mana, but there was a small chance a child possessing mana could be sired from parents who didn't have any.

Milteu's population far surpassed that of the Tuatha Dé domain, so the likelihood of finding a mage among the common folk was proportionally higher. With that in mind, I'd begun searching for someone with mana soon after I'd arrived, and I found Maha.

The orphanage she grew up in was run for the sole purpose of profiting off the orphans by collecting subsidies from the city. The children there were given the bare minimum amount of care needed to ensure they wouldn't die, and they were even sometimes abused.

Adopting Maha turned out to be rather easy. The director of the orphanage took her in only to make money, so all I had to do was procure him twice the amount he would have received had he supported her until adulthood, and he quickly agreed to let me take her.

At twelve years old, I was too young to adopt an orphan, but given that I worked at the Balor Company, and Balor was willing to sponsor me, I was able to meet the requirements, and Maha, Tarte, and I had started living together.

"Allow me to take your jacket, Master Illig," said Tarte.

"Ah, please," I answered, and Tarte nimbly took my jacket and put it away.

Tarte being here gave me more time to focus on what I needed to do, and while I'd never admit it out loud, her presence helped me relax, too.

My heart had been growing since I became Lugh, and I was beginning to feel new emotions that I'd never experienced in my past life.

Unfortunately, this also came with a weakness. There were times when I felt lonely, discouraged, and anxious. So long as Tarte was by my side, however, I was able to drive away those emotions.

Having a family truly was a wonderful thing.

"Tarte and I prepared dinner together tonight, Illig."

"I'm looking forward to it. Your cooking never disappoints, Maha."

"You're right to look forward to it. This is one of my best dishes."

Four months had passed since Maha first came home with me.

The abuse she'd suffered at the orphanage had left her feeling very weak. The poor treatment had also robbed her of the ability to trust most other people...which was exactly what made taking her in so easy. No one yearned for someone they could trust more than a person in that position.

I'd also been influencing her to instill affection and loyalty toward me using the same conditioning I'd employed with Tarte. As a result, she came to adore me as her older brother.

"Is work going well at the store?" I asked.

"Of course. I would never forgive myself if I did anything to sully your reputation, Illig," Maha replied.

After seeing to her education, I arranged for Maha to work at the Balor Company during the day. She'd been born into a merchant family and had received a fairly decent education before her parents had been killed during a burglary, so she was already quite intelligent.

Unfortunately, Maha had no sense for combat, so she wasn't suited for my assassination squad.

She was best put to use gathering information, procuring supplies, and offering logistical support. At the very least, though, I thought it best to train her to be able to defend herself.

"I think you have what it takes to become my right-hand woman as a merchant, Maha."

"If that's what you desire, dear brother, I promise I'll live up to your expectations."

Setting up Maha to work at the Balor Company was one step of my overall plan. After I left Milteu, I planned to have Maha stay behind.

I'd hand over to her the information network I was building, along with much of my work at the Balor Company. From then on, I'd be able to have her send me needed information and any goods I required while I was back in Tuatha Dé.

If Maha could learn the fundamentals of business, she'd be able to become my administrative assistant. There was a good chance that I'd entrust the operation of my brand to her in the future.

Maha placed soup, meat, and bread onto the table while humming cheerfully. She stared intently at me as the three of us started eating. It was obvious that she wanted to know what I thought of the cooking. I took a spoonful of soup to my mouth.

"Maha, the pork belly steak and the soup are delicious. Did you add the rendered fat to the soup?" I asked.

"That's exactly right. This is excellent pork belly, so I couldn't let the fat go to waste," she replied.

"I was entrusted by Master Illig to look after Maha, but I've learned so much from her that I'm starting to lose confidence in myself. But I won't lose. Especially not at cooking! Please try the pumpkin pie I baked!"

Maha and I laughed watching Tarte get competitive.

I'm glad I was able to find Tarte a friend her age.

Tarte had excellent reflexes, vision, and body control, all of which made her fit for my task force. On the other hand, she wasn't the best thinker, and she could be narrow-minded. As such, she was ill-suited for logistical support.

I found it quite interesting to see how cleanly she and Maha fit into their respective roles.

It was likely that during future assassination jobs, Tarte and

I would carry out the actual strike, while Maha would provide support.

The three of us engaged in idle chatter as we enjoyed our dinner.

"By the way, Illig, what kind of store do you intend to open?" Maha asked.

My decision had long since been made, but there were still some things I needed to get in order first. Specifically, I needed to meet two conditions.

First, I had to be sure the store would turn a profit. That much was unconditional. This business could not be allowed to fail.

Second, I wanted to sell products that appealed to nobility. That way the business would be valuable to my assassination work.

"My store is going to be aimed at women. I'm going to primarily focus on cosmetics, and I also want to sell confections that are sweet and keep well. That said, if I introduce too many products at once, it may hurt my sales, so I think I'll just focus on cosmetics at first."

The need to buy things was stronger in women than in men.

This was especially true for the daughters and wives of noble families, many of whom had a penchant for beauty products and sweet foods.

Beyond that, they loved being treated like they were special. If I became the representative of the world's leading makeup brand, I'd be able to visit the homes of noble families under the guise of bringing cosmetics and confections. They'd welcome me with open arms without so much as a second thought.

"A store selling cosmetics and sweets sounds wonderful!" exclaimed Tarte.

"That sounds like a good idea. The economy has been in good shape lately, and demand for cosmetics is high. However, there are a lot of cosmetics stores in Milteu already. You will need a very strong product, and even then, it'd likely be difficult to make... Consumers are careful with beauty products because you can't afford to be adventurous with what you put on your skin. Without a really enticing reason, most women are going to stick with the popular brands," Maha explained.

The girls seemed to like my idea. Once I had some trial products ready, I decided to have them try the items for me.

Maha did make some good points, however. There was no more difficult market to break into than cosmetics. When it came to beauty products, brand was more important than quality.

"I've given that some thought already. I'm going to make a product so attractive, the barrier of entry is not going to be a concern," I replied.

"Which means you're keeping it a secret," Maha deduced. "I'm looking forward to seeing what you have planned."

"If we can help make it better, please let us use it!" Tarte added.

I was coming to enjoy our dinners here in Milteu. The liveliness reminded me of my dinners back in Tuatha Dé. Despite running an assassination trade, the Tuatha Dé were a very warm family. My meals here with Tarte and Maha were becoming a very similar sort of environment.

Things were certainly warm and cozy now, but when I'd first adopted Maha, she'd been depressed and afraid. Things were tough for a while. We had what we did now because of the struggles we'd endured during those rougher times.

As we were finishing up dinner, a knock came at the door, and I called for the visitor to enter.

"Hey, everyone, it's me again! Sorry for dropping by so late." It was Balor's son, Beruid. He was my half brother, at least while I was still Illig, and was three years older than me.

The recent surgery I'd performed on Beruid had saved him from cancer, a disease that was otherwise a death sentence in this world.

Despite not yet being fully recovered, he still stopped by nearly every day with a box of sweets for Tarte and Maha.

"Good evening, Beruid. You have some excellent timing. We were just about to start class," I said. The main reason he came over was to sit in on the class I regularly held for Tarte and Maha.

Assassination required no small amount of knowledge and skill. To that end, I'd been teaching Tarte and Maha lessons on pharmaceuticals, physics, psychology, economics, and law. Little by little, they were gaining the knowledge they needed to serve me.

When Beruid had come by the house for his treatment, he'd happened to catch one of the classes and took great interest in them.

"What are you teaching today?" Beruid asked.

"We'll be continuing yesterday's physics lesson," I answered.

"That sounds fun. I really like physics. You can learn the reasoning behind the naturally occurring phenomena that we all take for granted every day, and learn how to realize those phenomena deliberately."

"That's the thrill of physics."

"Oh yeah, congratulations on being entrusted with a new store. I heard about it earlier today. That's a job only given to the most promising young employees in the company. If you're successful, you'll guarantee yourself a spot in management one day. If you ever need any help, just ask," Beruid said with a smile.

The only person who knew the secret of my true identity was Balor, so Beruid truly thought I was a bastard child. You would've expected someone in his position to feel jealous of a highly talented younger brother who suddenly showed up out of nowhere and received special treatment from his father. I'd expected some amount of resistance. Surprisingly, Beruid had taken quite a liking to me, even going so far as to seek out my instruction.

He was a difficult person to figure out, but adding him to the class didn't really take any extra effort on my part. I couldn't let him see the training that went on after class, of course, but I didn't mind if he listened during the lesson.

I didn't dislike him...and he could be useful.

Beruid was a skilled merchant, and he was the future head of the Balor Company. Being on good terms with such a person was hardly disadvantageous.

"All right, let's start today's lesson," I said.

I gave them each some handouts with today's material.

Teaching people in this manner was a lot of fun. My students were eager to learn, which helped make the lessons all the more rewarding. As I went through the day's education, I continued to think about my cosmetics store and my featured product.

While the item had been relatively commonplace back in my previous world, no one had ever seen it in this one.

After I introduced it to the market, it would surely become an essential part of the beauty routines of all women in this world.

The profits I would bring in were guaranteed to be astronomical, and soon there would come a day when everyone knew the name Illig Balor.

I'd decided to stay at home during the time I usually went to visit headquarters so I could focus on preparation for the new store.

Relying on my memory, I was laboring to create a cosmetic that had yet to be invented in this world.

My recollection of the recipe was a little vague, but with my knowledge of chemistry, I had the ability to reverse engineer the ingredients based on their effects. This was actually an item I'd made before.

I'd made it as a gift for my mother once when she'd been upset.

I had many more resources available to me in Milteu than I did when I'd made this cosmetic back in Tuatha Dé, so I'd been improving the recipe.

Before noon, I was able to put together a list of needed ingredients to make the trial product.

Turning in the list to the Balor Company's supply department would mean they wouldn't arrive until tomorrow night at the earliest.

"I expected these to arrive tomorrow..."

Not long after noon, the materials I'd requested had been

delivered, despite some of them being scarce and difficult to procure.

"Think of it as a message from Balor telling you to hurry up."

*So Balor is responsible for this.* If he knew that I was requesting ingredients for a trial product, he'd probably summon me tomorrow and ask for a blueprint for the store.

Balor liked to move fast. He was the type who wanted prototype products made quickly rather than flawlessly. Often, he'd made it clear that he preferred his employees just explain their ideas to him, rather than spend time to make a carefully planned presentation.

This style of management allowed Balor to quickly dismiss ideas he thought would fail, and if he decided a concept had promise, he would have his company support the product while it was still being developed.

"...Merchants are a little scary," I muttered.

Without a moment to spare, I got to work. Among the delivered ingredients were high-quality olive oil, clean underground water, pleasant-smelling essential oils extracted from different types of herbs, and a variety of medicinal compounds.

With these, I could finally manufacture my killer product.

Olive oil and water obviously did not normally mix on their own, so I had to procure another substance to get them to blend.

At last it was time to start crafting. The various herbs I'd procured afforded me the ability to create an infinite number of variations. Finding a good balance between aroma and effect promised to be quite difficult. I wouldn't reach the best combination by the end of the day, but I was sure to have a high-quality product before meeting with Balor tomorrow.

Come the next day, I made my way to Balor's office to see him at the appointed time.

Yesterday I'd contacted Balor, telling him that I'd completed a trial run of my store's main product and that I wanted to talk. I also asked him to bring his wife, Mira.

When I entered the room, Balor grinned and gave me a slight bow, while Mira narrowed her eyes in displeasure. It was to be expected; she believed me to be her husband's illegitimate son, sired from a prostitute.

"Father, Mother, thank you for making the time to meet with me today," I said.

"I knew you were a fast worker, Illig, but I never would've expected you to have your featured product ready in just two days," Balor said.

"This product had better be something truly amazing. If you went out of your way to call me here for something boring, I'll never forgive you," Mira snapped.

Having someone show such open malice toward me was almost refreshing. It was far preferable to an enemy who smiled to your face and then stabbed you in the back.

Mira was hiding her face under a scarf. I'd asked her to come today without wearing makeup, and someone with her level of vanity would never have allowed her face to be seen that way.

"I assure you, my product will live up to your expectations. The main offering at my new store will be cosmetic products," I explained.

"I'm not thrilled to hear that. When it comes to cosmetics,

brand matters more than quality. It's a very difficult market to break into. Even if you manage to land a hit in the industry, products don't stay popular for very long, making long-term profit difficult." Everything Balor said was true—I would've expected nothing less from such a successful businessman.

"That's true... For existing cosmetic products anyway. The purpose of makeup is to enhance a person's physical attractiveness, but that comes at the price of damaged skin. Laboring with soap to remove makeup before you go to bed at night results in damaged skin the following morning. Isn't that right, Mother?"

"...I won't deny it, but I still want to look presentable."

In this world, lipstick, foundation, blush, and many other such products were widely used, but there was no custom yet for using moisturizer or face lotion.

In other words, while the concept of using beauty products existed, the idea of using something to protect the skin from the damage of those products did not.

If you applied makeup without first using moisturizer or face lotion, it would harm your skin. Removing cosmetics from the face also required a lot of soap, which caused the skin to lose excess oil. A lack of oil hurt water retention as well, resulting in the flesh becoming dry and damaged.

Compounding things further was this region's warm climate. More makeup only made things worse on the skin.

"I truly respect the pursuit of beauty. But you're trapped in a vicious cycle. In order to hide your damaged skin, you apply even thicker makeup, which leads to even more damaged skin. I am going to free people from this concern. That is where my product comes in... I call it moisturizer."

At those words, Mira bent forward curiously. As someone who

clearly cared deeply about her looks, she understood my appeal better than anyone. There was no way she wasn't interested.

I produced a bottle full of moisturizer. Mira grabbed the jar, opened it, and scooped some out. Moisturizer was actually best used as a set with something called milky lotion, but I decided to sell only moisturizer.

In Japan, it was common practice to hydrate the face using both moisturizer and milky lotion. In America and Europe, most women used moisturizer by itself.

The culture of this land was closer to a Western society back in my first world. I was concerned that consumers would find applying both moisturizer and milky lotion annoying, so I decided to focus solely on moisturizer. By working to increase the water ratio and finding the most effective combination of ingredients, I'd attempted to suss out the most effective formula.

"It's kind of like liquid, but it's thick and adhesive. What is it?" Mira asked.

"It's a cosmetic product that moistens dry skin and keeps it in healthy condition. Makeup exists to exaggerate your beauty, but this is different. This is for healing and protecting your skin as well as bringing out its natural beauty. You'll understand once you try it. Please rub some on your face."

While clearly still suspicious, Mira was unable to resist the temptation of something that could make her more beautiful, and she removed her scarf.

Her skin was badly cracked and damaged from many repeated days of applying and removing makeup in a hot climate. She picked up the bottle again and brought the moisturizer to her face. As she slowly spread it on herself, her eyes widened.

"I can't believe this. I can feel this cream seeping into my skin and moisturizing it. I don't think I've had skin this smooth in over a decade," admitted Mira.

After seeing his wife's face, Balor took a bottle and scooped out some moisturizer himself. "This feels like oil, but...it's too soft."

"You have a discerning eye. Soft oil is exactly what this is. Using plain oil would've been terrible for the skin, but oil with water and other medicinal ingredients mixed in helps to soften and repair the flesh."

"This is incredible. I can already tell how happy my skin is. The moisturizer smells nice, too." With skin as cracked and dry as Mira's, of course it'd feel better after being moisturized. I also went out of my way to mix in ingredients that I knew she was fond of to bring about smells she'd enjoy.

"Moisturizer is like armor for the skin. Please try applying makeup over the moisturizer. With the oil's protection, your skin will become more resistant to pain even when using the same makeup you've always used..."

Before I'd even finished my explanation, Mira was already going through her bag and pulling out a full set of cosmetics. She painted her skin white with foundation and gave her cheeks a red tint with blush.

"Wow, everything went on so easily," said Mira.

"If you coat your face with moisturizer, you will cover up the unevenness in your skin, enabling other products to adhere more easily. So what do you think of my item?"

"I still despise you, but I have to acknowledge this is a great product. I'm going to take this bottle. And I want you to give me three, no, five more."

Mira stuffed the bottle in her bag. No matter what I said, I had a feeling I wasn't going to get it back.

"If my wife likes it, then I'm sure it's the real deal. Give me the prospects for its success," Balor said.

"This product will revolutionize cosmetics. All who wear makeup will come to need it. Both to heal and protect their skin."

I took a short pause for impact.

"This should not be thought of as a competitor for existing cosmetics. From now on, using moisturizer is going to become common practice everyone who wears makeup... You understand the value of that, right, Father?"

This was the reason I chose moisturizer. It could revolutionize makeup itself. My goal had never been to steal customers from existing markets, but instead to create a new practice for anyone who wore makeup.

It was impossible for this to not turn a profit.

"I can't say that I have a good understanding of makeup. Mira, do you think your friends would want this stuff?"

"I can't imagine a woman alive who wouldn't want it. I came here planning to mock and dismiss Illig, no matter what he made. After using this, however, I'm finding it difficult to do so. If it will get me more moisturizer, I'll even address this bastard child as my own son," admitted Mira.

"I see, it's that good of a product..." Balor closed his eyes and deliberated. He let out a slow breath. "Then the Balor Company will invest all of its resources into this new product. Mira, distribute these to your friends and do your best to spread the word."

"I have a lot of friends, you know." Mira did not seem eager to share the wondrous lotion with others.

"Mira, as long as we have stock, please continue to use it and tell everyone you know about it. Give a bottle to each person. If they want more, refuse and tell them that the moisturizer will be on sale soon. Illig, how many can you prepare in a week?" asked Balor.

"Until we can finalize a production system, I'll be making them by myself, so I can only create about two hundred in one week," I said.

"I've given you permission to hire all the staff you need, remember?" Balor said.

"The problem is that risks the formula leaking. It's likely other companies will attempt to make and sell moisturizer as soon as we launch this product," I explained.

"…That's not like me to get ahead of myself like that. You're right. Until we can establish the brand, we need to make sure we have exclusivity over this product. I'll assign two assistants to you whom I have full confidence can keep their lips sealed. Make as many as bottles as you can and send them all to me. Mira will then distribute them to the wives of noblemen and other such wealthy people. In this way, we can work to spread word of mouth among the upper class. Am I correct in assuming that's why you had my wife come today, Illig?"

"Exactly. A product won't sell on quality alone. Since the usefulness of moisturizer is so easily understood by using it, maximizing your wife's connections is the best way to spread word of it. There's no more effective form of advertising."

I needed Mira's help to show my target market the worth of my product. People were resistant to trying new products, especially when it came to items made to put on their skin. If trusted acquaintances used the product first, then they'd want to use it, too. The excitement that would build from hearing about such a useful item would undoubtedly snowball to create a large demand.

That was how business battles were won. It wasn't nearly enough to create some quality goods and then expect them to magically sell. Oral accounts were especially essential when the target market was upper-class women.

"How long will it take you to put together the production system?" inquired Balor.

"About a month, and there's a complication. A special drug is needed to make oil and water mix. It's a secret remedy of House Tuatha Dé, and it must be acquired there. Taking that into account, it will cost this much to make one bottle of moisturizer." I presented a document estimating the price of each of the ingredients that I needed.

"…The selling price of moisturizer is going to be cheap, but Tuatha Dé is quite far from here." Balor searched my eyes as if to gauge my true intention.

"That'll make it harder for the secret recipe to be discovered. I can't make moisturizer without this particular chemical. It may be possible for me to call an apothecary from Tuatha Dé to have it made here, but that would increase the risk of a leak. As long as the drug is produced in Tuatha Dé, I can keep the recipe hidden," I elaborated.

"I'll allow it, then. I'll leave the negotiation with House Tuatha Dé to you," Balor said.

"Understood."

This was my plan to ensure no one else could discover how moisturizer was produced.

The ingredient I used to mix oil and water was called lecithin, a naturally occurring substance found in soybeans.

To make lecithin, you first extracted oil from soybeans. You then filtered the oil to remove impurities and thoroughly mixed it with water until the paste-like lecithin separated from the oil.

Lecithin was used as a naturally occurring emulsifier, and it was capable of causing water and oil to mix. Without it, combining water and oil was impossible.

In the Tuatha Dé domain, I could have lecithin produced in an environment where the information was guaranteed not to leak. Without knowledge of that key ingredient, no other company would be able to replicate my formula.

More important than any of that, I was thinking of my long-term profits for House Tuatha Dé. Ensuring that the house had exclusive rights to production of a key portion of my moisturizer provided me with a good guarantee that the Balor Company couldn't push me out of the business.

"Illig, I know I'm repeating myself, but we're going to invest all of our resources into this product. If this succeeds, you'll become the representative of the new Balor Company brand, and you'll be famous worldwide. But if you fail, you know what will happen, right?" Balor asked.

"Of course. I will ensure this is a success. All right, I better get to work."

My main product had been decided, and I'd secured the full support of the Balor Company.

At this point, it seemed impossible to fail. It was only a matter of time until Illig Balor became known around the world as the person who built the Balor Company cosmetic brand.

With a reputation like that, I'd have easy access to any of my targets. Nobles would be fighting each other to have me visit their manors.

What's more, my success would grant me unlimited access to the Balor Company's information and distribution networks, plus I'd rake in massive sums of money.

Success was close at hand, ready for me to reach out and grab it. I just needed to stay focused.

I'd joked earlier that I risked becoming the target of assassination attempts myself if I grew too successful; however, it seemed inevitable at this point. Other businesses would seek to eliminate me; my coworkers could get jealous of my achievements; someone might even take me hostage to try to force the moisturizer recipe out of me.

*Let them come*, I thought. *It'll make for great combat experience for Tarte and Maha.*

A month and a half after the trial period, we went forward with our plans and opened the new cosmetics store.

I named the brand Natural You, and only half a year into its grand opening, it had become so popular, it was on its way to being a household name all around the world.

The store, selling moisturizer as its main product, quickly became a hit on a scale far larger than any of us could've imagined, largely thanks to the incredible publicity that'd started with Balor's wife. I'd seriously underestimated how quickly word traveled among the women of wealthy families.

Large lines formed at the store every day, and moisturizer was continually selling out the moment we got new stock. Despite my best efforts to increase production, we still couldn't meet the demand.

Every time I increased the manufacturing rate, word would spread, and the demand increased in kind.

Customers were not only coming from other cities, but other countries as well. The other day, Count Milteu received an official letter from a royal family in a foreign nation requesting moisturizer.

Underneath all this activity, however, a fierce information war had been unfolding.

Other companies were sending spies into the production factory or trying to bribe my employees, all for the purpose of discovering the production method for moisturizer. I'd raised security multiple times, but it'd quickly proved impossible to stop all of it.

Much of the recipe had been leaked, including the fact that it was made by adding herbs to a medicinal compound created by mixing olive oil and water. Some had even found out that there was a secret ingredient used to mix it all together.

Thankfully, the mixture of the herbs and the means of obtaining or producing the secret ingredient, lecithin, were still unknown. Thus, even with so much of the formula known to competitors, only the Balor Company still had the ability to make moisturizer.

Lecithin was still produced only in the Tuatha Dé domain, though Balor took care to conceal even that by faking its production in Milteu.

Even if word somehow got out that the lecithin was coming from Tuatha Dé, my father had taken extra care to ensure the production method would never be revealed, and the citizens of Tuatha Dé were already fairly tight-lipped. It wasn't especially hard to imagine what would happen if you were caught trying to sneak onto an assassin's property.

I was sure that everyone back home had their hands full.

The amount of lecithin required to keep up with the demand was far greater than anyone had expected. As a result, all of the soybeans in the Tuatha Dé domain had been used up almost immediately, but because ceasing production wasn't an option, Tuatha Dé had begun quietly buying up soybeans from other regions.

"Other companies want to sell moisturizer, but they have no

way of discovering the production method. It's only logical to expect them to get impatient and target people who know the secret."

This prediction of mine quickly proved correct.

Late one night, an intruder of decent skill sneaked into my house through the attic and made toward my room. "Decent skill" by my standards actually meant they were extremely talented, though this assailant still had no chance of catching me.

Dealing with them myself was sure to be easy, but I'd decided this was better practice for Tarte and Maha. I was content to just sit back and enjoy the show, though I did plan on stepping in to stop the fight if the girls were going to kill the intruder.

I heard someone stop directly above me. They bored a tiny hole in the ceiling. Most likely they were going to shoot me with a poison dart from a blowgun. Killing clearly wasn't the goal, as my rival businesses needed my information. This assailant wanted to kidnap and interrogate me to get my secrets.

*Hmm, how will Tarte and Maha handle this?* It didn't take long for me to get my answer.

Tarte entered the room and rolled up her skirt. A knife was strapped to her right thigh, a threefold metal rod on her left. She drew them both.

She connected the pieces of the rod together and attached the knife on the end to create a spear that she used to quickly jab at the ceiling.

Spears were the best weapon to use in close combat. When using a sword against one, it was said that you needed to be three times as skilled to win. Tarte was actually very skilled with polearms. So much so that I'd begun to suspect she had the Spear Arts skill.

I'd given her that concealable spear as a birthday present. Tarte immediately fell in love with it, declaring it a treasure, and she never slacked when it came to maintaining the weapon.

Tarte was capable of using both knives and spears depending on the situation and the distance between her and her opponent. She'd become skilled enough to be able to take down even the average knight in combat.

"You never stood a chance," she gloated to the intruder.

The intruder had the presence of mind to avoid screaming, but the blood spreading across the ceiling made it abundantly clear that they'd failed to dodge in time.

Tarte's strike had likely not been fatal on its own, but the scabbard for her knife had been laced with a neurotoxin. The poison was made from a Tuatha Dé secret recipe that I'd improved upon, and anyone who was so much as pricked by a blade coated in that substance would be rendered unable to lift a finger unless they had a very special physical makeup.

I chose this toxin because I wanted something that left my enemies alive but immobile. I couldn't have rival assassins committing suicide before I got them to say who'd hired them.

Someone lifted up a board of the ceiling, and Maha peered down into my room.

"We've caught him... I gagged him and tied him up so he can't kill himself," she said.

After detecting the intruder, Tarte had immediately stood guard and then intercepted before he could attack me, while Maha provided backup and blocked the escape route. It was safe to say they'd passed the test.

"Well done. That's no small feat detecting and dealing with an assassin of this caliber. I'm proud of you both," I praised.

Such speed of perception and action was commendable. They weren't perfect, of course, but it was clear they'd come a long way.

"Hee-hee-hee, I am so happy," Tarte giggled.

"Yeah, that was exciting. I feel like we can do anything," Maha added.

"You haven't had practical torture experience yet, have you? This is a perfect opportunity to put your classroom learning to the test. It would be very useful if you could get him to admit who hired him. See if you can devise a way to pry information out of him without a suicide. I've already taught you the necessary techniques to accomplish this," I commanded.

"I'll do my best! He tried to do something horrible to Master Illig, so I won't show any mercy," Tarte replied.

"Yeah, I have some anger I'd like to take out on him, too... If we do well, make sure to praise us, dear brother," Maha said.

The thing I was happiest about was that the two of them had grown capable of killing for me without hesitation.

Unlike me, they hadn't been given prisoners to get used to killing, so I wasn't sure they would be capable of it. Thankfully, it seemed their desire to make me happy had overridden any resistance they could've otherwise possessed.

Tarte and Maha had never looked more lovely to me than they did in that moment. I was certain they'd be great assets to me in battle.

While they diligently tortured the assassin, I cleaned the blood-spattered ceiling, then made some refreshments as a reward while I was at it.

It was going to be a long night.

Today was my day off.

Half a year had passed since I'd launched my Natural You cosmetics brand, but every day still felt like a war zone, and it didn't seem likely to calm down any time soon.

Even in such a busy time, rest was still important. Without it, you'd eventually break down. That's why I'd decided on taking a weekly one-day break from both my work as a merchant and from Tarte and Maha's training.

I told them to go out and enjoy themselves while I took my monthly trip out of the city.

Despite the identity of Illig Balor already being a disguise, I'd now disguised myself as someone from the Viekone domain in the neighboring country of Soigel. Viekone was over four hundred kilometers away from Milteu.

While it normally took around three weeks to make the journey from Milteu to Viekone, I could manage going there and back in just a single day. By implementing shortcuts and methods of travel above land, I'd shortened the time the journey took with each outing.

"Okay, I wonder if I'll break my record this time." Lately, I'd been making a game of it by timing myself. It made for great practice.

Less than half a day later, I arrived in the Viekone domain, and I sneaked into the courtyard of the Viekone estate.

I threw three pebbles at Dia's window. That was our signal. While risking being discovered as someone who'd illegally crossed the border and stolen into a foreign count's estate was dangerous, dealing with the official methods of immigration was a huge pain. That's why Dia and I had decided to meet this way.

She opened the window, and I used a wind spell to soar five meters above the ground. My eyes locked with Dia's as I reached the apex of the leap.

"Long time no see, Dia," I said.

"Yeah, it's nice to see you. Come in, I've got some delicious tea," she replied.

"Sounds good. I brought some candy from overseas."

"Well then, this is going to be a fun tea party!"

Before gravity pulled me into a fall toward the ground, I grabbed on to the rim of the window and pulled myself into Dia's room.

The room itself was not especially dainty. It was crowded with books about magic from all around the world, and staffs and other mana-boosting devices filled any other available space.

"I'm amazed every time I see this room," I remarked.

"E-even I know it's not very girlie, but I don't have any room for cute things. I do have another room for that kind of stuff, you know," Dia answered, flustered.

It was just like Dia to need another room because this one was too packed full of magical paraphernalia.

"It's fine like this. It fits you."

"I'm not sure how to take that comment, but I know better than to expect much from you in that department. Okay, here are all the spells I've written in the last month. I'm sure you'll find them interesting," said Dia, eyes sparkling, as she hoisted a stack of paper at me.

The pages were tightly packed with formulas written in the runic language of magic. In this world, only those with the Spell Weaver skill could truly give birth to new spells.

Anyone could write down a new formula, but if I didn't also copy it down, the incantation would fail. It'd become tradition for me to copy all the spells Dia had written in the month between our regular visits.

I easily grasped the meaning of each of Dia's spells as I wrote them down. This time they were especially complicated. Then something caught my eye, and I came to a full stop.

*...No way.*

"You were able to finish *that* spell?" I asked, incredulous.

"Heh-heh-heh, bet you didn't expect that. Ah, looks like you already wrote it down. All right, watch this." Dia began the chant. Her elemental conversion and incantation were as beautiful as ever. When she finished casting the spell, a nearby teacup began to float, bobbing gently up and down in the air.

It was a spell that manipulated gravity. Until now, the best we'd managed was doubling the gravity around something to increase its weight. This spell accomplished the opposite, causing a target to float. I'd tried to create this kind of magic myself previously, but I'd been unsuccessful.

I'd been after this kind of spell for a long time because it was a necessary component for the most devastating and powerful sort of magic I could think of.

Dia had come to my aid yet again. I certainly owed her a lot.

"Well, shoot. Looks like you beat me to it," I said.

"Your way of thinking is too rigid. In order to finish this spell, I..." Dia explained her thought process. It was plain on her face that she was having a lot of fun, proudly sharing her discoveries.

The girl never appeared cuter, or more captivating, than at times like those. We also happened to be sitting close together, and I could tell that she smelled nice.

"Lugh, are you listening?" Dia suddenly asked.

"Yeah, I am. That's an amazing idea. I hadn't even considered that," I replied.

"Hmm-hmm, does it make you respect your big sister a little more?"

Ever since the days when Dia had first served as my magic mentor, she'd enjoyed calling herself my big sister. I would've preferred we had a romantic relationship, but it was cute, so I allowed it.

"Yeah, I'm really impressed. I'd expect no less from you. How about some candy as a reward?"

"You said this is from overseas, right? ...It's so dark. It doesn't look very good."

"I guarantee you'll like it."

"Hmm. Ah, it's bittersweet—and really good. I like it. It goes well with tea, and it would probably taste amazing as an ingredient when baking things like cake."

"This candy is made from the seeds of cacao trees, which grow in countries to the south. Once my Natural You cosmetic brand slows down, I'm planning to start a confectionery line, and this is going to be the featured product," I explained.

The candy was chocolate—the ultimate sweet of my previous world. Just like with moisturizer, it was definitely going to make me a huge profit.

Selling chocolate as a limited wintertime product was an idea I'd been entertaining for a while. It'd probably fly off the shelves because of its long shelf life and perfect suitability as a gift.

"Wow, that sounds nice. If I lived closer to Milteu, I'd buy some," said Dia.

"Yeah, this is a little too far. I'll bring some more next month."

"I can't wait!"

If it was for Dia, I'd bring an entire sack of chocolate the next time I saw her.

We moved on to showing each other the results of our research since we last met. This was the thing I enjoyed doing with Dia more than anything, even if there was nothing amorous about it. Dia looked her best when she was talking about magic.

We quickly lost track of time, and the sun had started its descent into the horizon, which meant it was time for me to leave.

Admittedly, I was extremely reluctant to depart, but I had work tomorrow. Staying wasn't an option.

"...It's time to say good-bye already, isn't it? Whenever you have to go, I always think about how great it would be if you lived here," Dia said, clearly a little gloomy.

"I'd like that. What if I became your butler?" I offered.

"If you say stuff like that, I may actually try to make it happen, you know."

"Actually, becoming your butler would definitely be problematic for me... All right, time for me to go. See you next month."

"Yeah, see you!"

I jumped from the window, using wind magic to soften my descent. Dia leaned from the window and waved down at me. Our brief monthly visit was already over.

Though entirely too short, it had been a fantastic break nonetheless. I felt refreshed and ready to get back to work.

Two years had passed now since I'd first come to Milteu, and I was reflecting on the time I'd spent in the port city.

I was absurdly busy with all my work at the store, but through that, I'd been able to learn much about the world.

As the young prodigy who'd launched the successful Balor Company subsidiary, Natural You, I'd been invited to a wide variety of places and made a lot of personal connections. It also went without saying that I'd become incredibly rich.

As promised, I'd been receiving 5 percent commission on all sales from the Balor Company's cosmetic stores, and I was also still the manager of the flagship store, which held the highest sales out of any establishment in the chain.

I received all of my stores' profit after subtracting the Balor Company's cut and employee salaries. The business had done so well that I already had enough money to never work again for the rest of my life. For that reason, I'd taken to investing in a few things that'd piqued my interest.

The day to return home to Tuatha Dé had finally come.

The handing over of my responsibilities had mostly already been taken care of, and I'd said my good-byes to most everyone at the Balor Company.

A horse-drawn carriage was parked in front of the estate, and Tarte and I climbed in.

"Maha, I leave Natural You and the management of my information network in your hands," I said.

"I won't let you down, Lugh. I'll protect your base here in Milteu," she replied.

All three of us were fourteen years old now, and we looked quite a bit different than we did two years ago. Tarte had become very cute, and Maha was growing into a beautiful young lady. In the Alvanian Kingdom, fourteen was the age where you were recognized as an adult.

Though I'd tried my best with her training over the last two years, Maha had proved unsuitable for my assassination task force, as I'd expected. She'd grown to the point where I could confidently rely on her to manage logistical support, however.

I named her my administrative assistant in conjunction with the opening of a new store. She'd been working as Illig Balor's right-hand woman—and was becoming a very skilled merchant in her own right. While I was gone from Milteu, she was to assume all my responsibilities.

I also told her my real name and background. That's why she called me Lugh and not Illig on the day I left to return home.

While acting as the proxy representative of Natural You, she was going to carry out all the information gathering, capital provision, and resource procurement that I needed for my assassination work.

"I'm sorry I'm the only one who gets to go with Lord Lugh, Maha," Tarte apologized.

"I'd be lying if I said I wasn't jealous, but I'm proud that I can help Lugh in ways that no one else can... Tarte, please take care of him for me," Maha said back.

"I will!" responded Tarte. She and Maha exchanged a few encouraging words.

Maha then turned to me, tears forming in her eyes. Evidently, the separation wasn't going to be easy on her.

"Even if you can't stay for very long, please come visit me sometimes, Lugh," she pleaded.

"I promise I'll visit you, even when I don't have a business reason to come to Milteu."

"You'd better not forget that. If you go all the way to the Vie-kone estate every single month to visit Lady Dia and then never come to see me...it'll make me very sad, and I'll probably cry."

"Maha, you're an important apprentice and assistant to me. There's no way I wouldn't visit you," I said.

"Okay, I'll be waiting... Also, I found that thing you asked for—an uninhabited island located away from any merchant ship routes. Here's a map. What do you need this for anyway?"

"Two days ago, when I met with Dia, we finished some new magic. It's too powerful and dangerous to test anywhere other than an uninhabited island," I said.

This new deadly magic had been developed specifically for the purpose of killing the hero, and it held unfathomable power. The basic principles were complete, but it still needed a proper test run. Unfortunately, because of the spell's power and enormous area of effect, I couldn't risk testing it anywhere other than a place completely devoid of people.

The carriage departed, and eventually Maha fell out of sight.

I had at last completed my father's final trial. I'd successfully become a top-class merchant with wide-reaching fame.

There was no wife or daughter of any noble house that would not welcome Illig Balor with open arms.

Once I returned to the Tuatha Dé domain, I was going to start receiving real assassination jobs. I still had yet to kill anyone outside that underground prison. I wondered what sort of things this new me would feel when I killed.

The carriage clattered along the road.

I could tell from her face that Tarte was starting to feel a little homesick.

"Tarte, are you going to miss Maha?" I asked.

"…Honestly, yes. She's the first friend my age I've ever had."

I'd wanted to take Maha along, too, if possible, but I needed a representative in Milteu to manage my Balor Company information network.

Having a second location I could fall back on if House Tuatha Dé ever came under serious threat was a boon, too. In a worst-case scenario, I could fake Lugh's death and live the rest of my life as Illig.

"Really? Well, how about I leave the delivery of lecithin to you as often as I can. You'll have plenty of chances to see her," I offered.

Tarte had grown a lot over the last two years. She'd become extremely skilled with mana, and she was proficient with her wind affinity.

Her repertoire was comprised mostly of spells I'd created, and she was showing herself to be more than capable as an assassin's assistant. I don't think I could've had a more dependable guard or transport.

"That would make me happy. But I think Maha would rather see you," Tarte answered.

"You think so?"

"Yes. Maha loves you, my lord, and not as family or a friend. She loves you in, um, *that* way."

"I understand what you're saying, but I don't think you're right. Maha admires me. That's similar, but not the same thing."

"Sometimes the things you say are too difficult for me to understand, my lord."

"You'll understand someday."

Just then, the carriage came to a sudden stop. We'd been surrounded by wolves.

The driver jumped from the carriage and ran, abandoning his passengers. He was promptly set upon and became wolf food.

These creatures were far larger than normal wolves. Their claws seemed unusually large, and I could sense a small amount of mana emanating from their bodies.

These were monsters. Monsters were defined as animals that possessed mana. Just like with humans, animals also became stronger when enveloped in mana. Often, it resulted in mutations.

Typically, such animals were known to stay far from human civilization. It was strange to see them so readily approach people.

"This is perfect. May I use this as an opportunity to show off the fruits of my training?" asked Tarte.

"Ah, sounds good. I'll watch from here," I responded. Tarte then enveloped herself in mana to increase her physical strength, and she jumped out of the carriage.

All told, there were three wolves, and they quickly utilized the advantage of their numbers, encircling Tarte.

One of them bared its fangs and pounced. Before the wolf could bite into Tarte's flesh, a blade pierced through its mouth. Tarte was holding her spear. She'd lifted her skirt, removed the pieces of her weapon, and assembled it all in the blink of an eye.

The next wolf attacked from behind, but Tarte gave it a blow to the jaw and sent the creature flying through the air using the Wind Bullet spell.

The majority of sorcerers could cast magic only from the palms of their hands. Such was the way the formulas bestowed by the gods were written.

However, by modifying equations, Dia and I had made it so that you could cast magic from any point within a few dozen centimeters of your body.

Tarte could cast magic about forty centimeters out from herself. As soon as her opponents entered her range, she could knock them out instantly with a quick Wind Bullet to the jaw. Even the very best swordsmen would be caught unawares by such an attack because most everyone else was still under the impression that mages could cast magic only from their hands.

It was admittedly simple, but it made for a nice surprise attack.

The last wolf ran away too quickly for Tarte to be able to catch it on foot, but before the wolf could get very far, Tarte's spear pierced its back. She'd thrown the spear using the power of wind, giving it the speed of a bullet.

"That was impressive," I commented.

"It's all thanks to your training. I've become very capable in battle, my lord."

While Maha was working as my administrative assistant and sharpening her skills needed to handle my logistical support, Tarte was accumulating combat experience.

She looked proud of herself as she returned to the carriage, and she smiled contently when I patted her on the head.

"…Looks like it's about time for the hero to start showing up," I muttered.

I'd been allowed to reincarnate specifically for the purpose of killing the hero. After the hero overthrew the Demon King, he was supposed to go mad with power and bring ruin upon the world.

It had been long said that once monsters began to increase in number, demons would soon appear, followed by the Demon King and the hero, in turn.

Monsters appearing on a main road like this was likely a sign that demons were coming.

I needed to hurry. Thankfully, I'd been doing more these last two years than just simply working as a merchant. Lots of my time had been spent training Tarte, my combat partner. I'd also raised Maha to function in a non-battle support role from her place in Milteu.

I'd even had a major breakthrough in my efforts to create the ultimate weapon designed to kill the hero.

I was eager to experiment; my tests on the uninhabited island couldn't come soon enough. I was certain that not even the hero could withstand something that powerful.

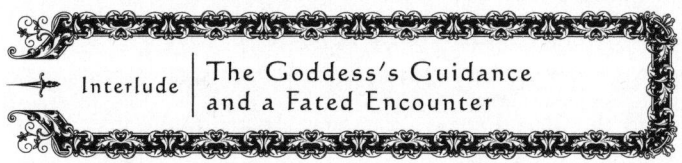

Interlude | The Goddess's Guidance and a Fated Encounter

In an alabaster room, a goddess wreathed in white sat down with a blank expression.

She looked like a doll, appearing inhuman and emotionless. Her persona didn't at all resemble the energetic and playful attitude she'd assumed when meeting with that other world's greatest assassin. That'd been nothing more than a personality simulation deemed most likely to put the assassin at ease.

The goddess was nothing more than a tool designed to watch over and protect worlds.

You could see her as a cold, cruel realist, but those words didn't accurately get at the heart of what the goddess really was. In truth, she was but a simple mechanism. Possessed of no emotion, she only pretended to have such feelings when the circumstances demanded it.

"An intervention in fate. Aid to Lugh Tuatha Dé successful," whispered the goddess in a dispassionate voice.

The assassin currently named Lugh Tuatha Dé had a very difficult mission.

His current odds of success were only 8 percent at best. That's why she was giving him extra support.

Even with the goddess's level of authority, however, there was a limit to how much she could intervene. If she had the ability, she would've directly removed the hero herself.

She didn't have the ability to increase her number of pieces, nor could she alter them in any way. Instead, she was focusing all her efforts on guiding her existing pieces down the right path.

If you wanted to put it in romantic terms, you could say she was setting up fated encounters.

Whether Lugh noticed these encounters or was able to take advantage of them was up to him.

"Depletion of Lugh Tuatha Dé's assigned support confirmed. Demanding additional resources… Dismissal of request by superior being confirmed. Grant of additional resources is dependent on the achievements of Lugh Tuatha Dé. Leaving this matter for now. Beginning phase two."

The goddess had hopes for Lugh Tuatha Dé, but she couldn't trust him.

He was nothing more than the piece that currently had the highest odds of saving the world.

Knowing this, the goddess was already moving on to the next piece. As long as the world was saved, it didn't matter which piece got the job done.

The goddess, robotic and emotionless as ever, continued to observe the world.

Illig was sleeping in this morning.

…Apparently, his real name was Lugh.

Certain circumstances had led to him pretending to be a person named Illig.

I loved watching him sleep.

While awake, he was handsome, kind, always on guard, and a perfect person in every way, but while sleeping, he just looked like a sweet, innocent young boy.

I asked if I could sleep in his bed because I was lonely, but that was just an excuse.

I just wanted to be with him so I could see his cute, sleeping face up close.

"Dear brother, would you wake if I kissed you?"

I really wanted to try, but I didn't have the courage.

Illig was like a father, a brother, and a teacher to me. He'd given me so much affection, and I could never thank him enough for that.

I wished he would see Tarte and me as members of the opposite sex, though...

The reason he wouldn't was because he already had his heart set on someone else.

It was frustrating.

If I'd met him sooner, perhaps I could've been the apple of his eye instead.

I wasn't going to give up, though. I still had time. The human heart is fickle.

Right now, the girl named Dia was the object of his desire, but that was only for the moment. Who could say what would happen in the future?

"Maybe I should get a little sleep, too."

Watching Illig's cute sleeping face made me sleepy.

It was cold outside, just like it'd been on the day I first met Illig.

## ~Lugh and Maha's Encounter~

Everything was stolen from me.

*"In order to trust someone, you must first doubt them."*

Whenever I was having a hard time, I recalled my father's favorite phrase.

He was an excellent merchant. Leaving his small hometown to find work, he ended up founding a company that grew very successful in only a single generation.

Father's belief was that "in order to trust someone, you must first doubt them."

It was impossible to unconditionally trust another person. First, it was best to be wary of them. Only decide to trust them once they'd done enough to earn it.

Blindly trusting others wasn't a virtue—it was simple carelessness.

I think those words are the reason I'm alive today.

...Through a plot orchestrated by Father's right-hand man, my parents were both killed.

They'd been on the way to an important business meeting when their carriage was assaulted by a large group of thieves.

The thieves knew ahead of time when the carriage was coming, and they waited for it in full armor. The escort Father hired had also turned out to be entirely made up of disguised thieves.

There was no way that was a coincidence. It was a plot by Father's right-hand man to take over the company.

After the funeral, that man approached me and started crying over my father's demise. He hugged me, saying that he would protect me and the company.

I'd just lost my parents, and he was a friend of Father's and an acquaintance of mine, so I put my head to his chest and cried.

I doubted his intentions nonetheless. If I'd really believed his words, I probably would've been killed, too.

In the midst of my despair, I still managed to recall my father's most important lesson.

I didn't have a family. The only person I had to rely on was this man, Father's friend and former adjutant.

I resisted the temptation to entrust myself to him and did some investigating. Through that, I discovered that he was the one who killed my parents, and in order to take the company, he was going to kill me next.

So I ran.

I barely got away. He'd assigned a guard to watch me, one who didn't hesitate to try to kill me once he saw I was running. If I didn't have mana, I doubt I would have been able to escape.

Father had always told me to hide my mana.

Being a mage came with a variety of perks, but in exchange, you ended up saddled with a lot of responsibility. If I was to inherit the company someday, it was far better for me to hide my mana. Concealing it had been the thing that saved my life.

I escaped the guard, took all the money I could hold, disguised myself as a simple town girl, and headed for the large city of Milteu, where I hoped I wouldn't be found.

A bit of fortune found me as I purchased goods from a traveling merchant for higher than market price, and I was given a ride in his carriage in exchange.

"I'll be back someday," I said while hiding among the merchant's goods as the carriage left town.

I wanted to protect Father's company, but it was due to the education my parents had given me that I knew I had to leave.

My safety could never have been guaranteed in that town. No matter what I did, I surely would've been killed.

If I wanted to protect my father's company, I had no choice but to run to prolong my life, and return once I'd become stronger.

That's why I left.

Gathering my resolve, I swore to myself that I'd focus on becoming stronger in Milteu, then return to my hometown someday to take back Father's company.

Life in Milteu was rough.

Even though I had knowledge as a merchant, no one would hire a child without any relatives.

One night a burglar broke into the cheap inn I was staying at and stole all of my possessions aside from my wallet, which I'd made sure never to let go of.

That unfortunate event ended up lighting a fire under me, inspiring me to start a new business using the street children who lived in the slums.

I gathered orphans, picking the smart ones who could read and write, and used the money I had on hand to get them some nice clothes. Then I had them act as tour guides.

I sent the kids in the best physical shape into the mountains to collect snow and ice from the caves in summer, and firewood in the winter.

Milteu was a large city and saw a lot of tourists. As such, there ended up being a demand for the exhaustive knowledge of the city that street children could provide.

One thing I was surprised to discover was how knowledge-able the kids were about good restaurants in the city, thanks to all the garbage they regularly rooted through while looking for their next meal.

The snow and ice we sold in the summer ended up being popular products, and there was high demand for the firewood in the winter. I sold our products below market price to target the poorer population of Milteu, which led to some impressive sales.

I was able to run a reasonably successful business employing kids I found on the streets.

If you had the ability to read demand and put your employees in the right place to succeed, then you could run a business. Father's teachings ended up saving me.

*When everyone reaches adulthood, I'll start a small company...* That was the naive dream I'd started clinging to.

Unfortunately, things soon went bad for my business, thanks to philanthropic efforts seeking to give aid to orphans.

After receiving some sudden inspiration, Count Milteu's wife took an interest in welfare and started to invest large sums of surplus tax revenue into relief for the poor.

Orphanages started to pop up all over town, each one after the large subsidies being offered. Thus, orphan hunting began. My street children were the first to be targeted, and we were all sent to orphanages. That marked the end of my business.

Just like that, my naive dream was over.

◇

Life at the orphanage was miserable, and that was putting it mildly.

It was so awful that my time spent with the other kids on the street seemed like heaven in comparison.

As the orphanage was opened for the sole purpose of reaping the benefits, the director, unsurprisingly, thought of nothing other than reducing maintenance costs. All he needed to do was keep the children alive to ensure they could keep lining their pockets.

We were given the cheapest food imaginable, all of which tasted horrible.

Children were regularly beat to silence them when they were loud, and the abuse only got worse from there. It was an everyday occurrence to see children bound and gagged with rags stuffed into their mouths.

There was only one other adult working at my orphanage, probably to keep labor costs low.

His sole job was to keep watch. He wasn't tasked with educating or taking care of the children in any way. The kids had to do all of the chores and look after the smaller children themselves. We were even forced to take on various odd jobs, and any who dragged their feet at work were hit. Any money we earned went straight into the pockets of the orphanage.

Once the good-looking children were deemed mature enough, they were forced to start taking customers.

A girl one year older than me named Noine returned to the orphanage one day and, likely because she'd been so traumatized by a client, took a knife and slashed her face repeatedly so that no customer would ever approach her again.

She'd been such a beautiful girl, but after that, she was unrecognizable.

Some children tried to escape, but that wasn't tolerated.

If the number of children in the orphanage dropped, so would the subsidies. Such a thing would incur the wrath of the director.

A failed escape attempt meant a kid would be mutilated both to ensure they would never be able to run again and to serve as an example to the others.

Nothing had ever made me hate my own powerlessness more.

Violence and fear ruled that place. My intelligence, and everything Father had taught me as a merchant, was worthless there.

While doing laundry in the garden one day, I overheard the director and the guard speaking.

"Do you think Maha will be able to take customers soon? Lately I've been getting the urge to pin her down and take her myself."

"That's a great idea, boss. She's a real looker, and a virgin, too. She's sure to fetch a good price. I'm reaching out to the perverts in the nobility who like them young."

"Hmm, don't give her away for cheap. Virgins can sell pretty high. Her price will drop if she's too scrawny, though, so make sure to feed her a well-balanced diet."

"Don't worry—I've been doing just that. She's already starting to put on a little meat."

"Once she sells, I might have a go at her. Sounds like she's growing into a fine young girl."

Feeling like I might scream, I covered my mouth with my hand and sat down on the ground.

They were going to make me take clients. Just thinking about it was making me sick, and I couldn't help but picture Noine, her face slashed beyond recognition.

*I can't end up like that. I won't end up like that*, I thought, but I knew I didn't want to take clients, either.

Unless I escaped, I'd be forced to suffer something terrible. There are no words to describe how scared I was.

No one at the orphanage knew I had mana. Regardless of how big and scary the adults were, if I could take them by surprise, I was sure I could get away.

I made a plan, devoting all of my time to preparation. I had to escape before they made me do the unspeakable.

Careful not to give away that I knew anything, I did my best to act as I usually did. There was no telling what they'd do to me if my scheme was discovered.

The night of my breakout had arrived.

A frenzy suddenly fell upon the orphanage.

Apparently, the son of the head of the Balor Company, who also happened to be one of the company's executives, was coming to the orphanage and looking to adopt.

Other children were excitedly talking about how if he found someone he liked, he'd adopt them and have them work at the Balor Company. Not only would the child who got adopted be able to escape this nightmare, but they'd also be set up with a job at the biggest company in the city.

This was the chance of a lifetime, the rope dangling down to the bottom of a pit. Everyone was abuzz, discussing ways to appeal to the visitor.

If I was chosen, I could get out without taking any risks. Working at a big company was also very appealing. Saving up money would put me toward the goal of getting my father's company back, plus it would afford me some invaluable experience.

Was it really all right for me to be chosen, though?

I had mana, a power that gave me a chance of escape. I'd already been working on a plan to run away. The other children didn't have that option. Without mana, they had no hope of getting out of here.

I let out a long sigh, looked at the ceiling, and decided that I would do my best not to catch the Balor Company man's eye. It was better to leave that opportunity to one of the other kids.

For a moment, I wondered if I'd become too soft. I couldn't help but feel sympathy for all the other children stuck in this wretched place with me.

Later on, the rumored executive of the Balor Company arrived at the orphanage.

Everyone was surprised to discover that the executive turned out to be a young boy the same age I was.

I was struck by how handsome he was. He wasn't just good-looking—he also had a certain elegance about him, and he radiated confidence.

"He's my prince," I muttered without thinking. I understood that he was special and that he was cut from a different cloth than I was.

Other kids quickly got over the shock of his age and hastily swarmed him, each one begging to be chosen.

"My name is Illig Balor. I'm looking for someone who could be my future assistant. Please tell me about yourselves."

The prospect of working so closely with a major player at the biggest company in the city only made the children more excited.

I watched the scene play out a few steps behind the other kids, while the greedy director fawned over the boy. He was probably offering a lot of money for the adoption. The director acted like that only toward people who were going to fill his pockets.

The boy closely examined the children one by one, asking each of them questions. He was well-mannered and had a wonderful smile. All the girls were looking at him as though he were a prince who'd come to whisk them away.

I was tempted to go to him, but I just stayed back and watched.

Then, after a little time passed, the prince pushed his way through the crowd of children and walked straight up to me. Looking me up and down with those unusual eyes of his, he smiled at me. My heart pounded in my chest.

"I found you. I have need of your strength. Will you come with me?"

He extended a hand...and I grabbed it.

Even though I'd said to myself that I wouldn't steal this chance from the other kids, I'd been unable to resist. I'd taken his hand almost unconsciously.

"Yes, I'd love to."

I don't think I'd intended to say yes, but the prince was so much larger than life, so handsome, that he'd stolen my heart before I knew what'd happened.

...*I'm sorry*, I apologized silently to the other kids.

I needed to do more than that, though. I resolved to one day return to that orphanage and save all of those poor children. With the support of an executive from the Balor Company, that should've been possible.

"Director Torran, I want to adopt this girl."

"An excellent choice. Unfortunately, this girl is a bit of a special case, so I'll have to double the price we discussed earlier... Actually, no, I'm going to need even more than that."

"How much are you asking for?"

The director then proceeded to give an outrageously high price. He was probably just trying to start negotiations with a high price, expecting a counter.

That kind of money could buy you multiple slaves.

"Very well. Here you are."

The prince coolly motioned for his attendant to take out some gold coins and stuffed them into a leather bag. Eyes wide in shock, the director eagerly accepted the money while bowing profusely.

"I-it's a deal. However, I'm afraid we can't hand her over just yet. We need to give Maha some time to prepare, so please come back in three days."

"Understood. See you in three days."

It wasn't time to prepare. The director wanted to sell me to some noble for a night to make a little more money while he still could. He likely wanted to have his turn at me himself.

I nearly called out to the prince to save me, but I ended up swallowing the words. The director was glaring daggers at me with bloodshot eyes, warning me not to say anything out of line. Fear gripped me, and I stayed quiet.

The prince looked at me and smiled. It felt like he was telling me that everything would be okay.

"Director Torran, I will come to adopt her in three days, but our contract is complete, and I am now her guardian. Make sure not to forget that."

"Of course, my good sir. I'll treat her with the utmost care."

It was a lie, of course. Once again, the director was warning me not to say anything. Even without him threatening me, I don't think I could've said anything. I didn't want the prince to think of me as defiled.

My hunch about why I was detained for three days was quickly proved right.

The very night I'd been adopted, a customer was lined up for me. The director had probably rushed to find a customer because the prince was coming to collect me in a few days.

Unfortunately, my customer was a nobleman, which reduced my chances of escape.

After being washed and dressed up in the nicest clothes I've worn since I ran away from home, I was loaded into a horse-drawn carriage.

The guard and the director sat next to me. Unless I did something, I was going to be raped.

My customer was the same person who'd treated poor Noine so horribly that she'd mutilated her own face afterward.

All of the kids who'd been forced to take clients always said that nobles were the roughest.

*I'm scared, I'm scared, I'm scared.*

All I had to do was endure this for three days, and then I could be with the prince. The image of his face came to mind. I couldn't stand the thought of being violated before I went to him.

It really wasn't like me to have such thoughts; they made me feel like a young maiden out of a fairy tale. I'd been focused on survival for so long that I'd forgotten those kinds of emotions. While I began to wonder what had changed in me, I quickly realized the answer.

It was love at first sight.

Honestly, I was surprised at myself for still being capable of such a feeling. It certainly explained the strange thoughts I was having.

I thought that if I managed to jump out the carriage window, ran to the first Balor Company store I could find, and then called his name, the people there would surely help me.

I had two choices. The first was to do as I was told and go to the prince in three days. The second was to risk danger and go to my prince still a maiden.

To me, the decision was easy.

"It's a shame," the director said with a sigh. "If that boy had only come a month later, I could've had my fill of this girl."

"...!"

The director reached over and rubbed my leg with his greasy fingers. I pretended to be scared so I wouldn't tip them off. Meanwhile, I measured the best time to escape.

The carriage turned on the road and swayed, causing both the director and the guard to lose their balance and tip to one side.

It was the best chance I was ever going to get. I opened the window and leaped out.

As I landed, I rolled along the ground to soften the impact. My dress was ruined in the process, but I didn't care. I even ripped the skirt to make it easier to run.

During my time working with other street urchins, I'd gained plenty of physical training, and I'd learned the back alleys of Milteu very well.

There was no reason to hide my mana now, so I ran with all my power. Sadly, it wasn't long before I was caught.

"How...?" I gasped.

I'd run into an alley but was able to make only two turns before the guard from the orphanage had caught up to me. No normal person should've been able to do that.

"You weren't the only one hiding your mana, little girl. Awww, I'll have to punish you for ruining your dress like that. Hyuk-hyuk-hyuk, not even the director will see us here. As long as I don't leave a mark, I can do whatever I like. I'm always getting stuck with the director's leftovers, so it'll be nice to break one in myself for a change."

This was terrible. Trying to escape into an alley had back-fired.

The guard swung his arm at me as hard as he could, and I closed my eyes to brace myself for the impact. To my surprise, the strike never came.

I slowly opened my eyes and saw that someone had caught the guard's arm.

"Y-you little bastard..."

"I believe I made myself quite clear. 'Our contract is complete, and I am now her guardian. Make sure not to forget that.' Maha is my little sister. What exactly were you about to do to her?"

My prince was there, standing right before my eyes. The guard cowered at the boy's glare alone and backed away.

"How did you...?" I managed to say.

"When I left, I could see your eyes begging me to save you, so I did a little research on Torran. It didn't take long for me to realize his intentions, so I kept an eye on you."

I was suddenly overcome with emotion, and my heart began to beat dramatically.

"But that was dangerous," I said.

"It may have been, but you're part of my family now. Family members protect each other." The prince let go of the guard's arm and stood in position to protect me. "Let's get out of here." He draped a coat over me and smiled.

Suddenly aware of my state of dress, I looked away shyly.

The guard was standing there paralyzed. He seemed unsure if it was okay for him to hit an executive of the Balor Company. Then the director appeared in the alleyway, and I stifled a gasp.

"Well, this is problematic. Your adoption of Maha was supposed to be three days from now," he said.

"I don't like being made to repeat myself. This girl is a part of my family. I won't overlook her being endangered," the prince replied.

"…Then you leave me no choice. I already have your money, so I don't need to kiss your ass anymore. I'll put you in your place, you little shit!"

"Y-you sure about this, boss? Illig Balor is the son of the head of the Balor Company. This'll make us enemies of theirs."

"You think I care? I'll just make him disappear. I'll sell him off in some foreign country as a male prostitute!"

The guard sneered at the villainous proposal. Clearly, he was glad for any justification to beat on the prince.

"Please run. That guy is a mage!" I pleaded.

"Yes, I know." The prince seemed surprisingly calm despite my warning.

He easily dodged the guard's punch and lightly brought his arms down on the guard's shoulders.

With a dull sound, the guard's shoulder joints separated, and the prince rammed into him while he was off-balance. He then stepped on the guard's knee, causing it to bend in a direction no knee rightly should have.

"GYAAAAAAAAAAAAAAAAAAAAAAAAHHHHH!!!" the guard screamed, writhing in pain.

The prince turned to the director and smiled. He closed the distance between them in an instant and pressed a knife against his throat. A line of blood trickled down the director's throat where the knife pricked him.

The director couldn't even manage a response.

"E-eek…"

"I never had any need to make a deal with you, you know. I could just as easily take her by force… To be honest, force is where I excel." The prince was smiling the whole time, but I could feel some kind of cold, dark aura emanating from him. It sent a chill down my spine.

The director, facing such a fearsome sensation head-on, wet his pants and was unable to move or respond.

"All right, Maha, let's go home. I already have a room prepared for you." The prince reached out his hand to me again, just like he had at the orphanage.

One thing I was certain of now was that this boy was not normal. If I took his hand, I'd cease being normal, too.

"Take me away, my prince."

But I didn't look back.

No matter how unusual he was, I fully believed I'd be happy anywhere as long as I was with him.

First, I had to doubt him, though. I would have to investigate who and what this boy was. Only then would I decide if he really was worthy of trust.

He may have been my prince and the savior I'd so longed for,

but I still needed to be sure. That's what my father had taught me, and that ideal is what had kept me alive through all my troubles.

## ~The Night Before Lugh's Departure~

Illig, whose true identity was Lugh Tuatha Dé, was to return to his real home tomorrow.

In preparation of his departure, we were going through final checks to transfer control of his cosmetic brand, Natural You, to me.

"And we're done," I said.

"Great. I leave it in your hands," Illig replied.

"I won't let you down. I'm confident I have the skill to protect your brand, but I won't stop there. I'll grow the brand even larger," I declared.

"With you in charge, that wouldn't surprise me," Illig said with a gentle smile.

"I'm also thinking of expanding beyond this city. There is a very promising store in a nearby town. It's the property of a company that used to be very successful but has fallen into decline since a change in management."

That "promising store" was one of the establishments in Father's old company.

Ever since Father's right-hand man took over, the company had suffered failure after failure and quickly fell into financial trouble. It was one of the smaller stores, and it had been put up for sale after being judged as not particularly important.

However, it was the first store my father had built. As such, it held many memories for me. I was going to take back Father's company. Taking that first shop was the first step toward that goal.

"Do as you like. I trust in your skill. I won't tell you to keep personal feelings out of this, but if you do decide to follow your heart, make sure you succeed," Illig instructed.

"Of course. I am your assistant, after all."

Illig probably knew everything about my past and how I was trying to take back my father's business. We hadn't openly spoken about it, but I was certain he'd done thorough investigations on my origin.

Even with such knowledge, he still trusted me.

For that reason, I was determined to see my personal goal realized while also making a profit.

*"If you do decide to follow your heart, make sure you succeed."* Hearing Illig say that only made me love him more.

Choosing to follow this abnormal boy down this strange road was definitely the right choice.

"Master Illig, Master Maha, I brought some tea."

"Thank you."

The kid who brought us tea had previously lived with me in the same orphanage and had even been one of my business partners back when I'd lived on the streets. Recently, I'd been rescuing different children from the orphanage by hiring them into the Balor Company.

"About that thing you asked me for. If I can get it, will you go on a date with me?"

"Only if you don't try anything afterward."

"That's unfortunate."

Illig and I laughed.

My lifelong dreams were at last within my grasp, and it was all thanks to my dear brother. That's why I'd decided that no matter what the future held for me, I'd dedicate the rest of my life to helping Illig, even if that meant dying for him.

I hoped that perhaps one day, once I'd achieved my objective, Illig would see me not as his assistant but as a lover.

For that purpose, I resolved myself to work hard to meet his expectations.

After a long time away, I'd finally returned to the Tuatha Dé domain as Lugh.

"It's changed so much in the last two years."

The most obvious change from two years ago were the vast soybean fields.

The little legumes could be grown in thin soil without much time and effort. They even helped replenish the nutrients in the dirt as they grew. However, because most people only regarded soybeans as food for livestock, there wasn't much demand for them. This was why so few people grew them.

Once House Tuatha Dé began buying up the crop as an ingredient for moisturizer, the price of soybeans inflated to the same price as wheat. Now that they'd become an easy source of money, there were soybean fields all over the domain.

Tarte leaned out of the carriage and looked around outside. "We've finally returned. It's so nostalgic. But I feel like the city life in Milteu fits you better, my lord."

"Did it really seem that way? I feel like this a better fit for me. I'm more at ease here."

My dyed hair had at last been allowed to return to its natural silver color. As the carriage trundled toward the estate, citizens of the domain began to approach and wave.

"Welcome back! You sure aren't called a wonder boy for nothing. Soybeans sell for an amazing price now, and my job turning the soybeans into that weird paste pays super well."

"Thanks to our boy genius, I was able to buy two cows."

"Even when you're not here, you continue to work for our sake!"

"I'm grateful for all you've done, but sure enough there were many times when I'd wished you were here."

It seemed that Father had explained to them that I was the one responsible for the increase in the selling price of soybeans. Everyone was telling me how much easier it had made their lives.

Once again, I was glad that I'd decided to export lecithin from the Tuatha Dé dominion.

In all reality, the Balor Company had probably noticed that the secret ingredient was made from soybeans. The reason they hadn't done anything with that knowledge was likely because they still didn't know how to turn soybeans into lecithin. They were probably also afraid of upsetting me, or perhaps they were simply showing respect for the person responsible for all this success.

Despite being a merchant, Balor was a compassionate man. During my time as Illig, he treated me as if I'd truly been his biological son.

Even that gentleness was a calculated business strategy on his part, however. It was a common misconception that the best merchants were the ones who coldly ignored the emotions of others and sought only efficiency.

If that was how you operated, then people would be unlikely to want to cooperate with you long-term and your business would suffer. The very best merchants were able to use their hearts to make important decisions, and they invested time and money accordingly into whoever needed it. I learned as much from Balor.

"Lord Lugh, this is for you!"

"Please take this as a token of my gratitude."

A number of people approached, handing me crops, cheese, meat from hunting, smoked fish, and more. I accepted them all without turning anyone away. Tarte and I quickly ended up with our hands full.

"They all love you so much, my lord," Tarte said as proudly as if she were talking about herself.

"Yeah. That's exactly why I want to bring prosperity to this domain, just like my father and his father before him."

I was reincarnated into this world to be an assassin, but more important, I was the heir of House Tuatha Dé.

Not long after my return to the estate, Mother came up to me and gave me a big hug.

"Welcome hoooooooooooooome! I was so lonely without you here, Lugh! Ahhh, I missed your smell. You're terrible, you know that? Last time you came home, you only talked to Cian about work and then left without seeing me!"

"...Can you not do this where people can see us? I have a position to maintain."

"Impossible. I haven't seen you in so long! Hmm-hmm-hmm-hmm, I was so, so lonely. Lugh, you can't leave us again. Whew, I've had my fill. Welcome home to you, too, Tarte. Thank you for staying with my boy. You can see how much I worry about him."

"N-no need to thank me. I would've missed him even more than you did."

"Is that so? Please continue to look after him! This boy always tries to do everything on his own, so I'm relieved he has someone like you around."

"I-I'll do my best!" Tarte stood up straight, her face blushing deep red.

I felt like she was taking my mother's words the wrong way.

"Mother, where is Father?" I asked.

"Oh, that's right. He wants you to meet him in the study. While you're talking to Cian, I want Tarte to tell me all about your time in Milteu. You never told me anything about yourself in your letters, Lugh!"

"O-okay, I'll tell you everything in full detail!" Tarte replied.

Hearing everything from Tarte, a girl who was closer to me than most anyone else, was sure to embarrass me. Saying anything to Mother about that would be a waste of my breath at this point, though, and Tarte easily relented when pushed, so telling her not to say anything wouldn't do much, either.

So I resigned myself to my fate. All I could do was pray she didn't talk about *that*.

*How did I let that happen to me?* I wondered. I supposed that, despite this being my second life, I was still in my teens. I was no more immune to the urges of nature than anyone else.

I left Tarte and went to the study.

Father took stock of me as soon as I entered, clearly evaluating me. He obviously wanted to see how much I'd grown over the last two years.

"Lugh, you've become a man," he said at last.

"Yes, I reached the age of adulthood a month ago."

Fourteen was when you graduated from adolescence in the Alvanian Kingdom. I was now an adult in the eyes of society. That meant I was of marriageable age.

Among nobility, it was common to arrange marriages far in advance while kids were still young and then hold the ceremony when they both turned fourteen.

However, only five years ago, a certain set of circumstances led to it becoming common practice in this country to wait until both partners turned sixteen.

"That's not what I mean. Unfortunately, this country is overflowing with children who have long since reached maturity. You have become an adult in the true meaning of the word... Becoming a successful merchant was part of your trial, but I'd never imagined you would take that this far. There isn't a single noble who doesn't know of Natural You, the cosmetic brand of Illig Balor."

"I invented moisturizer, a product capable of earning me a famed reputation as a merchant, and then made a plan to spread it...but everything that happened after that was thanks to Balor. He weaponized the popularity of moisturizer by attaching the brand to existing cosmetic products. In doing so, he rewrote the entire landscape of the cosmetics industry. His prowess was stunning to watch up close."

I'd envisioned using moisturizer to bring about a revolution in the world of cosmetics, but things had advanced so much more quickly than I'd expected. Despite being there for every step of the process as the person in charge of the cosmetics project, I'd still been completely taken aback by the incredible support I'd received from the company.

Now Natural You was becoming one of the most popular brands in the world, and it was known for more than just moisturizer.

"That man is as skilled as a merchant can get. Just having the chance to compare yourself to him is a valuable experience. Before your trial, I explained that my purpose for sending you to Milteu to work as a merchant was so that you could learn about the world, build another identity that will be helpful to you as an assassin, and build personal connections. None of that was a lie. But I did have one more reason. Do you know what that was?" Father asked.

I shook my head. For once, I had no idea what it could've been.

"I wanted you to find a life outside of the Tuatha Dé clan. Lugh, you are capable of having a successful career as a merchant. There are many who desire that life. Balor even recommends that you leave our clan of assassins and devote yourself to being a businessman. If that's in your best interest, then I... He's not just saying that, you know. He told me that you brought in revenue worth twenty years of this domain's tax revenue. It seems he wants you to support him as the second-highest executive in his company, and then one day support his son as well. If you choose that road, I won't stop you."

"What are you saying? The only reason I gained all that experience as a merchant was to better myself as an assassin," I replied.

"Lugh, at this point it's too late for me to choose any other way to live. You haven't yet bloodied your hands with murder. You can still find another way... We Tuatha Dé have protected this country by removing harmful influences, but it will not do the same for us. If we're ever revealed for what we are, the royal family will dispose of us as criminals to appease the nobility. Our loyalty to the country earns us no reward." Father's words were soft, and there was no charged change in his intonation. Despite the calm delivery, I still felt a chill run down my spine.

"I'll be clear. Being disposed of if our assassin trade gets discovered is also part of our duty. It's even possible the secret could leak from our employers' side without us doing anything wrong... Preparing other identities as early as one's birth is a form of insurance. When the country casts us aside, we'll be able to escape and live as different people. I just want you to know that I'd understand if you quit this unforgiving life now in order to choose an easier way to live. So I'll ask you one last time. Do you still choose to live as Lugh Tuatha Dé?"

Ever since I was young, I'd always been taught the value of the work House Tuatha Dé did. It was the members of House Tuatha Dé who were responsible for protecting the Alvanian Kingdom. Now, despite all his teachings, after all this time, my father had chosen to share with me this harsh reality.

Perhaps this timing was the very reason why he'd chosen to say anything in the first place.

Father wanted me to grapple with this question after I'd spent two years learning about the world but before I got started as an assassin and was unable to back out.

Before my reincarnation, I'd been raised only as a tool for killing. Not once had I ever spared a thought to the way I was used. I'd lived as a simple blade, devoid of doubt.

Things were different with Father, though. He'd raised me as an assassin, but he'd also taught me how to love.

Long ago, I'd decided to no longer live as a tool. I'd chosen to walk a path of my own free will.

"Father...no, Dad. I choose to live as a Tuatha Dé. I have something I need to do that I can only accomplish as a member of this family."

I'd decided to call him "Dad" instead of "Father." That was my way of showing him that I'd made this decision as a man. Now that I was older, I didn't feel the need to be so formal with him anymore.

"Is this decision coming from a sense of justice? Are you saying you have the conviction to throw your life away for the sake of the country?" asked my dad.

"...That's not it. I'm not that admirable of a person. It's just that the people of Tuatha Dé and my acquaintances in Milteu are special to me, and I want this country to remain at peace. I don't want the happiness I've gained to fall to ruin. That is most important to me. Even if the country does cast us aside, that'll be no problem for me. I trained under you, so there's no way I'd be so easily caught. After being outed, I'm sure I'd still be able to live as Illig if I needed to. Knowing that, I'm okay with the thought of being cast aside."

That's right, I wasn't trying to assassinate the hero because someone ordered me to. I was doing it of my own volition—and for my own happiness.

Allowing myself to be pushed around as I had in my previous life was no longer an option.

Whether my client was the royal family or a goddess, I wasn't about to follow anyone blindly. Never again would I allow myself to be killed.

Dad watched me without saying anything. I continued to speak.

"I do have one other reason. There is something I won't be able to do if I leave House Tuatha Dé."

"And what would that be? I can't field a guess."

"I am in love with Dia Viekone. I'm exchanging letters with her even now, and admittedly I have been crossing the border and sneaking into her estate to meet with her once a month. Slipping through the security at both the border and the count's estate is excellent training. I'm thinking of marrying her someday...and you need a certain rank in order to marry a count's daughter."

I'd made time to meet with Dia even when I was in Milteu. So strong was my desire to see her that I'd even made use of Rapid Recovery, my massive mana capacity, and brand-new spells to increase my speed to the point where I could get all the way there and back in just one day.

I loved talking about new spells with her, watching the elation on her face, and writing down all the spells she had invented.

"Bwa-ha-ha-ha-ha-ha-ha! I've always thought you too perfect of a son. I never would've expected you to do something so foolish. I see. Dia. If that's what you want, then by all means, welcome to the clan of assassins. I'll get you started right away... This is an important job. There is a noble we must get rid of. He's a wretched piece of work who's selling military secrets to foreign nations in return for narcotics, and then spreading them throughout the country. The people are suffering as a result. He must be removed."

It was almost unbelievable to me that a man could both be selling military secrets and subjugating his own country to drug addiction.

"I'll take care of it. Two weeks should be all I need."

"He's all yours. I'm not going to give you any advice. Eliminate however you see fit."

This was to be my first assassination in this world, and my target was a particularly harmful noble, at that. I was itching to put my skills to the test. This man was going to be disposed of efficiently, without so much as a trace left behind.

A much simpler target than the hero, of course, but it wasn't bad for my first job.

The day I returned home, there was a grand celebration for me having reached adulthood.

The next morning, I sensed someone in my room, and I opened my eyes to see that my mom had sneaked in. As a trained killer, I had the ability to immediately wake up no matter how tired I'd been.

I pretended like I was sleeping, and she stared at me for a long time… Mainly at the lower half of my body.

Mom really hadn't changed in the last few years. I'd grown a lot while I'd been gone, but she hadn't visibly aged at all. I don't know how she managed to look twenty-five years old despite actually being over forty. Perhaps the Tuatha Dé family had some sort of secret for preserving youth.

Were that true, it'd probably be a bigger hit than the moisturizer I'd created.

I sat up in bed.

"Good morning. Mom, what are you doing in here so early?"

"Drats. Nothing happened this morning."

From that one sentence, I knew that Tarte had told her about the darkest moment of my life.

"…I've developed a countermeasure so I won't have to deal

with that again. Besides, if that happened every day, it'd be a serious illness."

"Well, that's disappointing."

"Hold on, do you really want to see that kind of thing from your son?"

"I really want to see it! It's proof that you've become an adult."

I smiled reflexively.

Regarding that "darkest moment"...

It was fall of my thirteenth year. Tarte and Maha usually tried to hide this from me, but they were clearly starved for affection, prone to loneliness, and yearned for family.

Such a yearning was understandable, especially because they both lost their families at very young ages. Occasionally, the loneliness would become too much for them to bear, and I would let them sleep with me.

There was nothing lewd about it. All we did was sleep in the same bed. Feeling someone else's body heat helped them to relax.

This custom also helped bring us closer together. The trouble was, I hadn't quite understood the desire of my developing teenage body. That's not to say I lost control to the point where I did anything stupid like put my hands on either Tarte or Maha, though.

One ominous day, Tarte and Maha had coincidentally both asked if they could spend the night with me, and we all ended up sleeping together. We all happily greeted the morning together. That's when everything went tragically south. Tarte sniffed a few times and said that she smelled something weird. Maha agreed and craned her neck, and then I panicked upon realizing the sticky state of my lower body.

There couldn't have been a worse time to have a wet dream.

I hadn't had many of them in my first life, and this had been my first ejaculation as Lugh Tuatha Dé, so it took me a bit of time to realize what had happened, which is why Tarte and Maha had caught on first.

I knew I'd never forget the looks on their faces. They both blushed deep red and looked away, shyly peering toward my mess.

I'd always regarded the two as family and acted as both a father figure and a brother to them, and then I'd allowed something that disgraceful to happen. I wanted to smash something. Or die.

I could feel everything I'd built crashing down around me.

For some reason, the fact that Tarte and Maha didn't hate me for it but instead were clearly concerned for me made it so much worse.

"Master Illig, um, please ask for my help from now on! I'm your retainer, so I can give you that kind of service as well! It will be so hard for you if you just let it build up! This is a necessary service!" Tarte insisted.

"...Dear brother, even if you call me your sister, your body doesn't lie. Sometimes I wonder whether you want me to be your sister or your lover. Isn't it possible for me to be both?" Maha asked.

I couldn't believe they were so considerate as to be able to make jokes at a time like that. As a result, that horrifying scene had ended with laughter, and I was able to maintain my dignity as their father figure and older brother. After that, they'd asked to sleep with me much more frequently, for reasons that continued to elude me.

From then on, I took special care to ensure that shameful incident would never occur again. I didn't want Maha or Tarte to have to see anything so unsightly. I even devised a countermeasure to prevent any future explosions.

My own body sure was annoying. The sexual appetite of a young adult was truly something to behold.

Not even an assassin could escape the shackles of the human body.

Mom refused to leave the room when I was trying to change, saying she wanted to "see my grown-up body," so I chased her out, got ready, and went to the dining room.

The breakfast Tarte prepared for me was waiting on the table, and once I sat down, she stationed herself behind me. Unsurprisingly, the girl's cooking was as tasty as ever.

This meal was extra enjoyable because it'd been made with Tuatha Dé ingredients, which made me feel nostalgic and increased my appetite.

After I'd finished eating, Mom walked into the room with a wide smile on her face. She handed me a proposal for a wife.

There were no digital photos in this world, so hand-drawn portraits were sent before meetings that arranged to judge compatibility for marriage.

As it happened, this was actually the fourth girl Mom had brought to my attention. All of the girls so far had been beautiful, held good social standing, and were close to my age. From an objective standpoint, they'd all been perfectly fine candidates.

Although Tuatha Dé didn't have the highest annual tax revenue, it was well known that we made a lot of income through the medical trade. The family also had strong connections with major noble families. As such, we never hurt for marriage proposals.

Tarte, still stationed behind me, seemed to be in something of a bad mood.

"Mom, I've told you I don't need these. I have no plans to take a marriage interview."

I was already in love with Dia, so I didn't need to meet anyone.

Tarte breathed a sigh of relief.

Most noble families used the marriage of their oldest son as a tool to make connections or increase their family's rank among the noble hierarchy. Undoubtedly, many investigations were conducted to find the most suitable partner for any one candidate. My parents and I didn't have an interest in that kind of thing, however.

If our family rose beyond the rank of baron, there'd be an increase in responsibilities. Doubtless, we'd have to attend more annoying social functions. The current size and standing of the domain suited Tuatha Dé just fine.

The reason Mom was bringing me these marriage proposals was probably because she was excited to have new babies to dote on.

"Oh, come oooon, Lugh. I found a really good girl this time. I want to meet my grandchildren!"

...*Just as I thought.*

Tarte looked like she wanted to say something, so I allowed her to speak.

"I think it's too soon for Lord Lugh to marry."

"It's not too soon! He's already an adult. If he takes too long, I'll be an old woman before I have any grandchildren. Oh, wait, could you have his babies, Tarte?! ...Hey, that would work, actually. You have mana, and you're not a noble, so the number of annoying parties we have to go to wouldn't increase. That's a good bargain. I have a feeling you'd be able to have children right away, too."

"Wha—? U-umm…if that's what my lord desires." Tarte blushed deep red all the way to her ears at my mom's relentless teasing.

There was no need for her to take that joke so seriously.

"Mom, stop picking on Tarte."

"I'm not picking on her. And, Lugh, I've been meaning to bring this up, but you've been talking back to me quite a lot lately! What kind of tone is that to use with your mother?"

"I'm an adult now, so I feel like I should speak like one. I'm not a little kid anymore."

I'd considered continuing to play the good child in front of Mom, but…parents needed to be able to let go of their children.

"Awwww, come on, Lugh. I can't take it! My cute little baby has become so brash!"

Evidently, my mom took no notice that treating me like a child was going to make me want to behave the way she wanted even less.

When night fell, I released two pigeons into the sky.

A letter had recently arrived from Maha, who was still in Milteu. She was running my cosmetic brand, Natural You, in my absence.

It was a lot for her to handle on her own, but Beruid was helping out as her assistant.

Beruid had received a high-quality education from a young

age, and he had connections in various places. He had a wealth of real-world experience, too. Often, he'd sat in on my classes for Tarte and Maha, and proved to be a fast learner. That played no small part in enabling him to become the skilled businessman he was today.

Even though I was the representative of the overwhelmingly successful Natural You brand, I'd still been surprised to learn that he wanted to take classes from me, considering that he was heir to the Balor Company.

I told Maha to make effective use of him—and to learn from him, too. Just as he had a lot to learn from me, I was sure there was a lot that could be learned from Beruid.

My letter of reply contained two orders for Maha.

The first order was to gather information on Count Azba Venkaur, my current assassination target. Count Venkaur's wife was a Natural You customer, so the company likely had some intel on her already.

I wanted Maha to use that as a starting point and perform a thorough investigation into Count Venkaur.

With this job, I wasn't sure if it was wise to take my employer's information at face value. That's why I needed my own reports on the mark.

My second order was to send a letter to Count Venkaur's wife informing her that Illig Balor wanted to visit her to show her a new product.

If Count Venkaur had anything to hide, he was likely to be extra wary, making it difficult to get near him. His wife, on the other hand, was sure to welcome Illig into her home, as he represented Natural You.

The requested data arrived four days later.

Maha had ended up sending me stacks of files, all of which had been transported via horse-drawn carriage to conceal them as a mere cosmetics shipment.

Natural You performed regular shipments of goods to members, and because my mom was a member, there was nothing unusual about a delivery arriving from Milteu.

Creating a membership program with regular home deliveries had been one of my proposals. The shipments included products a grade above what could be found in the store, and they were delivered monthly. It was a service targeted at the truly wealthy and, as a result, came with a heavy price tag.

The service transported reliably high-quality products in exchange for large, regular payments. The system gave Natural You a steady source of revenue from wealthy clients, and it had worked to successfully prevent the resale of products.

If you could afford this service, then you could avoid the war zone that was the storefront every day. What's more, being sent special products most people couldn't obtain gave the buyer a sense of superiority that upper-class people couldn't resist. The number of members quickly exceeded capacity, and being a Natural You member had even become a symbol of status.

"Maha works quickly. So he really is spreading narcotics. This guy really is something."

The size of the Balor Company information network was truly incredible. Count Azba Venkaur had previously caught the attention of the Balor Company while up to some criminal activity in Milteu, and they'd been keeping files on him ever since.

Narcotics brought misfortune to all but those who sold them.

Count Venkaur would get young nobles addicted by inviting them to try the drugs at secret parties, and it appeared he also made use of a criminal network to spread them throughout cities.

In particular, the narcotic he sold was derived from an evergreen shrub called vieze. Technically, it was a stimulant.

Stimulants increased activity in the brain, heightened the senses, and caused a state of excitement. Put simply, they made you high. In exchange for the feeling of euphoria, your body ended up becoming extremely dependent on them.

Milteu was able to prevent the narcotics from entering the city, but neighboring towns ended up suffering deeply from the addictive nature of the drug.

"Guess there's no choice but to kill him."

This count was selling narcotics in such a roughshod manner that he'd already ended up on the Balor Company's radar. It was only a matter of time until his actions went public.

However, when accused of being responsible for trading narcotics, Count Venkaur feigned ignorance about the whole thing, saying he was unaware of the mafia transporting the drugs through his domain. He ended up arresting a small-time criminal and pinning the blame on him, thereby crediting himself for solving the problem.

Large bribes to a high-ranking official had likely also helped him get away with it.

Since such an excuse had actually worked, Count Venkaur likely had enough support from other nobles that the royal family was unable to touch him.

The steady increase of narcotics being dealt bothered me. If left alone, the entire Alvanian Kingdom risked being plunged into addiction.

Since the law couldn't bring him to justice, there was no choice but to remove the pest through assassination.

Such was the duty of House Tuatha Dé.

Our carriage bumped along the road.

Countess Venkaur had eagerly bit at the invitation Maha had
sent her to see a new product, writing in her response that she
definitely wanted me to come.

I'd dyed my hair black and put on glasses to take on the image
of Illig once again. While in disguise, I had to make sure to act
like Illig Balor all the time, even if no one was watching.

Maha was sitting next to me. She was cheerfully humming
despite her usual reserved personality.

"We haven't seen each other in so long, dear brother," she
said.

"It hasn't even been a month."

"For me, ten days is way too long a time to go without seeing
you."

Behaving like a spoiled child, Maha leaned on me.

"You didn't need to come, Maha. As the true Natural You
representative, I could've done this alone."

"That may be true, but I wanted to see you. I was careful to
make proper preparations to ensure the company would be fine
without me for a day. Beruid is there, too, so there's nothing to
worry about."

"Guess that won't be a problem."

"...By the way, Illig, it looks like I'll be able to get one of those things you asked for."

A while back, I'd asked Maha to look into finding a divine treasure.

In this world, there existed weapons and items that could not be forged by man and possessed unfathomable strength. They were made with technology and materials that exceeded current understanding. As such, they were referred to as divine treasures.

One such item was the magic spear Gáe Bolg, a weapon wielded by a man who was known by the nickname Kran's Hound. Coincidentally, that guy was one I'd judged to have the highest probability of becoming the hero.

Another example was the magic blade Fragarach, an ancient sword wielded by a legend from a great war fought many years ago.

Such weapons were undoubtedly going to make killing the hero much easier. That's why I'd been spending some of my excess funds in an effort to obtain at least one divine treasure.

I was also hoping that once I was able to set my eyes on a real divine treasure, I'd be able to study it in order to create stronger weapons and spells.

"I can always count on you to help me out, Maha. Thank you," I said.

"You're welcome... So, Illig. Have there been any developments with Tarte since you went home? In a girl-boy sort of way?" Maha asked.

"Of course not."

Maha sighed in exasperation at my words.

"Really? Hasn't it been difficult? Up until now, you'd been going to a brothel in order to relieve yourself, but isn't it going to be torture for you without brothels in the Tuatha Dé domain? Every time you went to see Dia or went to a brothel, Tarte looked like she was going to cry, you know. I'm sure she'd be happy to help you out herself."

I stifled a gag, both because Maha had found out about the brothel and because of the way she'd worded that last sentence.

"Why are you trying to push me into that kind of relationship?" I asked.

"It just bothers me that you're trying to run away from your romantic feelings for us," Maha explained.

"We're family. We've been that way for years now."

I'd been raising them for a number of years now. I could still vividly recall the early days after I'd first met them both. Surely Maha was mistaken.

"When we were younger, we definitely thought of you as our dependable older brother. But we're growing up. And when you grow up, you develop these types of feelings. If a girl has a guy as attractive as you in her midst every day, how could she not fall in love? ...The worst thing about it is how you continue to ignore us. Tarte is the type to bottle up all her frustration without making a single complaint. If you continue to take this attitude with her, she'll explode." Maha spoke in a serious and earnest tone.

*Ah, I see. So she's doing this for Tarte.*

"Fine. Just once, I'll throw away my preconceptions and give Tarte some attention. That doesn't mean I can return her feelings, though," I explained.

"Because of Dia, I'm sure. I don't think that would be a problem, though. Tarte might always be second place for you, or a girl you only see occasionally, but she'd be fine with anything as long as you loved her. There's no more convenient arrangement than that, you know. She's also cute and well-endowed, besides. You're a nobleman—it's expected for you to take a few mistresses."

"Is that so?"

"Of course it is. So are you finally able to wrap your head around the fact that you have two girls who love you?"

"Wait, *two* girls?"

"I'm in love with you, too, but my all-out attack is going to have to come a little later. I'm going to continue to grow the Natural You brand and perfect the information network, and once I become completely indispensable, I'll use that as a pretext in my negotiation. It's like you taught me, dear brother. You must be on equal terms with your negotiating partner, or you won't get the deal you want."

Maha certainly had put an astounding amount of effort into it all. The truth was that the girl was already a supremely vital asset. If she became any more important than she already was, I would never be able to get along without her.

"You really are an excellent apprentice," I said.

"That's right, so you'd better prepare yourself," Maha replied, glancing up at me with a smile. Such a flirtatious gesture actually caught me off guard for a moment.

That young girl I'd found at the orphanage was becoming a woman. Failing to notice something that obvious meant I still had a long way to go.

We arrived in the Venkaur domain.

The region was quite lush, with farmland that stretched for miles. In some ways, it resembled the Tuatha Dé domain.

Apart from the dangerous-looking men carrying swords out on patrol, that is.

A few of those guards approached our carriage.

Count Venkaur was probably employing this kind of private army because he had something to hide.

One of them opened one of the carriage's windows and greeted me with a wide smile.

"What business do you have in Venkaur?" he asked menacingly. I grinned in response.

"We are representatives of Natural You, good sir. We came to offer Countess Venkaur an exclusive look at a brand-new product. This is the invitation we received from her ladyship."

Once I showed him the letter, he told us to follow them. It seemed like the guards had been made aware of our coming.

The sight of the estate took me by great surprise.

While the land felt similar to the Tuatha Dé domain, the manor could not have been more different. The building was grand and luxurious, different in every way down to the material used to build it. There was no way this kind of place could've been built on money from this domain alone.

"Oh, look who it is! Welcome, welcome, my dears. I've been waiting in great anticipation for this new Natural You product."

The lavish front door to the mansion opened, and a short, round woman walked up to greet us wearing a glittering dress that brought to mind the image of a goldfish.

A number of rings clinked together on both of her hands, and a giant sapphire hung from her necklace. She was also wearing makeup so thick that *gaudy* wouldn't even begin to describe it.

"Countess Venkaur, thank you very much for your invitation.

I'm particularly proud of this new product, and I wanted a true lady as beautiful as yourself to be the first to use it," I said.

"Ooh, you flatter me. Please come in! My skin has been in such great condition ever since I started applying Natural You's moisturizer. I'm sure this next product will be just as wonderful."

Just like that, we were in the house.

The new cosmetic product I'd prepared was actually a new form of moisturizer.

I'd added a smidge of almond oil to the olive oil that was used in the recipe. This helped to enhance the scent while also improving the coloring of the skin when applied. I'd also improved the medicinal ingredients.

They were admittedly minor changes, but with the kind of person the countess was, the special treatment of getting to try a brand-new product before anyone else in the world did was going to outweigh the quality of the product.

Maha and I complimented Countess Venkaur relentlessly.

"It is exactly because you understand quality, my lady, that I wanted you to be the first to try this product," I would say.

"If it meets the approval of Countess Venkaur, other women will be dying to use it themselves," Maha would add.

Throughout the conversation, we continually peppered in such comments. The countess fell hook, line, and sinker for the simple compliments and quickly became cheerful.

*This really is too easy.*

With the countess in such a friendly mood, all we needed to

do was make idle conversation that would extract the information we needed via seemingly nonchalant questions.

When we asked her how the economy in Venkaur was so prosperous, the countess answered that it was because business with foreign nations had been going well. She said she didn't know any details about the trade itself, however, and it didn't appear that she was lying. The countess was truly ignorant about her husband's dealings.

That came as a relief. If she'd known, I would've had to kill her, too.

Maha and I continued to gather information.

"My husband likes nothing more than to enjoy a glass of wine on the balcony at night before he goes to bed."

Such a seemingly innocuous statement was actually an incredibly useful bit of intel.

"It's truly great that my husband's business has been so successful. It was only two or three years ago that we were a poor noble family that couldn't afford much in the way of luxury. I'm so happy that I can dress so beautifully now. So happy indeed!"

"Yes, we'll have to thank him as well. It is because of his success that we were given the privilege of seeing you in such exquisite form, Countess Venkaur," I said.

"Oh, you're making me blush... Oh-ho-ho-ho!" Countess Venkaur laughed jovially.

She really had no clue. This woman was utterly ignorant to how many soldiers had died as a result of the information her husband had sold to foreign countries. She lived unaware that people throughout the country had been reduced to hollow shells because of crippling drug addiction.

As in my previous life, I was an assassin. But this time, I was not a simple tool. Who I killed and when was up to me. If there'd been any doubt in my mind before, the conversation with the countess had erased it.

I was going to kill Count Venkaur.

Three days later, I returned to the manor with Tarte.

While Tarte had been absent during the initial visit, she was my assistant, and I was going to need her for the job.

The estate was in a fantastic defensive position, but as I'd expected, finding a spot to hide three hundred meters from the building proved to be quite easy.

The security was tighter than it was three days ago, which probably meant Count Venkaur had returned home.

I'd hidden in the thick grass of a small hill with a good view of the estate. Using earth magic, I'd dug a shallow hole in the ground, laid down in it, and then covered myself in grass.

The sun had already set, so no one was going to notice me at such a distance.

Without the information I gained three days ago, Tarte and I probably would've had to camp out for a few days while we waited for the count's return, and killing him would've been much more difficult, as we would've had to sneak into his estate.

Thankfully, his wife had ended up happily volunteering both the day he would return and the information that would allow me to kill him without entering the manor.

I clutched a gun made from magic. It was already loaded with tungsten bullets.

Mages always had their bodies enveloped in some amount of

mana, even when they weren't intentionally doing so. This made them stronger than normal people, so normal methods wouldn't be able to kill them.

Such was true of Count Venkaur, but even then, Gun Strike was more than enough to end his life.

My Tuatha Dé eyes allowed me to clearly see the second-floor balcony, even from such a great distance. Gathering my focus, I drove everything but that veranda from my field of vision.

Tarte was there to stand guard while I focused on the assassination. Her presence was what allowed me to concentrate entirely on sniping the count.

After about ten minutes, a fat middle-aged man wearing a bathrobe and holding a glass of wine walked out onto the balcony. He looked up at the moon with a contented smile. It was the face of a man who thought himself to be the happiest person in the world.

*"My husband likes nothing more than to enjoy a glass of wine on the balcony at night before he goes to bed."*

The countess's words had proved true. It was thanks to that unknowing woman that her husband was going to die.

Count Venkaur stood there just staring at the moon, totally still and totally defenseless. Admittedly, it made him a very convenient target.

There was hardly any breeze that night. At a distance of three hundred meters, there was no way I was going to miss.

I caused an explosion in the cylinder using fire magic.

There was a special cushion covering the barrel that acted as a silencer. As a result, my shot made almost no sound.

The extremely heavy and hard tungsten bullet rocketed from the rifle close to the speed of sound, reaching its target in less than a second.

With such overwhelming force that it took the count's head off his shoulders, the bullet easily penetrated the skull.

"Time to withdraw."

"Yes, my lord," answered Tarte, and we escaped into the mountain.

No one would've thought to look for assailants along the mountain road, and it allowed us to easily emerge on the high ground from the other side of the peak.

This world was devoid of the concept of sniping. Shortly, they'd be looking for an assassin in the estate who was never even there. We'd be able to escape without issue.

The bullet penetrated both the target's skull and the wall, so it wouldn't even be found at the scene of the crime.

My first assassination in this world was a success.

I'd decided on my own that the assassination had been necessary, and I'd performed it of my own will.

My former self didn't feel anything after a kill, but how did my new self feel?

Though only slightly, I could feel my heartbeat speeding up. Then, for some reason, I came to a complete stop, unable to move. It was a strange feeling, one I couldn't understand.

Tarte turned around, concerned. She slowly walked toward me and gave me a hug.

"Tarte, why?" I asked.

"I don't know. You just looked scared."

"...Did I?"

I gave myself up to instinct and hugged her back.

Tarte grinned cheerfully and held me tighter. She smelled nice. Somehow the action calmed me down. Tarte's softness and warmth enabled me to regain my senses.

...I finally understood what Maha meant when she'd said that Tarte was growing up.

I took a deep breath, and suddenly everything was okay. I was back to my normal self.

"Sorry about that. Let's go," I said.

"Okay!" Tarte replied cheerily.

The two of us promptly resumed our escape down the mountain road.

Count Venkaur's wife would surely hate whoever killed her husband. He'd been an ideal husband in her eyes, and she'd known nothing of his many illicit activities.

I never came to regret what I did that night, but I made a point not to forget it, either.

That's what was required of Lugh Tuatha Dé.

My first assassination as Lugh Tuatha Dé had been executed to perfection.

Just as the royal family asked, I'd killed my target in a way that ensured that anyone who saw him knew it had been murder. The royal family had wanted to make an example of the count to send the message that this was what would happen to any noble who dared to think they could get away with anything they wanted.

Without any evidence of connection to the royal family, no one would be able to point fingers to the ruling party, either. At the same time, the general feeling was that the royal family was behind such assassinations, but without proof, no one could say anything. In this way, many nobbles toed the line out of fear that they would be next.

"If only killing the hero could be as easy as this was," I muttered while running down the mountain road.

I had high hopes for the new formula that I was going to test in three days on the uninhabited island that Maha had found for me. The magic I'd devised was strong enough to obliterate anything for hundreds of meters in all directions. That's why it could only be tested somewhere without people.

I had high hopes that it might even be able to kill the hero.

It'd now been three months since my first assassination.

I was relaxing on a hill with a really nice view. This had come to be my favorite spot.

In the last three months, I'd been busy with training, magic development, raising capital, and expanding the information network as Illig Balor. I'd even performed two more assassinations.

That many kills in such a short amount of time was an absurd pace. I suppose it was a good indicator of how rotten the Alvanian Kingdom had become.

Nobles were left mostly to do as they pleased, so long as they paid their due in taxes to the royal family. They were allowed so much freedom, it enabled them to make laws within their respective domains.

Their other duties really only included conscription of soldiers and the contribution of funds and food during times of war.

This excess of time and money inevitably led to many nobles growing overambitious.

Many nobles even saw themselves not as subjects of the king but as the rulers of their own little countries. Unless drastic measures were taken, more upstarts like Count Venkaur were likely to crop up.

"I defeated Ronah today, my lord! With that, I'm now up two wins to one."

A cheerful Tarte addressed me as I was lying on the hill, breaking my train of thought. Judging by her heavy breathing, she'd probably run all the way here right after her fight with Ronah, hoping to earn my praise.

"Beating Ronah means you're probably able to handle any of this kingdom's knights. Was he angry?" I asked.

"...Only a little. I've got a message from Ronah, actually. He said he wants to train under you, because he's interested in the training regimen that made a girl like me strong enough to beat him," Tarte replied.

"It must've been a shock to hear someone as proud as Ronah ask for help with training. But you did great."

While only a member of the branch family, my cousin Ronah was a mage and was still a bearer of the Tuatha Dé name. As such, he was already receiving high-quality training. Two years ago, he'd possessed enough power to rival the strongest knights in the country, but since then, he'd succeeded in becoming even stronger.

It was actually because I'd judged Tarte and Ronah to be of relatively equal strength that I'd ordered Tarte to challenge my cousin to some practice fights.

Tarte had lost the first, narrowly won the second, and easily won the third. She really was improving quickly.

"I'm your retainer and assistant. I have to be able to handle at least this much! ...Huh? Isn't that Maiya? It looks like she's calling us."

Maiya was one of our longest-serving retainers. Judging by her panic, it seemed like something serious had happened.

We hurried back to the mansion, where I was greeted by the smell of blood. Most of it had been cleaned up, but there was enough left that my nose caught the scent.

There was no sign of a fight. The blood instead seemed to

have come from a heavily wounded guest who just arrived at our estate. Whatever was going on, it wasn't likely to be very pleasant.

I entered the study to find my dad. His face was usually rather expressionless when he was working, but today it appeared especially rigid.

"Lugh, we just received a request. I want you to handle it," he said.

"Is it of the behind-the-scenes sort?" I asked.

"Of course. It's okay if you refuse the job. Honestly, it's one you'd be better off not accepting, but I'll leave it up to you... The request is to assassinate a count's daughter in the neighboring country of Soigel...Dia Viekone."

I felt my heart drop.

Dia was my magic mentor as well as my friend. Not to mention I had feelings for her.

*I'm being asked to kill her?*

"There are two things I'm unclear on. First, wouldn't it be problematic to interfere in the affairs of a foreign country? Second, the Tuatha Dé clan only performs assassinations for the benefit of our nation. I can't see how killing Dia would benefit anyone."

"This hit holds none of the honor of our usual work. It's a hit born purely of self-interest. That's why I'm leaving it up to you. This job is not just for the good of the country. We risk this blowing up into an international incident if our involvement is in any way exposed."

It was true. If it ever came out that we killed a high-ranking member of a foreign country, it could ignite a war.

"...Give me the details. Why do we have to kill Dia? Does it have something to do with the civil war in Soigel? Count Viekone sided with the king and lost, but his house paid its indemnities and should have been left alone after the war."

With the Balor Company information network at my disposal, there was no way I wouldn't have known about such a large event, even if it'd been in another country.

Soigel suffered from the same problems as Alvan. Namely, the level of power retained by the nobility and the growing ambitions of many of its members.

The difference was that Soigel had no Tuatha Dé clan.

As a result, the upper class had grown exceedingly impudent, and finally, many had one day declared the king an incompetent and negligent ruler. Declaring themselves the proper rulers of the kingdom, the nobles banded together and started a rebellion… which they won.

As soon as I'd heard about the civil war, and that House Viekone had picked the side of the royal family and lost, I'd rushed to Dia to see if she was okay. I told her I was prepared to use Illig Balor's influence to ensure asylum for her whole family.

Dia had responded by saying that they were fine, and she told me not to come back until things had settled down.

"Oh, you know that much already? Then I'll continue from there. Count Viekone lost and surrendered half of his wealth and land just as he was told… However, things didn't end there, unfortunately. Dia draws a lot of attention. She's beautiful, and she also possesses very powerful mana. As mana is inherited from one's parents…you'd be hard-pressed to find a greedy nobleman who wasn't trying to get ahold of her."

Evidently, paying the indemnities hadn't been enough to ensure the Viekone family's safety. I'd naively underestimated the greed of mankind.

As I thought about it, there had been something strange when I'd talked with Dia about the revolution.

*No way. Did she know this was going to happen, and prepare herself for it?*

"Count Viekone planned to do whatever he was told. Likewise, Dia also wished to avoid needless bloodshed. The trouble is, their vassals couldn't accept that. One thing led to another, and they ended up killing an envoy who'd arrived to take Dia away. At the same time, all the vassals tendered letters of resignation and announced they were going to fight back. They even went as far as to gather volunteer soldiers from among the citizens of the domain. Now they're barricading themselves in the castle and holding Count Viekone and Dia inside. Indirectly though it may be, House Viekone has started a second rebellion. An army has already been dispatched their way, and fighting has begun."

Count Viekone and Dia seemed to have been truly beloved by their people. Normally, citizens of a domain couldn't care less who their lord was, thinking that had little effect on their day-to-day lives.

Admittedly, all the nobles whom I'd killed had been replaced with puppets of the royal family, and there'd been no disapproval from the citizenry. Despite this more commonplace indifference, the commoners of the Viekone domain had resolved to take up arms and fight for their rulers of their own accord, all in an attempt to protect Dia.

"So we've been asked to end a war in its early stages by killing Dia and her father, therefore removing the will of their citizens to fight... Is that what you're going to say? Who in the world requested that? This doesn't seem like the kind of thing the Tuatha Dé clan should get involved in," I said.

"Our client is Count Viekone himself. His loyal retainer gave his life to convey this request," my dad explained.

"Why?"

"Listen to the end. The details of the request are to fake Dia's assassination and get her to safety. Even if their vassals win this battle, enemy reinforcements will soon arrive, effectively rendering their efforts pointless. This is the only way to save Dia, and we're the only ones who can pull it off."

Now it made sense. The deaths of those who'd started the rebellion were unavoidable at this point. Vastly outnumbered, Dia and the count couldn't be saved, no matter how they fought. In such a case, faking Dia's death was the only way she was going to get out of there alive.

"I understand the situation, but what I still don't get is why you accepted this request. I never would have thought you the type to forgo our family creed," I stated.

"You're overestimating me. I have strayed from our tenets once before. I don't doubt you've had your suspicions about this already, but Esri is a daughter of House Viekone. Which makes Dia your cousin. I have to repay my debt to Count Viekone. If he wants to save Dia, then that's what I want, too. I owe that to him," Dad explained.

"And what if I refuse?"

"The job would be impossible to complete. I would go, but I am not fast enough to make it. By the time I got there, it'd all be over. It has to be you, Lugh. Don't think of it as a job. This is simply a personal request from me to you. One that also happens to deviate from our family creed."

If the heavily wounded messenger who'd delivered this request was anything to judge by, the fighting had begun already.

Soigel bordered the Alvanian Kingdom, but the Viekone domain was over three hundred kilometers away, on a path that crossed two mountains.

Increasing your physical capabilities had a limit, and anyone with a normal amount of mana would've run out long before they got there.

It would've probably taken my dad two days, with him needing to take breaks along the way. On the other hand, I could get there in a few hours. It probably took the vassal three days to get here, but with my speed, I knew I could make it back in time.

Taking on this task was a bad idea. There was no defendable cause, and there was even a risk it'd bring harm to the Alvanian Kingdom.

I had to laugh. Hadn't I decided that I wouldn't repeat the mistakes I'd made in my first life? I wasn't a tool. I made my own decisions.

That's why I had to follow my heart.

"Dad...I accept this request."

"Tell me your reasoning."

"I have three. First, I owe Dia a debt for teaching me how to use magic. Second, I'm in love with her. Third, I made her a promise to come running when she calls for me. She's definitely calling for me right now."

I grasped the Fahr Stone necklace that Dia had given me when she'd left Tuatha Dé.

*One more thing. Remember when you said you would do anything I want as thanks? I'm asking for that favor now. If I ever need to see you, promise you'll drop everything and come running to me!*

There was no doubting Dia needed me now. It was time to fulfill that promise.

It was undoubtedly a very dangerous situation to walk into, but I had to follow my heart.

"Is that so? ...Only one time in my life have I used my blade for anything other than our family's service to the Alvanian Kingdom. Do you know what that was for?" asked my dad.

"No. I can't imagine you doing that sort of thing."

"It was for Esri. I never would've imagined my son would end up doing the same thing. I didn't think you were anything like me, but it seems we're similar in the most unexpected of ways... Good luck."

I nodded, then felt a wave of emotion come over me. My dad had also strayed from our family's beliefs for my mom. We really were alike. This was the kind of thing that deepened familial bonds.

Leaving the room, I had a brief conversation with the foreign vassal who was being treated in a neighboring chamber. Once finished, I hastily departed.

This was an assassination to save Dia's life, and I was going to see it done.

When I left the mansion, Tarte was waiting for me, dressed and ready to go.

"I brought your equipment, my lord. I'm also ready to head out."

With all possible speed, I took the gear and donned it. Tarte had been eavesdropping on my conversation with Dad. We'd both been aware, of course, but we'd allowed it. I'd trusted that Tarte would use that information to prepare for departure.

"Our destination is over three hundred kilometers away. I'm going to head there at my full speed. You won't be able to keep up."

My work was much easier when Tarte was with me, but I couldn't rely on her this time. Unless I moved as fast as I could, I wouldn't make it there in time.

"I know we can't go together, my lord. But I can at least help you along until I run out of stamina. Even with Rapid Recovery, your stamina and recovery rate won't keep up when you go that quickly. Let's go!"

Without waiting for my reply, Tarte used an original wind spell I'd taught her.

This spell redirected airflow to create an aerodynamic wind barrier, thereby reducing air resistance and allowing you to move at higher speeds.

Tarte took off at a full sprint, while I followed behind her.

Wind resistance was a big deal. Once an object exceeded forty kilometers an hour, its kinetic energy was halved as it expended energy to push air out of the way. As speed increased, air resistance increased exponentially.

Running at my full strength would've normally expended more stamina and mana than my Rapid Recovery skill could keep up with.

With Tarte redirecting the airflow in front of me, I could avoid that. This enabled me to move at a pace near my full speed while consuming stamina and mana at a rate that Rapid Recovery could handle.

Tarte was really giving it her all. It was undoubtedly taking serious mental energy and stamina to create the wind barrier while still running to keep up with me at the same time.

Even from behind, I could tell that Tarte's breathing was pained and that she was drenched in sweat. Still, the girl refused to slow her pace. She managed to carry on like that for around an hour, and when she finally came to a stop, her legs were trembling.

It was clear that Tarte had hit her limit. Actually, she'd likely reached her natural maximum a while back. Sheer force of will had driven her beyond that point, but even that had only been able to keep her going for a finite amount of time.

"I'm sorry. This is all I can do for you," Tarte forced out in between heavy breaths.

I walked up from behind her and put an arm around her shoulders.

"Thank you, Tarte. Because of you, I was able to preserve some of my strength."

With the energy I'd saved because of her efforts, I could go all out now without depleting my strength.

"…You really love Dia, don't you, my lord?" she asked.

"I do," I answered.

"Then I wish you luck. Please bring her home safely. I'll be waiting for your return." Tarte smiled, gave me a light push on the back, and sat down on the ground.

Despite the grin, she looked like she was going to cry.

"There's no need to worry. I'll be back."

Leaving Tarte behind, I took off. If I'd stopped then, it would've only been a waste of her efforts and words of encouragement.

I charged forward with everything I had.

As I sprinted across the land, I took hair dye out of the backpack that Tarte had prepared for me and colored my hair. I then disguised my face and wrapped it in a scarf to conceal it.

The hope was that such a facade would prevent the small chance of House Tuatha Dé's involvement being discovered. The path to the Viekone estate wasn't as the crow flew—it required you to cross winding forest trails and mountain roads.

I caught sight of the first of the two mountains you have to cross. This was the most difficult part of the journey.

If I wanted to get to the Viekone domain in just a few hours, I couldn't afford to cross both mountains on foot. Dashing along, I climbed to the summit of the first mountain. With a running start, I leaped from the cliff while performing an incantation.

*"Wings of Steel!"*

Just like Gun Strike and my other spells, this was an original spell I'd created using Spell Weaver.

I produced a lightweight hang glider made of aluminum. This was a shortcut I'd devised. By jumping off the summit of the first mountain, I was able to drift through the air and skip over the second mountain entirely.

The wings of the hang glider caught the wind, and I soared through the air.

The wind brushed against my cheeks. The glider didn't have any sort of power of its own—it was simply riding on the air.

Without an updraft, my altitude would slowly drop. If it fell too much, I wouldn't be able to cross the second mountain. Since I wasn't getting any wind, I decided to simply make some of my own.

*"Summon Wind!"*

As I rode the updraft I'd created, my altitude rose spectacularly.

In no time at all, I'd made it past the second peak. I was nearly there.

Once I'd landed, I slipped past the border into Soigel and began to sprint. On the way, I ate some provisions and used magic to summon water to quench my thirst. It took me just over five hours to cover the 322-kilometer distance.

There was a reason I'd been able to arrive so quickly, and while avoiding detection at that. It was because I'd made this journey many times in order to see Dia.

Without my regular trips, I would've been forced to rely on the crude maps of this world to find my way. I would have never made it in time using such a method. Getting to Dia's place during my very first trip had not been easy. Never would I have thought that my monthly secret meetings with Dia would come in handy for such an unexpected disaster.

When I at last arrived, I quickly found that much of the domain and the town that surrounded the Viekone estate had become a war zone.

I hid myself in the woods at a safe distance from the fighting.

Dia's father was a count, and as such, his manor was so large, it was better described as a castle. The fortified building sat on the outskirts of town, guarded by a large rampart.

Making use of that barrier, the vassals of Count Viekone had somehow managed to successfully keep the army of the enemy noble faction at bay.

The miraculous defense was unlikely to last much longer, however. The opposing force outnumbered the vassals far more than I'd expected.

Even with the advantage of the rampart, the defending group was made up of only two hundred soldiers, while the attacking force boasted fifteen hundred. Mages could make up for a deficit in numbers, but no one stood a chance when they were outnumbered that badly.

Thus far, the noble faction's army had been kept from entering the castle, but only just barely. The estate was likely to fall at any moment.

*Wait, that doesn't make any sense. How have they been able to last this long?* I thought.

Using my Tuatha Dé eyes, I could see that the invaders boasted far more mages. People with mana shouldn't have had any trouble just jumping over the rampart.

There was something else that seemed odd to me, too. The noble faction seemed very focused on a particular window of the castle.

"Ah, that explains it," I said, finally catching on. Dia was the reason the castle hadn't been taken yet.

I remained hidden in the darkness of the woods, being careful to avoid detection.

Before sneaking into the estate, I wanted to cause a disturbance that would weaken the attacking force's assault. It didn't look like the vassals were going to last much longer.

"I need to be strong… To save Dia, I have no choice but to kill those who are trying to steal her away."

I wanted to kill as few people as possible, but in such a situation, there was no method to save Dia that didn't involve murder. Her safety was my first priority, which meant my hands were going to get a little bloody.

I produced a gun using one of my spells.

Using a silencer was a waste of effort this time. With the gun's level of firepower, which was high enough to kill battle-ready mages, there was no way their mana-enhanced ears wouldn't catch the sound.

I channeled mana into my Tuatha Dé eyes.

In battle, it was said that a single mage was the equivalent fighting force of a hundred soldiers. To rephrase, this meant that killing a single mage was the same as taking out a hundred ordinary swordsmen.

My Tuatha Dé eyes allowed me to sense mana. Normally, you couldn't sense an opponent's mana unless you were relatively close to them, which made picking out mages difficult.

Thankfully, I was more than able to tell who among the invading force could use magic.

I drew a deep breath, and as I released it, I used fire magic to create an explosion within the iron gun. A tungsten bullet shot from the barrel and cut a large hole through the chest of a mage who'd been on the front lines.

*That's one.*

I loaded another bullet and another body hit the ground.

One after another, they began to drop as I killed them efficiently and without emotion.

At the death of the fourth mage, the army took on a noticeably different formation.

Anyone who could use magic positioned themselves behind the ordinary soldiers for protection. They'd also clearly identified the direction my projectiles were coming from by way of the sound of the gun and which mages had been killed. Soldiers were dispatched in my direction, and the archers loosed a volley of arrows.

With no small urgency, I left that spot and, taking a large detour, began to move toward the opposite side of the battlefield.

"Just as I thought, they already know about the guns," I muttered.

The army's response had been too quick. Had they never encountered firearms before, they would've been far more confused. The explanation was simple enough: Dia had already been using Gun Strike. Perhaps that was the reason the vassals had been able to hold the estate against the noble faction for three days.

Dia could reliably hit a target from a distance of up to three hundred meters. She'd been able to prevent anyone getting over the rampart from her spot at the castle window by using Gun Strike, as the spell had enough force to kill a mage in a single shot.

It had reduced the enemy numbers, of course, but her shots had also caused the attacking soldiers to shrink away in fear of being the next one to take a bullet.

Almost all mages were of proper nobility or came from a branch family. Such social standing and battle prowess meant the noble faction couldn't afford to keep throwing away the lives of their mages by having them try to scale the rampart.

While it was true that the mages might've been able to use magic to get multiple ordinary soldiers over the rampart at the cost of a few deaths, Dia sniping with Gun Strike kept that from being a viable strategy.

So long as the mages from the noble faction stayed away from the front lines, the Viekone mages would be able to handle the enemy soldiers who didn't have mana.

Using wind magic, I picked up sound from the battlefield.

The noble faction soldiers were yelling about how there was someone other than Count Viekone's daughter who was using the strange iron stone magic.

The enemy's response was visibly too late.

Normally, four people being killed among so many soldiers wouldn't have been a problem. The reason it had created such an uproar was because four mages had been singled out.

Now was the time to take advantage.

Stealthily, I made it to the other side of the battlefield, and while hiding in the woods, I produced a bow and some arrows made out of metal.

The arrows each had a special attachment on the end containing a jewel filled with red light.

"I didn't want to play this card yet, but...I don't have much choice."

The jewels were actually Fahr Stones. Each stone was filled with mana to the point where it would very nearly explode.

Fahr Stones had the ability to store mana and were typically used to measure a person's mana capacity.

But if you filled one past its limits and then broke it, the entrapped mana would explode outward.

Years ago, I almost destroyed the Tuatha Dé estate with one of those stones.

After much testing, I'd discovered that filling the stones with 70 percent fire mana, 20 percent wind mana, and 10 percent earth mana resulted in the highest destructive force.

I poured more mana into a Fahr Stone to push it beyond its capacity. The stone made a high-pitched noise as cracks began to form on the little sphere's surface.

I drew an arrow—and released. Leaving a red trail of light, the arrow slipped through the trees and made impact in the middle of the noble faction's army. Seven seconds later, light overflowed from the stone, and then it exploded.

Flames burst forth from the fire mana, which then exploded in combination with the wind produced by the wind mana. The earth mana became countless iron scraps, which then shot forth in all directions like bullets from the force of the explosion.

The blast itself was about two hundred meters wide, and the iron scraps caused additional damage for another few hundred beyond that.

Dozens of people were injured or killed from the explosion, burns, or the flurry of shrapnel.

I'd stored mana equivalent to the capacity of three hundred

ordinary mages, and when the stones exploded, this was what happened.

My mana capacity was over a thousand times higher than the average mage's, but instantaneous mana discharge was much harder to increase. Truthfully, mine sat only around seven or eight times higher than a regular mage's.

Fahr Stones changed everything, however.

I fired three more Fahr Stones into crowds of enemy soldiers, and then after using Gun Strike to take out one more mage, I decided to move again. Remaining where I'd been hiding for much longer was likely to be dangerous.

I suppose you could say that even that type of large-radius attack was a form of assassination.

Assassination was defined as killing someone without showing yourself and without your target being aware of you. The mages I just killed with Gun Strike and the soldiers who died from the Fahr Stone explosions died without realizing who their attacker was.

An assassin did not devote themselves to assassination merely out of pride—it was simply because they were unable to rely on other means. That was not to say it didn't have unique benefits. The use of covert methods helped me send the battlefield into a state of confusion and take out multiple soldiers without ever showing myself.

After four Fahr Stone explosions, the entire noble faction looked ready to flee.

Even the mages were getting increasingly scared because they didn't know what they were fighting. It'd also grown quite clear that they were being specifically targeted.

"The Viekone soldiers are well-trained. It looks like they understand the opportunity they've been given," I observed.

Count Viekone's soldiers, who had been stuck on the defensive for the last three days, now opened the castle gate and charged.

Even after having lost a decent number of soldiers, the noble faction still retained a strong advantage in numbers. Their heavy state of panic, however, was what allowed Count Viekone's people to take the offensive.

With their mages leading the way, the count's soldiers began to rout the enemy.

Very quickly, the battlefield descended into a state of mass confusion, and there was no longer any need to fear the castle falling.

I hadn't actually planned on changing the outcome of the battle all on my own. All I'd been trying to do with that series of attacks was create a diversion.

To avoid enemy attention falling on Dia and me, the battle had to be turned from a one-sided fight into a difficult struggle where the noble faction soldiers didn't have the luxury of turning their focus anywhere else.

Employing the Fahr Stones had been for a second purpose as well. They were part of my plan for saving Dia.

With a ground battle unfolding, sneaking into the manor was sure to be quite easy now. It was time for a rescue mission.

I killed a large number of soldiers as I went along.

Not all of them had been bad people. Many had merely been ordered against their own will to wage war.

Such a thought pained me. I never would've cared about something like that in my previous life.

After the diversion had been created, I'd resolved to kill anyone who tried to steal Dia away. Rescuing her would've been impossible had I refused to do so. There was no time for regret. If I felt the need to repent, it was going to wait until after Dia had been secured.

"At least the worst-case scenario didn't happen."

The enemy force laying siege to the castle was larger than I expected, but I'd feared something even worse.

Using the Balor Company information network, I'd been gathering information to try to find the hero and seek out divine treasures. With some effort, I found intel on a man I believed to have the highest chance of becoming the hero, as well as the divine treasure he wielded.

It was a man known as Kran's Hound, and the powerful magic spear he carried was called Gáe Bolg.

That man was known to be in Soigel.

His involvement was my speculated reason for the noble

faction's rebellion having been so successful. While there wasn't much proof to that, I had hit upon some evidence.

If my theory was correct, there was a chance that a man with a divine treasure and a tremendous amount of strength could've been present on that battlefield.

Thankfully, my fears went unrealized. If Kran's Hound had been there, he surely would've shown himself already.

"Now things get tricky," I said. Sneaking into the castle had been easy because of all the confusion on the battlefield, but getting to Dia was going to be difficult.

The true nature of Dia's assassination could never be publicized. Only a very small number of vassals knew that her death was to be faked.

Even with my help, House Viekone could not escape defeat. Many of the vassals were going to be taken prisoner, after which they'd be subjected to questioning and execution. The reason so few people knew about this plan was to prevent the secret from getting out.

For that reason, they needed someone who could sneak into this castle. A castle that the noble faction failed to infiltrate after three days of siege.

It would have been impossible for a normal person, but I could manage it using my skills as an assassin.

During a stealth operation, it was imperative that you did everything you could to avoid detection. This was much more difficult than it seemed, and it involved more than just staying out of sight or ensuring you made as little noise as possible.

No matter how covert you were, it was impossible to stop yourself from breathing, or to keep your body from emitting heat or any sort of scent. So long as someone was alive, they continued to leave traces of their presence.

True stealth required you to repress those giveaways to the best of your ability while using your skills to avoid detection by others. Success demanded that your awareness and perception had to be superior to anyone else's.

To erase anything that would alert another to my location, I used one of my custom spells.

Wind began to flow around me.

The flood of information being carried to me by the wind would be enough to fry the brain of a normal person. However, I dealt with a level of information that would break a normal person on a daily basis. Plus, Rapid Recovery and Limitless Growth had worked to increase the capabilities of my brain. As a result, I could bear any intel my magic brought me.

The spell I used had created a gust of wind. By altering the flow of that breeze, I could obtain three-dimensional visual information for places that were otherwise beyond my sight.

Coupled with this bit of magic, I also got a sense for my surroundings by picking up on certain sounds, listening for breathing and heartbeats, and using body heat to read the movements of those around me. These were all tricks I'd picked up in my previous life.

With so much information on my enemies at my disposal, it was almost like being able to see the future.

Using my many skills, I discerned the best route of infiltration. It was time to begin.

I sneaked through the mansion, weaving through gaps in those keeping watch.

There was only one place she could've been. The Fahr Stone explosions hadn't only been to turn the tide of the battle—they'd also been a signal for Dia.

I was confident that if I used Fahr Stones, Dia would notice that I'd arrived, and she would stick her head out her window. As anticipated, she had done just that after the fourth explosion. That was how I knew what room of the large estate she was in.

Without giving away a hint of my presence, I arrived at Dia's room and put my hand to the door.

It was locked, of course, but that was hardly a problem. Manipulating the metal mechanism by way of magic, I picked the lock.

The door opened to reveal Dia and a middle-aged man.

"Lugh! You really came for me!" Dia threw herself into my chest, with her beautiful silver hair trailing behind her.

It was only in that moment that I realized I'd finally surpassed her in height, a fact that made me a little happy.

I hugged Dia tightly, basking in her warmth, her smell, her softness.

*Dia, my love. I'm so glad you're safe.*

Her face looked ghostly pale, however. With my Tuatha Dé eyes, I instantly understood the reason. She'd used almost all of her mana. Any more, and she would've collapsed from mana deficiency.

Dia had probably been giving everything she had to protect her vassals, even if she knew saving them all was impossible.

"I promised, didn't I? That I would come running when you wanted to see me," I said.

"...You remembered that promise, after all this time," Dia replied.

I nodded. There was no way I was going to forget my promise to her.

The middle-aged man watched us with a mixed expression on his face.

There was nothing showy about his dress, but his dignified demeanor betrayed his status as a nobleman.

"I've always thought her to be a virtuous girl, but to think she would have her heart stolen by someone like you. It's nice to finally meet you. I am Dimor Viekone, Dia's father."

"I am Lugh Tuatha Dé. I came here to fulfill your request."

"While that was my request, this isn't exactly what I had in mind... If only my vassals had listened when I told them to leave us and run. They said they couldn't abandon me and Dia, and once they found out I was planning to surrender, they shut us away in here," he explained softly. The count sounded proud, sad, and a variety of other emotions all at once.

One of the biggest reasons he wanted Dia spirited away to safety was surely because he didn't want his subjects to fight. If Dia died, there would be no reason for his people to remain. They would be able to leave this losing battle and escape to live another day.

"What do you plan to do, Count Viekone?" I asked.

"I'll be able to manage on my own... After watching all this fighting, I've built up a bit of an urge to get in on the action myself. I'll cause as much destruction as I can in order to draw enemy attention away so others can escape. Once they're free, I'll make my own getaway. I plan to lay low for a while and make preparations to expel the traitors from these lands so that one day this country can be returned to its rightful ruler."

As expected, given the man's high-ranking position as a count, Dimor Viekone was a very strong mage who had a lifetime of training behind him. My dad even considered him a good friend.

If his plan involved his own survival, I had no doubts he was capable of pulling it off.

"Understood. Count Viekone, I'm going to start a fire in this room. We're going to make this look like a suicide. I even brought a small corpse that could pass as Dia."

"So *that's* what that large bag you've got is for. There's really a corpse in there...?"

My third reason for using the Fahr Stones had been to obtain a burned cadaver. I'd collected one of the bodies that'd been sent flying from the explosion and altered it a bit to pass for a double of Dia.

"That's right. I'm going to put the ring that Dia always wears on this body, and once it's fried to a crisp, no one will be able to tell that it's not her."

In my previous world, this kind of trick wouldn't have worked because of dental records. This world didn't possess such identification methods, however, so it wasn't a concern.

"I'm jealous of Cian for having such an amazing heir," Dimor admitted.

I pulled a container of oil out of my backpack. Starting with the bed, I doused the entire room.

"The last part requires a bit of performance on your part, Dia. I want you to open the window and address your vassals. These

266    The World's Finest Assassin Gets Reincarnated in Another World as an Aristocrat

are the lines I've prepared for you. 'I can't stand anyone else getting hurt for my sake, and I will not become another's property.' Once you finish that, close the window. That's when we'll start the fire."

"Hmm, that sounds like it could work. Those taking command on the front lines know that we're faking your death. They should be able to take advantage of the situation and get the others to safety. It's best for you, too, Dia."

"Yes, Father."

Not all of the vassals were going to make it out safely. Once they stopped fighting and tried to run, some were undoubtedly going to be captured, and any who did escape faced a rather uncertain future. Still, escape held more hope than continuing a losing battle.

Dia didn't object to the plan because she understood that. The girl was determined to do what was best for her people. There was likely still some part of her that wanted to win, and she had to have known victory would've been possible if I went all out.

With the spell we'd designed to kill the hero, we could've wiped out every last one of the invaders. Dia must've been dying to ask me to use it on the noble faction's forces. I knew she wouldn't request such a thing, though, because Dia understood that winning this battle would solve nothing.

My plan was the one that would save the most lives, after all.

"Lugh, I'm ready when you are," Dia declared. With determination in her eyes, she turned around and put her hand to the window. She opened it and confidently began her performance.

With this, my work was almost done. All that remained was

to return to the Tuatha Dé domain with Dia. So long as there were no complications, we were going to get out just fine. No sooner had that thought crossed my mind than a chill ran down my spine.

I raised my mana as high as I could, grabbed Dia by the shoulders, and pulled her behind me.

*This is bad.*

As soon as Dia had opened her mouth to deliver her message, I was struck with an ominous sensation. It was an unexplainable, sixth sense kind of feeling. My experience as an assassin had given me a special sense for danger, and my alarm bells were ringing.

Driven by instinct, I grabbed Dia by the shoulders, pulled her behind my back, filled a Fahr Stone with mana to near bursting, and stuck my body out the window.

A good distance from the rampart, a large man turned toward Dia and hurled a long spear.

He had spiky red hair and the physique of a bodybuilder. The savage, bestial smile he wore suited him almost uncomfortably well. The air around this strange person was rich with mana so sinister, it seemed unnatural.

*Is this guy human?!* I thought, utterly incredulous.

By using my Tuatha Dé eyes, I could tell right away that the spear was loaded with an enormously high instantaneous mana discharge that far exceeded anything I was capable of.

I drew an arrow with a Fahr Stone that had been filled to the brim with mana and fired.

The spear transfigured as it traveled through the air, increasing in speed as the tip divided into multiple points. Such swiftness far outstripped the speed my tungsten bullets traveled at via Gun

Strike. Without my Tuatha Dé eyes, I don't think I'd ever have been able to spot the incoming projectile.

The force of the spear gouged the earth as it sailed through the air. Soldiers of the noble faction and Viekone vassals alike were indiscriminately torn to shreds. Numerous invisible blades formed around the spear, causing additional damage.

This was more than some polearm—it was a weapon of mass destruction.

The red-haired man's spear and my Fahr Stone collided.

I'd used a special sort of Fahr Stone that'd been made to focus its blast forward when it detonated.

The spear, now traveling at supersonic speed, collided with the Fahr Stone, releasing an explosion born of a force equivalent to the mana of three hundred mages. The iron scraps formed by my earth mana went flying in all directions.

Undaunted, the man's spear slipped through the blast, reduced the rampart to rubble, and pierced halfway through the wall of the castle.

Had it not been for my counterattacks slowing it down, that attack would have reduced the entire estate to rubble, and we would've been in dire straits.

The spear began to rattle, then pulled itself out of the castle wall and returned to its owner.

…*So this is the power of a divine treasure.*

I'd been gathering information on such objects and had recently started the preparations on finally purchasing one, but this was the first I'd ever seen in person.

The man and I locked eyes. He was about six hundred and forty meters away, a distance technically within Gun Strike's range, but hitting a target that far with any sort of reliable accuracy was impossible for me.

Such was not the case for the red-haired man.

Perhaps that could've been chalked up to the divine treasure, but that wasn't all. His skill and impossibly large instantaneous mana discharge were what had made the attack possible.

I entertained the thought that it would be nice if it turned out that the man's only abnormal capability was his instantaneous mana discharge, but I knew that was wishful thinking.

It wouldn't have changed my course of action anyway. I needed to retaliate—and soon.

Chanting a spell, I created a cannon. Against an opponent of such strength, it was clear a gun wasn't going to cut it.

The weapon I created was a 120 mm cannon with rifling carved on the inside.

The barrel of such a weapon was very thick, and the bullets were equally large—each one was about the size of a milk bottle.

Such a dense barrel enabled it to withstand more intense explosions. I trusted this one could even take an explosion born of my full strength.

"Both of you, cover your ears and open your mouths! *Cannon Strike!*"

This was the fourth deadliest spell in my magic arsenal.

An extremely hard and heavy bullet shot toward the man. It spiraled rapidly from the rifling.

Gun Strike couldn't compare to the strength of Cannon Strike. If the former was at the power of a rifle, then the latter held the force of a tank cannon. The firepower needed to push out a tungsten bullet of that size could be achieved only with a full-strength explosion.

People commonly had this the other way around, but large cannons were actually more accurate than rifles. The faster speed of the bullet meant it took less time to reach its destination, reducing the effect gravity had on it. Furthermore, the larger kinetic energy and mass of the cannon's ammunition reduced the effect of other factors like wind. It was because of such factors that the attack held greater accuracy than a smaller round.

Gun Strike was effective only from about four hundred meters away, but with Cannon Strike, I could reliably hit a target from a distance of up to a kilometer.

The only hitch was that such a weapon was a little too abrasive for assassination.

Bullets fired by Cannon Strike had an initial velocity of 1,650 meters per second, and they reached Mach 4.8.

The bullet reached its destination in just 0.4 seconds, where it landed over six hundred and sixty meters away with a thunderous roar that kicked up a giant cloud of dirt.

While the cannon's spike and anchor had been fastened to the floor, the force of the explosion had torn cracks in the walls and shattered all nearby windows.

Dia and Count Viekone stared with their mouths agape.

"Whoooooooaaaaaa, it's been a while since I've seen your Cannon Strike! There's no way there's even a trace of that guy left," Dia exclaimed.

"What in the world was that?" asked her father.

"An assassination trick of mine. I use it to kill long-distance targets," I answered.

"That's not like any assassination technique I've ever heard of..."

While I'd hoped it had indeed been enough to kill the red-haired man, it didn't take long to get my answer.

When the dust settled, the man was still standing and looking mostly none the worse for wear. Blood was running down his face from a spot on his forehead, but the same savage grin was still plain on his face.

It was enough to make me want to laugh. If only I'd missed. At least there still would've been some hope then.

This man had survived a direct hit from Cannon Strike, an attack with strength that rivaled a tank cannon.

"THAT HUUURTS! This is the first time I've ever felt pain. Not bad!!!" He was yelling so loudly, I could hear his every word even from so far away. His tone was both menacing and joyful.

Dia was trembling in fear.

The man's already enormous muscles began to swell until they burst through his clothes, and the horns of a demon sprouted from his head.

I was certain I recognized those visual cues to be part of Berserk, an S-Rank skill.

Triggered by rage, Berserk increased your physical strength and mana. An aura of rage also further enhanced your attack and defense. It could activate only under a certain condition, but it made up for that by far surpassing the destructive force of other S-Rank skills.

Another Cannon Strike wouldn't so much as scratch that guy now.

"Lugh, grab Dia and run. With him here, we no longer

272 The World's Finest Assassin Gets Reincarnated in Another World as an Aristocrat

have time to fake Dia's death. That man ended the civil war. The royal family surrendered because no one could stop him. You're looking at one who has the strength to end wars by himself. I hadn't expected him to show up so soon," said Count Viekone.

If it was true that the man ended battles by himself, it still made him inferior to House Tuatha Dé. We ended such conflicts before they could even begin.

Still grinning from ear to ear, the man continued to shout in our direction.

"I came all the way here 'cause I heard some girl was using some troublesome magic, but holy shit, I did not expect to find something this amazing. Hey, you! I could kill every person here, or we could end this with a duel, like knights! If you win, I'll have the entire army withdraw and never touch the Viekone domain again! Don't you even think about running. If you pull something like that, I may not be able to restrain myself! I've finally found an opponent who can give me a real fight!"

This kind of person was easy enough to understand. He'd been dispatched by the noble faction because they were getting annoyed that the Viekone domain had managed to hold out for more than three days. He then got bored because he was too strong and felt like this fight was beneath him. The ecstatic look on his face was because the red-haired man had finally found someone who could pose a threat.

His was a spirit that had long yearned for a proper duel. To such a person, finding a worthy opponent must have been akin to a child opening presents on Christmas.

I believed that arrogance could be used to catch him off guard, however. This man thought himself invincible, but I'd discovered a fatal weak point.

"Count Viekone, Dia, his mind is set on me. His attributes are significantly higher than mine, so running isn't an option. I have to accept his challenge."

"Lugh, please don't… You *can* win, though, right?" Dia asked, sounding helpless.

I slowly shook my head.

"There is a one hundred percent chance I'll lose. If Cannon Strike couldn't kill him, then I have no hope of beating him one-on-one. I wouldn't last ten seconds."

I produced a two-handed tungsten spear. The metal's natural weight made the weapon weigh more than a hundred kilograms. After I'd created the object, I added two spells to it.

"If that's the case, then why are you so calm?! If you lose, you'll die, you know?! This is a stupid idea. I'll fight with you."

"I only said I wouldn't win in a duel… I'm going to announce that I accept his challenge, but I don't plan on actually meeting him on even ground. That's why I'm doing this with a spear."

I hurled the weapon out the window.

Tears began to well in Dia's eyes.

She probably thought I'd lost it after seeing me throw the weapon I'd just made straight out a broken window. The action was not without a good reason, however.

"Dia, I'm not a soldier or a knight, and I'm certainly not the hero. I'm an assassin. I don't agree to fair fights. Assassination is the only thing I can do, and that's precisely the plan here," I explained, flashing a smile to comfort her.

There was more than one way to go about assassination. Even

against such an overwhelmingly powerful opponent, I still had a viable option. My preparations were nearly complete.

"Count Viekone, please follow me. If he wants to decide this battle based on a knight's duel, we're going to need you present," I said.

Surprisingly, in this world, it wasn't all that rare to entrust the outcome of a war to a single knight.

In a conflict where both sides held a similar amount of military strength, a proper war was liable to drag on and lead to devastation on both sides. To prevent that, both sides would occasionally pick their strongest knight to decide the outcome of such conflicts through a duel.

Truthfully, I'd never expected such a thing to happen during my rescue of Dia. To think that a knight's duel would be how my operation ended... My plan had truly gone off the rails. My line of work demanded expecting the unexpected, however. Improvisation was a very necessary component of assassination.

Saving Dia was all that mattered. What methods I employed to that end didn't matter.

"Understood. Let us go. I apologize for dragging you into this, Lugh... I could use the last of my strength to give you and Dia time to escape," offered the count.

"That would be a bad idea. You wouldn't last a minute against that man. It won't be necessary anyway. As I said, I'm going to kill him."

I couldn't help but wonder how that red-haired guy had gotten so impossibly strong. If he turned out to be the hero, his death was going to make things very problematic in the future. Unfortunately, he had to die here if Dia and I were going to live at all, so it was hardly much of a choice anymore. I didn't have the luxury to consider what was going to happen after that.

The assassination had to come first. Only afterward would I spare time to think about anything else.

As a professional killer, that was the best I could do.

Turning away from Dia's troubled gaze, I walked out onto the courtyard with Count Viekone.

"All right. I accept your challenge," I declared.

The man threw back his head and laughed with delight at my agreeing to the duel.

As I paced toward him, I counted down the remaining time.

*Four hundred forty-three more seconds.*

Both camps had stopped fighting, almost as if the hard-fought battle of the last few days had never even happened.

The frightful man's exclamations alone had brought the conflict to an end. He truly was a monster.

I walked a few hundred meters from the castle to a level plain with a nice view of the land around us, then turned to face my enemy. There he stood, with his spiky red hair and two-handed spear so long, it dwarfed its wielder.

His already muscular body had swollen to abnormal proportions thanks to the S-Rank skill Berserk. A faint glow could be seen in the man's eyes, and horns were protruding from his head. Faced with such a sight, anyone would've thought him a demon. I could almost see the flames of his fighting spirit bursting forth from around his body.

Something was off, though. Berserk was supposed to grant

overwhelming strength in exchange for losing the ability to reason. While my opponent was clearly hungry for a fight, it seemed he was still in possession of his mental faculties.

There was a skill that negated the side effects of Berserk, but I thought it impossible that someone could've been fortunate enough to have been awarded both. If the goddess had allowed him to choose his skills like she'd permitted me, it would've been feasible, but the odds seemed too low for such a powerful combination to have occurred naturally.

*Two hundred twenty-one more seconds.*

"Give me your name, kid," the man demanded.

"Feri Marconi. My family are distant relatives of House Viekone." There was no way I could give him my real name, so I offered a fake one instead.

"Feri. I won't forget it. Thanks to you, I was able to taste my own blood for the first time." At those words, the horned man wiped blood from his forehead and licked it.

The wound itself had already healed. Even as a mage, such an injury should not have closed after only a few minutes.

His robust body had been enhanced by Berserk, affording him unbreakable defense, but some other skill allowed him to retain his intelligence. Both mind and strength were in top form. I couldn't think of a more dangerous foe to face. As if that hadn't been bad enough, the man also appeared able to recover from superficial damage almost immediately.

It almost made me want to call him a cheat.

"I'm glad to hear it. Since we're about to duel, it's only proper to give your name in return. A knight's honor demands such," I replied.

Truthfully, I couldn't care less what the man's name was, but if he wanted to play knights, I was more than happy to go along with it. The more distracted he was, the easier it would be to kill him.

"Ah, sorry about that. I'm Setanta Macness. This is good. This is what it's like to show respect to your opponent before a battle."

The Macness family was known to have connections to the Soigelian royal family. So why had Setanta allied himself with the revolting noble faction?

Setanta was also the one known as Kran's Hound, the very same person I'd previously reasoned had the highest chance of being the hero. Seeing how he'd used his spear to such deadly effect had done little to lessen that suspicion.

"Setanta, I have something I want to confirm. If I win this duel, will the army actually withdraw?" I asked.

"That's what I said, didn't I? We'll pull out, and I'll never touch this domain again. If anyone else tries to interfere with this land, I'll kill them myself. Wanna make it a geas?" Setanta inquired, shrugging. Evidently, he was offended that I hadn't taken him at his word.

A geas was an oath offered to the gods.

"I believe you. But if I win, I'm going to kill you. I don't see how you'll be able to keep your promise." My bold words were meant as a provocation.

"You've got a big mouth, kid... You're the first person dumb enough to talk to me that way. Hey, Dilmura! If I die, make sure to uphold my oath in my place! Satisfied now?"

"Thank you. One more question. What will happen if I lose?"

"If I win, then we'll take Dia and kill everyone here. I don't feel great about it, but that's what's gonna happen. Gets you even more fired up, though, huh?"

"Yeah, you're right. There's no way I can lose now."

"Then let's go ahead and get this started. I can't wait any longer. I've been waiting my entire life for someone strong enough to give me a real fight."

To be honest, speaking with Setanta wasn't easy. I couldn't relate to his feelings at all.

"Before we begin in earnest, can we get the soldiers around us to move back? I'm afraid we won't be able to avoid harming them during our fight. If I win, the war will be over. There's no need for any more unnecessary death," I said.

"You're such a nice boy. Did your parents teach you those manners?"

"That's right. I'm the product of very strict discipline."

Both camps heeded the command and gave us a wide berth.

While I'd decided to kill anyone who obstructed my path to rescuing Dia, I still didn't want any unnecessary bloodshed. Plus, this was a perfect excuse to stall for time and get Setanta into position.

Little by little, I moved our starting position away from the estate, telling him that it would be easier for us to fight out in the open without any obstructions.

Setanta fell for it, and I guided him precisely to where I wanted him.

I produced four titanium-alloy knives. I placed two of them at my hips and gripped the other two in my hands.

*Forty-four more seconds.*

"Sorry, could you give me a second to prepare?"

"Go ahead. This won't be any fun if you're not at your full strength. So you're a dual-wielder? Those knives are puny. How do you think you're gonna stop my spear with those?"

"You'll see once we start fighting. Actually, you probably won't."

The little blades were nothing more than a distraction. I was using them to attract Setanta's attention to ensure he didn't notice my real attack.

"What do you mean by that?"

"I mean that I'm going to end this duel without needing to deal with your spear."

*Nineteen more seconds.*

"That mouth of yours is starting to get on my nerves. I can't figure you out, and that's only making me more excited to kill you. What should our starting signal be?"

"How about we start when this coin hits the ground?"

"Works for me."

I flicked a coin with my finger, and it spun through the air.

Setanta focused on the coin. In a real one-on-one bout, nothing was more important than the first strike. That's why he was watching the coin so intently, to make sure he didn't miss the moment it hit the ground.

The man was so focused, he'd lost sight of everything else around him.

*Eight more seconds.*

He had no idea that he was about to be assassinated. If I had to pin down the exact meaning of that word, I'd define it as killing someone via an unexpected method without a target being aware it was happening.

Even while I stood right in front of Setanta, I had devised a way to kill him that fit that definition.

"I am not a knight. Honor and respect have no place in my line of work. Die."

The count hit zero.

The moment the coin hit the ground, Setanta's fighting spirit and mana surged, but the man suddenly disappeared.

It wasn't that he'd suddenly moved at such a high speed that he'd appeared invisible, although that's what he'd tried to do. Unfortunately for him, I'd killed him before he ever got the chance. My own attack had been so quick that not even my Tuatha Dé eyes had been able to keep up.

A hole that went down for miles had been gouged into the earth. It fissured and began to spread as the ground shook.

I directed all of my mana to my legs and leaped backward. I then shifted it toward defending myself.

So powerful was the spell I'd used to kill Setanta that I risked ending my own life with the aftershock. I focused everything I had on defending myself.

That's when the ground exploded.

Shock waves accompanied by a tsunami of sediment radiated out from the spot where Setanta had been standing.

I was swallowed up immediately. Totally buried by dirt, I was helplessly thrown around in all directions as the blast wave carried me away.

A conjured barrier of wind maintained my supply of oxygen. I fought desperately to maintain my mana output and protect myself. Letting up for a moment would've spelled my death.

I had no idea how far the tsunami carried me, but the shaking finally stopped, and I came to a stop.

Both of my legs had broken, the result of jumping back with more force than my body could handle. I also had a few cracked ribs, and my left arm had snapped. My legs and ribs had thankfully broken rather cleanly, so I used mana to connect them back together. My left arm, however, had a compound fracture. If I tried to heal it as it was, the risk was high that it would connect in an unnatural way. I decided to hold out for medical treatment.

Using earth magic, I pushed myself free from the mountain of dirt and rock.

I was shocked to see where I'd ended up. The force of my attack had carried me from the site of the duel all the way back to the demolished rampart.

"That was Gungnir, the formula I developed to use against the hero. That was the magic that killed you, Setanta."

What remained after my assassination was shocking.

A yawning abyss at least a few kilometers deep had been gouged into the earth where Setanta had been standing. Its bottom was too far down to see. Dirt from the explosion had been kicked up so high, it was raining down on the castle roof.

This was only the aftermath. Setanta had taken a direct hit. There was no way he'd survived, and I sensed no sign of him.

Many soldiers in the surrounding area were buried in dirt. The Viekone soldiers were assisting those who needed help, while the noble faction soldiers were running away with looks of confused terror.

*Good thing I had them all stay back*, I thought.

Had anyone else been within two hundred meters of my attack, they would've almost certainly perished.

That was Gungnir—the spell I'd designed to assassinate the hero.

When I'd tossed the tungsten spear out the window, the assassination had already been 80 percent complete.

There was an earth spell that doubled the target's gravity.

I studied the formula for that spell and discovered that you could adjust the multiplier both positively and negatively.

I multiplied the tungsten's gravity by -2, which caused the spear to accelerate upward at 19.8 meters per second squared.

The amount of time my mana allowed me to maintain that reverse gravity spell was three minutes. The spear accelerated upward for that entire time, and even once its gravity returned to normal, its kinetic energy continued to carry it upward until it came to a stop at 1,023.5 kilometers aboveground.

Naturally, what came up had to come back down.

With a spear falling from 1,023.5 kilometers, it would reach a speed of 4,480 meters per second.

The spear weighed one hundred kilograms and fell at a velocity of Mach 14, which created a force of $3.6 \times 10^9$ joules.

Considering a tank cannon fired with kinetic energy equal to $9 \times 10^6$ joules, the spear fell with four hundred times the kinetic energy of a tank cannon. The heavier the object, the more force with which it would fall, but the problem was that a greater mass depleted my mana quicker when inverting its gravity. This significantly shortened the length of time I could maintain the spell.

At present, that was the limit of my power.

My inspiration for this attack was a weapon that had been developed back in a country from my former world known as America. Commonly, they were called "rods from God."

Rods from God was an idea for a weapon that would drop metal rods from satellites orbiting in space. Upon impact, the rods would rival the power of nuclear weapons.

There were problems with actually realizing this weapon, though. The cost of placing objects of that mass in space was prohibitive, and even if you did get the projectiles into space, keeping them from burning up in the atmosphere before they reached the ground was an issue as well.

The magic of this world made getting around such complications rather simple.

I lifted my spear a thousand kilometers in the air merely by reversing its gravity, and a convenient spell called Windbreak dealt with the friction of entering the atmosphere by repelling air.

Gungnir was the most power I could manage, which made it the ace up my sleeve.

"I already knew this, but putting its power aside, there are a lot of drawbacks."

The biggest problem was how long it took to prepare. A total of ten minutes was needed for the spear to make its trip up and then back down. Another problem was the difficulty of aiming the shot.

Normal mages would be killed simply by being caught up in the explosion of the impact. That meant the death zone extended as far as two hundred meters out, so long as the target was a normal person. I doubted the hero was likely to die unless he took the hit head-on.

Even without the concern of air friction because of my wind magic, I still had to account for the rotation of the planet, among many other calculations. Even if I got all of the calculations right, if the spear was off by even the tiniest degree, it would probably fail to kill the hero.

Thankfully, I'd been able to practice the attack a few times on an uninhabited island. If I hadn't, I probably would've missed. I really owed Maha for having found a spot where I could practice.

This time the spear had landed exactly where I'd calculated it would, but I still had adjustments I could make to the formula.

"For the time being, I need to check for his corpse."

Using wind magic, I scanned the area for Setanta. While it was likely he was dead, I couldn't be sure until I saw the body myself. At Mach 14, Gungnir had been too fast, even for my Tuatha Dé eyes, to perceive.

I searched every inch of the surrounding area, but I found no sign of the red-haired man. I even tried searching underground with earth mana, but that turned up nothing as well.

In addition to not finding any trace of a body, something else was curiously absent—Gáe Bolg, Setanta's divine treasure. Even after an impact that big, it shouldn't have disappeared.

If the weapon wasn't there, did that mean that Setanta had somehow escaped with it?

"That's impossible," I said to myself. If he'd been able to grab the spear and escape, he doubtlessly would've tried to continue the duel.

Dia came running toward me.

The noble faction army had already pulled out. Actually, it would've been more accurate to say they fled to safety. I doubt they wanted to fight a monster capable of both causing so much destruction and killing Kran's Hound.

"Lugh! Thank goodness you're safe," Dia cried.

I caught her as she flung herself at me.

It seemed like Dia had a hugging habit. She kissed me on the cheek, then blushed deep red and turned away.

Overcome with love for her, I turned her face toward mine, and this time I kissed her on the lips. She accepted the motion, although she was forced to balance on the tips of her toes in order to reach me, an effort which only made her more adorable.

It was really only a peck; our lips barely touched. But that did not diminish the joy I felt from the act.

"Well, that was a surprise... But...not an unpleasant one."

Dia's every mannerism was cute.

My elation was short-lived as I realized the successful assassination had created a new problem. Since the entire noble faction army had run away, the plan to fake Dia's death wouldn't work anymore.

This was my first ever failed assassination.

Things certainly could've turned out worse, though. While I prided myself on my flawless success rate as an assassin, I cared far more for Dia's safety.

Such a way of thinking would've been impossible for my former self.

A lot happened after the duel.

Despite further time devoted to searching for him, neither Setanta nor his spear ever turned up.

Even though the noble faction had withdrawn and promised to uphold Setanta's oath, Count Viekone decided the risk of the nobles seeking revenge was too high. As such, he distributed his wealth among his surviving vassals and ordered them to leave the domain.

Count Viekone said he'd rely on one of his many personal connections to hide, build up strength, and then one day return to have his revenge.

Dia was going to live in the Tuatha Dé domain, beginning life as a different person.

Dad got to work creating a foolproof new identity for her, and Count Viekone had said he had a way to trick everyone into thinking Dia was still in Soigel.

Perhaps it was selfish of me, but the idea of spending time with Dia every day was very welcome, and our spell-development research was sure to progress much more quickly now that we could see each other all the time.

Unfortunately, I'd revealed an ace in the hole I'd been hoping to save for the hero—and in front of a large crowd of people, too.

I doubt anyone understood the theory or nature behind Gungnir, but I didn't think it prudent to continue to trust it as a guaranteed win anymore.

I was going to need new magic—something even stronger than Gungnir. To that end, Dia's cooperation was likely to be extremely necessary.

Carrying Dia in my arms, I made my way back home.

Running like this was more tiring than carrying her on my shoulders, and my left arm still hurt a little after receiving surgery and further self-healing. I still preferred to hold her in my arms, however. That way I could enjoy her warmth and her softness.

"Dia, are you okay with all this?" I asked.

"...I'm sad that things ended up the way they did, but thanks to you, we avoided serious tragedy. Thank you," she replied softly.

In the end, House Viekone lost its land, wealth, and retainers. Even if it had come at a heavy price, the worst-case scenario had still been avoided.

"It may be hard for you until you get used to the Tuatha Dé lifestyle, but you'll be fine if you hang in there."

"There's no need to worry about that. Remember, I once spent two weeks there. I love the Tuatha Dé domain. And you'll be there, too." Dia spoke as cheerfully as possible, likely so as not to cause me any more concern.

*Dia is a tough girl*, I thought.

The sun had already set. It was the perfect time for our escape across the border.

"Hey, Lugh. Why did you risk your life to come and save me? House Tuatha Dé probably had nothing to gain from it."

"I did it for you. I promised I'd come running if you ever called for me."

"…You did, didn't you? Thank you, Lugh. I'll have to do what I can to return the favor."

"There's no need for that. I made that promise to return a favor I owed to you in the first place. If you try to return it, we'll be stuck in a never-ending loop."

I'd made my promise to Dia after asking something unreasonable of her, saying I would do anything in return. After all these years, I'd finally paid her back.

"That's true, but exchanging favors for the rest of our lives sounds kinda cool."

"You're not wrong."

While the haze over my heart had not yet cleared, I did feel like a little light was starting to break through.

Somehow, we made it back to Tuatha Dé.

It truly was fortunate that I had the Rapid Recovery skill.

Dia had fallen asleep in my arms at some point during the trip. She must have been exhausted after pushing herself so hard during the battle.

My ears caught the sound of footsteps as soon as I returned to the Tuatha Dé estate.

Tarte approached, her eyes welling with tears as soon as she saw me. She clapped her hands together over her chest.

"Welcome home, my lord. You came back safely! I'm glad. Truly," she said.

"Don't tell me you haven't slept this whole time?" I guessed.

"No, that's…not true," Tarte lied. Anyone could've seen she'd been up for the entirety of my absence.

To have not slept for this long after giving everything she had to help me preserve my stamina on the way to the Viekone domain was ridiculous. Unlike me, she didn't have Rapid Recovery. Still, this was hardly the time to get angry and scold her.

"Thanks, Tarte. Your help was what enabled me to keep my focus until the very end."

Gungnir was magic that pushed me to the very edge of my limit. The calculations were complicated, and the spells required fine precision. I couldn't allow the slightest deviation when releasing the lance, and I needed to guide my target to the exact spot the spear was going to land. It all required an enormous amount of mental energy.

If my concentration had slipped for even a second, I would've failed. Tarte's help had allowed me to take it easy during that first hour of travel to the Viekone domain. I was sure that extra energy was what had allowed me to triumph.

"Yes, my lord! It was worth it... This is Dia, I presume."

Tarte had heard about Dia many times from me, but this was her first time seeing her in person. She looked her up and down with great interest.

"I'll introduce you once she wakes up. It looks like she's going to be living here," I said.

"She's so beautiful, like a doll. I'm so jealous," Tarte said with a sigh.

Tarte was quite beautiful herself, so she really had no reason to be envious. Saying something like that would've been embarrassing, though, so I kept the thought to myself.

I sensed someone else enter the room, and I looked over to see Dad.

"I see you've completed your mission. Great job," he praised.

"I'll give a detailed report later, but unfortunately, this was my first ever failed assassination."

I was supposed to get Dia out of Viekone and take her here after faking her death, but all the enemy soldiers had fled after my duel with Setanta, so we'd been left with no witnesses for the staged suicide.

"If Dia is alive, I should think that is good enough. You didn't make any mistakes that exposed your identity or where you are taking Dia, did you?" asked my dad.

"Definitely not."

"Good. You should get some rest... You have my thanks for fulfilling a request that I, your worthless father, could not." My dad paused for a minute before continuing. "Moving on... I have an urgent message to deliver to you. After you left, we received word that the hero has appeared. He's a young man born here in Alvan. The appearance of the hero means that monsters will be on the rise, and demons will soon be reborn. I want you to keep this in mind, Lugh."

If there was word of such a person in Alvan, that meant Setanta couldn't have been the hero. It was good news, but it also made me uneasy. This turn of events raised the question of how Setanta had gotten so powerful.

It meant that something existed in this world that allowed a normal person to achieve incredible power. I would have to launch a thorough investigation into Setanta's history in the coming days.

"Yes, I'll be careful. What are we going to do about Dia?" I asked.

"I already have her identity prepared in the family register. She will live in Tuatha Dé. Dia's silver hair really stands out. The only people with silver hair in this country are you and Esri. That said, it would be really regrettable to have her dye it...so I'll use the little-sister identity I already have in the family register. I had prepared this for a different purpose, but we may as well use it now. It wouldn't be unnatural for your little sister to have silver hair."

I didn't get the meaning of making Dia my little sister. I understood that it'd make her silver hair less conspicuous, of course, but...

"Why little sister and not big sister?!"

"Have you forgotten that I prepared a little sister for you on the family register? It was for next month."

"Ah."

I had indeed forgotten. It would've been a problem if Dia assumed an identity that wasn't a younger sibling.

"Dia is short, her face is still childlike, and, hmm... Yeah, little sister will be just fine."

I made a point to remember that Dad said that after looking at Dia's chest.

She certainly did look like Mom.

"Understood. I'll inform Dia when she wakes up."

I expected her to be angry about being made out to be younger than me, but I trusted she'd come around once I explained things.

"Yes, please... One last thing. Word is the hero is the same age as you. If that's the case, you'll actually be meeting him at a certain place before very long," my dad said.

My heart began to pound in my chest.

There was a law that had been decided on in this country five years ago. As a result of that rule, nobles became unable to marry at the previously eligible age of fourteen years old. Instead, getting engaged at fourteen and getting married at sixteen became the norm.

If the hero was my age, and he followed that practice, we were definitely liable to cross paths soon.

"I'll do my best not to offend him."

"The hero will probably search for a companion while there. We have an obligation to this country. I don't want to invite any unnecessary trouble, but... If necessary, I wouldn't mind if that became your top priority. I doubt even the royal family would complain."

I was finally going to be able to lay eyes on the target I'd been assigned to kill.

I'd have to keep a careful watch on him. The hero wasn't to die until after he'd killed the Demon King. Until that time, I was going to focus on studying his every ability and work to uncover as many potential weaknesses as possible.

Concurrently, I also had a plan to search for a way of saving the world without killing the hero. Unlike my previous self, I wanted to avoid any unnecessary deaths.

There was also the matter of Dia, Tarte, Maha, and everyone else I'd come to know and love. If I had no choice but to kill the hero to save the world and everyone in it...I trusted myself not to hesitate when the time came.

If I was to assassinate the hero, it was only going to be because I had decided to do it of my own free will. That was how Lugh Tuatha Dé had chosen to live.

# Afterword

Thank you very much for reading *The World's Finest Assassin Gets Reincarnated in Another World as an Aristocrat*.

I am the author, Rui Tsukiyo.

Just as the title says, the world's greatest assassin finds himself reborn in another world.

He then works to combine his knowledge from his previous world with the magic of the new one to become the strongest he can be. His wish for his new life is to live for himself and to find happiness.

In his first life, he was nothing but a tool, and in the new world, he chases after the chance at happiness he'd missed out on the first time.

Please continue to cheer him on as the adventures of his second life continue.

Thank you, Reia, for your wonderful illustrations. They clearly communicate the hard work you put into them. As the author, looking at them fills me with joy. I will do my best to write interesting stories that are worthy of your illustrations.

Miyagawa, my lead editor, thank you very much for always giving me such quick and honest responses.

To the editing team; all involved at Kadokawa Sneaker Bunko; lead designer, Takahisa Atsuji; and all the people who have read this far, thank you very much!